I AM JUSTICE

I AM JUSTICE

D.P. WATKINS

STORY GRID

A STORY GRID EDITION: 0005
STORY GRID PUBLISHING LLC

STORY GRID

Story Grid Publishing LLC

223 Egremont Plain Road

PMB 191

Egremont, MA 01230

First Story Grid Publishing Paperback Edition November 2021

For Information About Special Discounts for Bulk Purchases,

Please visit www.storygridpublishing.com

ISBN: 978-1-64501-075-3

Ebook: 978-1-64501-076-0

To Lisa VanDamme, who taught me to read,
Jeremiah Cobra, who inspired me to write,
and Kate, the greatest storyteller I know.

I AM JUSTICE

PROLOGUE

I KILLED A DOG ONCE. When I was sixteen, a bull terrier took my leg for a snack and I just remember looking down and wondering why my dress had gone from yellow to maroon. The rest was a blur. All I know is eventually my hand found a rock and six swings later that was the end of Spuds MacKenzie.

I dragged myself four hundred yards across a snow-covered lettuce field before reaching our farmhouse. When I told Pop what happened, he just glared, then disappeared in the direction of my blood trail. He returned sometime later carrying the dog's limp body and told me to bury it behind the main barn. Never mind that I was still bleeding. Never mind that the frozen ground fought hard against the blade of my shovel.

I can't say how long I stood out there digging that grave. I have dug many graves, and even the smaller ones can take all day. All I know is, by the time I finished, the only light came from a crescent moon that hung in the air surrounded by the billions of stars that crowd the Michigan sky on clear nights.

I wandered back to the house, which was still and silent, and as my hand reached for the door, I stopped. Pop's muddy overalls were there, folded neatly on the porch. He had retired for the evening. For the first time in my life, I was outside, alone.

Pop had lots of rules, but one stood above them all. We

were not to venture into his office. He called it an office, but it was actually a barn.

Three barns stood on our property. The one closest to the house was little more than the rotted corpse of a shelter, the roof long ago caved in and the paint long ago worn away. Pop probably would have torn it down, except for the feral cats that called it home. The farm's main working barn was a few yards behind that, about two times the size of our house, with state-of-the-art everything.

Pop's barn was a more modest structure. Set about a hundred yards away from the house, it looked like most barns you see on small family farms. Red and white. Freshly painted each spring. Wide doors at the front. Lonely. Peaceful.

But we all knew what lived in there. Not feral cats but feral girls.

The Heiden.

To this day, I don't know why I did it. Maybe it was sheer curiosity. Maybe it was the feeling I had cheated death and for the first time sensed just how precious life was. Whatever the reason, I bent down and felt around inside his right pocket for a keyring, which held about twelve different keys. Keys that were never out of his reach. Keys I had never touched with my own fingers. I gripped them tightly and headed in the direction of Pop's office.

I walked quietly and carefully, stopping every few steps to look back at the house. Nothing moved. Nothing stirred. I kept walking.

The barn door was secured by an extra-large, stainless steel padlock. I fumbled through the keys until I found the one that fit and tried to open the lock. It took more effort than I expected, and I had to jerk my wrist hard to make the key turn. But once I did, the lock sprang open violently, clanging loudly against the door.

I stood there for minutes trying not to breathe, waiting and listening, waiting and listening. I expected to see the house lights turn on followed by Pop charging toward me. But it was still just me and the sound of the wind wrestling with the trees.

I slipped the lock off and placed it carefully on the ground. A few more deep breaths and I cracked open the barn door and slipped inside.

Pitch blackness. I fumbled around for a light switch, and as the room came to life, I had to cover my mouth to muffle a scream.

A dozen or more dog cages were lined up along the far wall, large enough for a person to sit in upright but not to stand. A few were empty. Most were not. They were occupied by young women, all about my age. Most of the girls still slept, but a few were looking at me, wide-eyed, lips quivering.

None made a sound.

I took in the rest of the room. The floor was soft and carpeted. To the left was a large bed, to the right an exam table with blue padding and black metal stirrups. Beside it, black leather straps dangled in midair, supported by a metal bar attached to the ceiling by a chain and a spring. It looked half like a swing, half like a torture device.

I had always known about the Heiden, but I had never seen more than one at a time, and then never without Pop and Anna Claire close by.

"Are you here to help us?" The girl was young, no more than fourteen, her blonde hair dangling down past her elbows.

I couldn't answer. I could hardly move.

"What's your name?" she said. There was no fear in her voice, and, it seemed, no hope. Just a gentle curiosity, as if I were an alien creature who might be able to explain to her what kind of planet she had crash landed on.

I walked hesitantly, then fell to my knees in front of her cage.

"What's that?" I said, trying to sound normal, though tears streamed down my cheeks and into the corners of my mouth.

"What do I call you?"

"Paige Marie," I whispered. I didn't ask her name. I kind of think I didn't want to know it.

She smiled then peeked past my shoulder. I flinched, fearful I'd find Pop looming over me, but then I heard her voice. It sounded awestruck.

"The stars!"

Her eyes were wide. Blue with flecks of brown around the edges. Then the eyes looked at me and they had a purity about them, as if they had never witnessed tragedy or evil. It seemed impossible. I knew what those eyes must have seen.

I jerked my head away and saw, traced into the dust just outside the girl's cage, a stick figure family. They were smiling.

I had always been taught that family was sacred. That you could not survive on this Earth without the protection of your kin. That loyalty and obedience were the highest virtues. But, deep down, I never believed it. To me, only one thing mattered. Innocence. I guess because it's something I never had—or because I had promised myself, on some forgotten night of my childhood, that I would rather die than betray the few scraps of innocence I still had. I decided in that moment that the girl who gazed up in awe at the stars did have a name. I named her Innocence.

I pulled myself to my feet and shuffled over to a filing cabinet near the bed. The top drawer was locked, but the next two slipped open easily enough. The first was filled with bottles of lotion and things of that sort. The bottom drawer had empty bottles of water and a large plastic container with mixed nuts. I brought the nuts over to Innocence.

"Here. Hold out your hand." I pressed a handful of almonds and walnuts into her palm, and felt her warm, fragile fingers curl around my hand. We held each other for a moment before she slipped an almond into her mouth.

"He lets you walk around free?" she said.

"I'm his daughter." The words made me queasy.

She nodded and I could see the memories wash across her soft, pale face, like film from a movie. "I miss my dad," she said. "He worries a lot, you know? This one time I snuck out of the house to meet up with this boy. We didn't do anything. He wanted to kiss me, but I think we were both too shy. We just sat on the playground swings and talked. But when I got home Dad was in my room crying. I'd never seen him cry. Not ever. I hope… well, Mom will take good care of him."

"How can you do that?" I said, and I was shocked by the sound of my own voice. There was anger in my words.

She cocked her head. "What?"

"You're never getting out of here. You know that. Right? He's not going to let you go. You have to understand that. When the moon is full, he's going to show up and Anna Claire is going to show up and I'm going to show up and we're going to go deep into the woods and you'll never be seen again. And you're worried about the stars and about your dad? What about you? Don't you want to live?"

She looked at me and said, her voice gentle, "I did."

"No!" I was on my feet, as if my body had made a decision before my mind. "This ends now."

My hands shaking, I switched off the lights, backed out of the barn, and shut the door, running to the house without reattaching the lock.

No more victims, I thought.

And if it costs me my life? My hands were squeezed tightly into fists and I thought about the atrocities those hands had helped commit.

So what if it costs me my life? I never had a chance to live. I never got to look up at the stars and love the world. But if I can just keep her alive. If I can just make sure she gets to wrap her arms around her dad one more time and maybe sneak down to the park again and kiss that boy…

I reached the house before I could finish the thought and crept inside.

Pop's room was upstairs, next door to mine, but my older sister Anna Claire and younger sister Laudie Mae slept together downstairs in a bedroom down the hall from the den. I crawled between their beds and jostled Anna Claire.

"Paige?" she said.

I didn't know what to say. What could I say? I sat there shaking my head, not crying, but just looking at her helplessly in the dim glow of a nightlight.

"What's wrong?" Anna Claire said.

"We have to save them," I whispered.

"What? Save who?"

I held up Pop's keychain. "The Heiden."

Anna Claire snatched the keys from me, her face drawn in

horror. She looked over at Laudie Mae, who was still sleeping soundly.

"There are so many of them. In Pop's office? I've seen them. There are so many of them."

Anna Claire looked over her shoulder at the clock. "Pop'll be waking up in a few hours."

"Then we have to go. Now."

She ran her fingers through my hair. "Okay, babe. Okay. Go to the barn and wait for me. I'll get everything ready."

A few minutes later I reached the barn door and hesitated. I couldn't make myself go back inside, so I waited, back against the barn, my stomach tight and my teeth clenched. Time passed slowly, but as soon as I heard the muffled clang of the house door shut, I stood breathlessly, trying to make out the sound of footsteps—and to count how many feet were moving through the frosty grass. I could hear nothing. Any sound was smothered by a steady brush of wind that strangled recalcitrant tree leaves.

I saw his face before I saw the two girls behind him. As Pop emerged from the darkness into the moonlight, Anna Claire dashed out with Laudie Mae in her arms. "He heard us leaving," she said, her voice soft but her eyes loud. *Prepare*, they said.

Pop didn't stop to speak to me but brushed past me as he reached for the door of the barn. Then he paused. Maybe it was only an instant, but it felt as if he stood there for a long time. Not like he was hesitating. Like he was savoring.

Then he pulled the door open and turned on the lights and said, his voice flat: "Inside, girls."

The three of us stepped into the barn. The Heiden were all awake this time. Most of them scurried to the backs of their cages when they saw Pop. A few sat there, hugging their knees. Innocence knelt at the front of her cage, bitter and defiant.

Pop stepped into the center of the room. "I'd like to introduce you all to my girls. The oldest one here is Anna Claire. The youngest is Laudie Mae. And this here, I guess you met her, this is Paige Marie."

Anna Claire reached out for my hand and pulled me close to her. The three of us stood there, shivering in the cool air.

Pop ran his fingers along the cages until he reached the filing cabinet in the corner. He pulled his key chain from his pocket and unlocked the top drawer. When his hand emerged, it was holding a pistol.

"Pick one," he said to me. I clung tighter to Anna Claire. "You can't have all of them, Paige. Pick one." Moments passed and he suddenly lurched in our direction. "Pick one!"

"Me." It was Innocence. Her voice wasn't pleading. It was unflinching and confident, even though she knew as well as I did she was not volunteering to go free.

I shook my head. "No," I whispered.

"She chooses me."

"Well?" he said.

I nodded, terrified that if I didn't consent, Innocence would not be the only girl who would have to pay for my sins.

"Good." Pop unlocked her cage. She didn't wait for his orders but crawled out and unsteadily pulled herself to her feet, only a few feet away from me.

Anna Claire was squeezing my hand so hard I couldn't feel my fingers, and even though I knew I shouldn't do it, I said to the emaciated girl standing in front of me, "I'm sorry."

"I'm not," she said. She closed her eyes, waiting. Pop lifted the gun and, before he pulled the trigger, Innocence opened her eyes one last time and said: "Run."

But I didn't run. Not that night.

Not for many nights to follow.

CHAPTER ONE
(SEVEN YEARS LATER)

CADENCE CAN'T STOP LAUGHING. She's captivating when she laughs. Her eyes narrow and her mouth opens wide, and it's like joy escaping from an overfilled balloon.

"You didn't," I say as we walk through campus in the direction of her dorm.

"Oh, you know I did. I jumped right up in my chair," she leaps onto a bench, "and I said, 'Kiss the ring, bitches. It's the start of a new era.'" She holds out her hand and there's no ring but I kiss it anyway. She deserves it. She's been vying for the top spot in the Black Students' League for more than a year.

Her smile vanishes and we've been best friends for so long that I know what she's looking at before she says the name. "Izaak."

I spin on my heels and feel Cadence's arm shoot in front of me, like a mother stopping short.

Izaak Lane is standing there, his face drawn tight with a look I can't quite read. His eyes are steely but solemn, filled with something that resembles remorse, only there's a hint of a smirk on his lips. Apprehension tugs at my chest and I realize I'm holding my breath. Even though I see him at school and Jiu Jitsu just about every day, it's been nearly a year since we last spoke.

"Congratulations, Madame President," he says to Cadence, though his eyes never leave mine.

"How the hell did you find that out?" Cadence says. "It just happened."

He looks at her. The remorse is gone, and he's all in on the smirk. "I got my ways. So what's on the agenda this semester? Deplatforming? Riots? Woke pasta in the dining center?"

"What does that even mean?" I say.

Cadence hops off the bench. "He's just trying to bait me. I swear, you *wish* some shit would go down on campus just so you could get famous writing for one of those conservative sites. Izaak. You're *black*. Just send in a video application and they'll make you editor-in-chief."

The smirk vanishes and I notice his long fingers tapping the side of his leg, as if he's trying to calm himself. It's subtle, and the most nervous thing I've ever seen him do. "Anyway, I'm not here about that. I need to have a word with Justice."

"Oh, hell no," Cadence says, inserting herself between us. "After what you did last year? You know people still give her shit for that? Still call her a slut and blame her for ruining Villanova's playoff season?"

Izaak's jaw tightens. "It was news."

Cadence is yelling now, and I feel invisible and exposed all at the same time. "News? Motherfucker, Kareem Hanley tried to rape her and if his dad wasn't who he is, you think she would've backed off her story? And you printed her *name*, Izaak. In the freaking *Clerk*. So unless you're here to apologize—"

"I am."

It stops Cadence cold. For a moment she watches him, her body tense, like she's about to slap his face. Then she glances at me over her shoulder.

"It happened again," he says. "I mean, it's just a rumor. No one's talking. Not publicly. So, yeah. I'm sorry. I'm sorry we didn't take him down last year when we had the chance."

So many thoughts are rushing past, like one minute I'm playing in a field with puppies, and the next I'm watching a tornado tear through and wreck the world around me. I try to steady myself, only my heart is racing and standing still feels harder than running at full blast.

Before I can say anything, Cadence tries to shove Izaak back, but instead it just turns into a smack on the chest. "You have no right."

"Maybe not. Or maybe I'm the only one here who gives a damn about what's right."

He reaches out as if to touch my shoulder but I swat away his hand. "Don't," I muster.

There's more I want to say. I want to fling words at him so sharp he'll collapse in a puddle of regret. I want to make him cry and plead and beg for something more than forgiveness—for mercy. But I don't. Because I know what I'm capable of—and I know what it actually feels like to watch a person beg for their life.

He pulls back. "I *am* sorry, J," he says. "If I hadn't… I thought you wanted me to do it." He looks at Cadence. "Apparently, I was wrong."

"I think we're done here," Cadence says. Izaak starts to say something but stops himself and just nods.

As he walks off, Cadence pulls me tight and guides me to

the bench where we sit, our boots nearly touching, separated only by the dust of a light snow.

Of all the things I've been through in my life, of all the wars I've fought, last year should have been the easiest. But it was like those movies I hate where you watch someone strive and battle and win—and then in the last scene they're randomly mowed down by a truck.

I had managed to build a life for myself. A life with friends and dreams and stability and a growing conviction that I might just end up somewhere close to normal. And then, overnight, it vanished. The only thing I didn't lose, the only person who stuck by me, was Cadence.

She shouldn't have. When I think of what it cost her—it was the reason she wasn't made BSL president last year—she should have said, "Sorry, girl, I love you but I'm not diving off a cliff with you." I even gave her an out. I told her I wouldn't blame her if she needed some time apart. But loyalty means everything to Cadence, and so here we are. The two of us. Alone. Together. As always.

"Forget about him," she says, hints of her perfume drifting off her neck. "Tonight, it's just you and me. Tonight..." She catches herself.

"Tonight, you and Mathis celebrate." I mean it to sound like a fact. It sounds like an accusation.

"Shit. You want me to cancel?"

I wipe away tears and let out a dramatic sigh, hoping to assuage her guilt by mocking it. "Don't worry about me. Cadence Jenkins is madly in love with the mysterious Mathis and little ol' Justice will just have to spend the night by herself. Like always. When am I going to meet this guy anyway? It's been like six months."

The mood has shifted—thank God—and Cadence punches me playfully. "It's been *three* months. And, like I said, it's… complicated. Anyway, I'm serious. You need me?"

"No, it's fine. I'm busy tonight anyway."

"Ah. So when am *I* going to find out what the hell *you* do every other night?"

I throw her a playful smile, but inside I'm flush with guilt that borders on shame. For the trillionth time, I try to make the words come out. To tell her about my job, and my name, and Pop and all the rest of it. But how can I? It would put me in danger. It would put her in danger. And even if it didn't… I can't risk losing her again. "Like I said. It's complicated."

"Hey. It doesn't even matter," she says. "You've got your secrets. I've got mine. But in the end, we're sisters. Right?"

We clasp hands, and though part of it feels like treason, another part of it feels desperately right. I say—the way we always say to each other before we part, "Yeah. We're sisters."

CHAPTER TWO

I HAVE TO THINK THAT strip clubs were invented by a man-hating feminist. Seriously, there is no faster way to fall into misandry than to dance for a living.

Start with the obvious. The jerks who come in, grab, complain, and don't tip. Or, the married guys who tell themselves looking isn't cheating, in which case, fine, but maybe ask your wife's opinion. Or, the pathetically lonely guys who think it's easier to pay for conversation and a lap dance than to, I don't know, ask a girl to coffee.

Here's what you learn dancing. Every man lies. Every man's a mark. A man's dignity ends where a girl's cleavage begins.

On the other hand...

Ask any of the girls who work with me at Night Shade, and they'll tell you they find the job empowering. They'll say there's nothing degrading about grinding on a guy's lap for twenty dollars; that's just society's Puritanism. They'll talk about how they love setting their own hours and earning more in a night than most people do in a week.

Less often mentioned: The half who don't use dope use meth, and the ones who don't do drugs at all occasionally take ecstasy.

Still, when anyone asks, I read from the same script. Only

I know full well that this place makes me feel hypocritical and less than human. I just don't have another choice. You want to stay off the grid, you need cash. You want to stay off the grid and still pay for a decent liberal arts college, you need a lot of cash. So it's either this or a life of crime. But crime attracts the cops and I already have enough reasons not to like cops.

The Uber drops me off in front of a three-story brick building in the south end of Philly where a red awning juts out over the sidewalk with the name "Night Shade" emblazoned in elegant white lettering.

I walk through an alleyway toward the back. It's a quarter to ten, and the parking lot is mostly empty. I expected it. The crowd won't pick up for another hour, but I like getting started when the club is quiet. I'm a good talker and talking tends to pay better when you can hear.

A quick stop in the dressing room and twenty minutes later, I'm decked out and standing in the doorway. I take three deep breaths. Something inside me changes and I step into the club lights.

The smell is the first thing I notice. It's cool and smoky and completely distinct. Every strip club smells like this, and no other place on Earth does. I march slowly past the main stage, and though I don't let my eyes wander, I'm instantly aware of everyone and everything.

Along the main stage are chairs and tables, where a handful of men are throwing small bills and taking in the pole dancing. Right now, it's mainly gawkers, the kind of guys who will toss you a few ones, more out of guilt than anything. Once the club gets busy, it'll be different. Stage-side you can typically find the party guys who dump money like it's confetti.

Early in the night, what you're looking for is the lonely guy with cash to burn. He's here for personal attention, and if you play it right, he'll be willing to shell out for dance after dance, just to sit and talk. I once made four grand from a lawyer who wanted to debate whether Stalin was worse than Hitler. How do you know if a guy has money? The truth is, you don't. I've seen flashy guys dead broke, and bums who ran hedge funds. Scarlett says you need to learn how to smell the money.

I see her walk in. Scarlett's redheaded, not naturally, and large-chested, also not naturally. Still, she's one of the few girls here who looks as good in real life as in the club. Part of me wants to say, "Good for you." Another part of me wants to say, "Who's your surgeon?" But, as it happens, Scarlett hates anyone not stuffing money in her g-string so I say nothing.

The DJ calls me to the main stage and off I go. Tonight's soundtrack has been early 2000s club music for the most part, and my song turns out to be Sean Paul's "Get Busy." I'm more of a nineties rock girl, myself, but you can't really shake your ass to Pearl Jam. Believe me. I've tried.

I strut down the stage and it's amazing how you can be in two places at once. I can see their faces, I can feel the movements of my body, I'm aware of everything—yet in my mind I'm looking at Izaak and thinking about all of the things I should've said but didn't. I hate him. I hate him in a way I have never hated anyone. Even Pop I can't say I truly hated. Maybe that's because the hatred is drowned in an endless bottle of fear.

And now fear is all I feel because three guys just entered the club. The two tall black guys I don't recognize. The white guy I do.

Vic Michaels is hard to miss. He's six-foot-four, though he looks shorter next to his friends, and has one of those faces

17

that's neither attractive nor ugly but unforgettable. Deep-set eyes, red freckles, and a chin the size of Chicago. We spent a semester together in class last year. We never spoke, but that doesn't matter. I'm unforgettable in my own way.

Mercifully, my song ends before Vic spots me and I start to rush offstage, leaving behind a good-sized pile of ones.

Here's the thing. I'm not proud of stripping, but that's not even the issue. The issue is that it goes against everything Cadence stands for. The issue is she stood by me, and as painful as it would be to hear people talk about the stripper whore who "falsely" accused Kareem Hanley of attempted sexual assault, to risk losing Cadence—or worse, humiliating her—would finish me.

I scramble down the stairs and I'm reminded of one of the two reasons you never see dancers run. First, running just isn't sexy. More relevant here, we wear insane heels that make walking damn near impossible. Before I know it, I'm on my ass.

Jewel rushes over to me. "Oh shit, you okay, Fantine?"

I manage to nod but all of my focus is on the three guys. I make myself look. Scarlett's with them, laughing her ass off. The guys seem uninterested. Vic looks my way, but I don't see the faintest hint of recognition in his face. Maybe I'm not as unforgettable as I thought.

"I'm all right," I say as Jewel helps me to my feet. The relief washes away any embarrassment, and when I see Scarlett lead the guys to the private VIP area I decide to finish my shift. It feels like tempting fate. But what choice do I have? I've got bills to pay.

CHAPTER THREE

"**GIVE IT TO ME,**" I scream, my voice echoing against the brick buildings that line Night Shade's parking lot.

Vic had recognized me. Not at first, but the pieces clicked at some point and he came over, drunk and friendly, to invite me to a party. I tried to play it off at first like he was confused. "No, my name's Fantine. What's a Haverford?" That sort of thing.

Then Vic's friend pulled out his cell and started playing a video. Of me dancing. Not even on stage, but off to the side. Naked and on the lap of a truck driver who probably has to pay for two seats when he flies. "I don't know, guys," Vic said, grabbing his friend's phone. "Looks a lot like that girl from school. Maybe I'll send it around. Ask for some second opinions."

I rushed over to one of the bouncers. But by then Vic was already heading out the door of the club. I chased after him and now here I am, trying to decide how hard I'm willing to fight to make sure that video never sees the light of day.

But I can't make a decision. I'm acting on autopilot, and I have no clue what I'm saying. Am I begging? Threatening? Are words even coming out of my mouth or just howls of anger? Only when I find myself planted on the ground, looking up at

Vic laughing, do I realize I must have lunged for him and he must have shoved me to the pavement.

On any other day I would've taken him down, but I realize I'm still in my heels. I kick them off, ready to jump back into the fight, when one of Vic's friends tries to pull him away. "Leave her alone, man. We don't need this shit."

Vic brushes him off and stands over me, handing the phone back to his friend. "Don't know what you're so afraid of. You got a sick body, Jay Bird. Kareem wasn't lying."

I pull myself to my feet, ready to have another go, but a car pulls up. It's Vic's other friend. "Yo, hop in, kid," he calls.

Vic gives me a last look, chuckles like I'm pathetic, and disappears into the Audi.

When I turn around, I notice a small crowd watching from just outside the front entrance. I rush over to Scarlett.

"What's their phone number? They said they gave it to you. What's their number?"

"Abe's going to have your ass," she says with a sneer. But she pulls a napkin out of her purse and drops it to the pavement. "Tell them I said thanks for the tips."

As the Uber brings me back to Bryn Mawr, I take a deep breath and send the text.

it's Justice… i've got money… just please don't send that video to anyone

Yeah, I need that money, but money can be replaced. A reputation can't.

I'm staring at the phone, waiting to see that Vic's read the text.

Minutes pass and it feels like hours.

He read it. He's typing. Then a reply.

I'm listening

I answer: *meet me at the Merion 9th hole in an hour*

At home I scramble through my things, pocket the seven grand stashed in my closet, and for a moment I consider bringing my pistol. I decide against it. It's not that I trust Vic. It's that I don't trust myself.

I call a Lyft this time and have it drop me off on the opposite side of campus. I decide to walk down Ardmore Avenue rather than cut through the school. Something about it seems safer and more anonymous. And something about staying anonymous seems important.

I pause as I reach the green. I can smell fresh pot smoke and see some trash littered on the edge of the course, just along the trees. I listen for voices, but whoever was here must've just left. Hanging out on the 9th in the middle of the night is sort of a thing at Haverford.

I check my phone for texts, thinking maybe Vic showed up early and bounced when I wasn't here. But just as my phone screen jumps to life and the light ruins my night vision, I hear faint voices behind me.

"Jay Bird!" It's Vic. He stops a few yards from me, his two friends from the club behind him. His voice is friendly, but the words are slurred. "Hey, sorry about what happened back there. I was just playing. You know I was just playing? Back there? At the club? I wasn't going to release that video. I told these guys. Guys, I told you, right? I wasn't going to send it to anyone."

He's not swaying, but he might as well be. He's hit that spot where you're so blasted that by the end of your sentence you forget the start of your sentence.

"It's fine," I say. "Can you show me?"

"What's that?"

21

"Just show me the phone so I know it's gone."

The taller of the two friends steps forward. "The man said he won't be showing the video to anyone. So we good."

"You know what? Fine." I shove past them, my cheeks burning with rage. The rage isn't directed at Vic, I realize, but at myself. Maybe it's because I'm giving in too easily. Or maybe it's because I've made myself vulnerable. Not just by coming here. But by letting myself be filmed. By putting myself in a position where I have to hide, not just from Pop, but from my closest friends.

I can hear the music from Night Shade in my head, hear the crowd laughing, and it's as if I'm reliving every moment of the last four years all at once. Only then I realize the sounds aren't in my head but are coming from a cell phone and from the three guys standing around laughing at a video of me dancing naked.

I charge at Vic and grab his shirt. I can feel his friends try to pull me away as I scream, "I said I'd fucking pay you! I've got seven thousand!"

"Seven grand?" He pulls out a wad of cash. "Man, I use seven grand just to keep my ten grand warm."

"Give me the fucking phone, Vic!"

He's still laughing, the way people laugh at a Chihuahua that thinks it's a Doberman. Fine by me. I like being underestimated. I leap forward, trying to drive my knee into Vic's solar plexus, but he's too tall and I end up connecting somewhere around his navel. He stumbles back, dropping his friend's phone. I start for it, then feel strong hands pull at my shoulders and drag me backward to the ground.

"Damn, Jay Bird," Vic says after recapturing his balance. "You got some fight in you." He starts patting his pockets like he's forgotten something. "Shit, guys, she made me lose my phone."

"Man, Vic, we had this conversation in the car," says a voice from behind me. "That's *my* phone. You forgot your shit back at your place. Remember?"

"He wasted," another voice adds.

Before the guys behind me can react, I spring to my feet and lunge to where I saw the phone fall. I feel the cool glass of a screen against my fingers and I pull the phone to my chest as I crash to the ground. Then come the sound of footsteps and I spin onto my back just in time to see Vic coming at me. I send the heel of my right foot toward his crotch. He jumps back fast enough that I miss him but he's so drunk he loses his balance and two hundred pounds of man falls on top of me.

"Fucking bitch," he says, shoving his hand around my neck. He looks down at me and his eyes are terrifying. Even in the dark I can see them—hateful and glassy and blank. Only it's as if they aren't seeing me but some vision or memory of their own.

My instinct is to grab at his wrists, but even drunk he's strong enough I'm worried he'll crush my windpipe long before I can tear them away. My free hand gropes blindly for something—a stick or a goddamn pinecone. All I feel is air and grass and a few crumpled bags left behind by the group that was here before us.

I hear so much yelling but I don't know where it's coming from or what anyone's saying. My mind is starting to fade and I've done enough Jiu Jitsu to know I'll be blacking out soon.

I keep clawing at the ground when I feel the sharp edges of a broken bottle, still wet with the remnants of what I assume is beer.

I point it at Vic's face, hoping to drive him back. He releases one of his hands, enough that I can feel some blood rush back to my head, and tries to swat the bottle away. Only he misses the bottle and loses his balance.

For a moment the world goes black and I think I've passed out. Only I'm still aware. I'm aware of weight and motion and a second later I see Vic scramble off of me.

It's over. We sit and look at each other, his eyes wide, and I think maybe he's about to apologize or congratulate me on my moxie.

But that's not what happens. What happens is I see him holding his neck and a dark liquid jet out from between his fingers. We stare at each other, neither of us able to process the moment but connected in some eternal way, as if he knows I will be his last memory, and I know this moment will be forever etched in my own mind.

One of the friends rushes over and asks Vic if he's okay, but Vic just keeps looking at me. The friend looks at his own hand, now covered in thick blood. "Oh shit. Oh shit! Warren, we got to get help."

"Yo, our scholarship. We can't be here. We got to call the man."

The friend looks at Vic, and for a moment I think he's going to lift him into his arms. Instead, he turns to me. "You okay?"

Startled, I look up at him and nod.

I can see it in his eyes. He's scared. As scared as Vic and me, and I think about this thing one of my professors once told us about some ancient economist who said most people would be more bothered by losing their little finger than the death of a million strangers in a foreign land.

The thought is erased by the sight of Vic slumping over, unmoving. Vic's friend—his *friend*—looks at me one last time. "I'm sorry," he says and rushes off.

I sit there in the damp, cold grass, trying to sob, only sounds won't come out.

Then I catch myself. This isn't over yet. If I stay here? If they find me? My picture will be on the news.

What if Pop sees it?

Then it won't matter what the law does to me because I won't be around long enough to find out.

I tuck the cell phone into my back pocket and crawl over to Vic. I know immediately that he's dead. I root through his jacket and his pants searching for his phone—the one with my text message telling him to meet me on the golf course. But it's like they said. He didn't bring it.

I reach into his back pocket and find his wallet. I make a note of the street address and then start running in the direction of my house.

CHAPTER FOUR

I SPENT THE NIGHT PACING around my room, trying to figure out my next move. Now here I am, standing on a doorstep in Ardmore, my toes curled tightly inside my Adidas, half wishing the door won't open. That'll mean Vic lives here alone, or in any case that I can make it in and out unseen. My stomach sinks as I hear footsteps from somewhere inside, but quickly panic gives way to conviction.

I have to find the phone.

The door swings open. A middle-aged man with worn skin and kind eyes is holding a phone to his ear, though not the one I'm looking for. Clearly Vic's dad. After a pause, he says, "Hey, I'm going to have to call you back. I do appreciate it, though."

He studies me a bit more than I'm comfortable with. "Can I help you, miss?" he says, a hint of Louisiana in his voice. He sounds weary but otherwise stoic, as if he still hasn't processed the news. But he's heard it.

My first thought is to say I'm a reporter for *The Clerk,* Haverford's student paper, and that I'm sorry for his loss, and I would really appreciate the opportunity to talk to him about his son. But looking into his eyes, I just can't bring myself to lie.

"You know my boy?"

I keep standing there, silently and stupidly. Finally, I just nod.

He glances past me and waves me in. "Come on, sweetie, come on."

The outside of the house looked like a neglected concrete box with green moss running up the sides and torn screens covering stained windows. Inside, the walls are pristine white and the floors are polished cherry oak. It's like Baltimore swallowed Beverly Hills, which isn't uncommon in this part of Pennsylvania. The Main Line region running northwest out of Philly is so expensive that I've met people pulling down six figures who you'd swear from the outside of their homes pay for groceries with an EBT card.

We head down the hall to the kitchen, the harsh notes of dark roast wafting through the air.

"I figured some of his friends'd show up," he says. He shuffles to the other side of an island where half a pot of coffee sits next to a 76ers mug. He tops off his drink and asks if I want a cup. I decline, but he continues fishing a second mug out of a cabinet.

The kitchen is small but smartly remodeled. Stainless steel appliances. Granite countertops. It has a cold feel, as if it were one of those show homes. The only personal touches are a framed picture of Christ on the wall and a fridge covered with photos of what appear to be high school basketball players.

"I'm Ron Michaels," he says, handing me the coffee, "but most people, they call me Coach."

"Justice," I say, happy he can stop calling me sweetie.

"Tell me about yourself, sweetie. How do you know Vic?"

"We had some classes together last year," I say.

"Never seen you around here. You live on campus?"

"I'm renting a place in Bryn Mawr. One of the duplexes

in Garrett Hill." Most people hear Bryn Mawr and they think of the multi-million-dollar homes tucked away in the woods. Garrett Hill is sort of like Versace for H&M—the low end of the high end.

"You grow up here?"

"More or less." Definitely not something I want to discuss.

"Vic and I, we came up from Louisiana. Plaquemines Parish, if you know the place. Most of it's under water, now. Funny, isn't it? When you're young, everything seems so permanent. Like it will be there forever and never change. Then time passes and you realize everything changes. Nothing's permanent. Not even the ground you walk on." He catches himself staring off into space and sends me a forced smile, seemingly more from reflex than from genuine emotion. "Got any roommates?"

"One," I say.

"That's good. That's good. You shouldn't be alone. Not after something like this." We stand there together, sharing silence. "Well, you'll forgive me, I've got to take care of some things. But you can go on and make yourself at home right here. I won't be long."

"Of course. I don't want to get in the way."

Ron Michaels plods down a hallway and I hear a door open and shut. I let a few moments pass and finish off the coffee. I'm not thirsty, but it gives me an excuse to put things off for just a few moments longer. When I'm out of excuses to delay, I slip out of the kitchen and into the living room, where a staircase leads to the home's second level. Every step jacks up my heart rate, and I start to worry my legs will buckle. Two thoughts battle in my mind. *I can't. I have to.*

At the top of the stairs I turn down a long hallway. I open

the first door I see. Clearly the master bedroom. Not what I'm looking for.

I reach a second door at the end of the hall, which creaks as I open it. I freeze at the threshold, listening for any hint of sound from downstairs. When I'm convinced no one heard me, I walk into a room that's lined with basketball posters and smells of boy. Vic's room.

I sense immediately the phone isn't here—or, if it is, it's hidden in the IKEA dresser to my left, or in the unmade bed to my right, or under the piles of clothes that cover the floor.

I look over the room again, more slowly this time. Something inside me collapses, and it takes a moment to realize why. Under the bed is one of those briefcase-sized fireproof safes. Fantastic.

I start by rifling through the drawer of Vic's nightstand. It's filled with random cables and magazines and empty packs of chewing gum. I close the drawer, ready to move on, then second-guess myself. *Be quick but don't rush.* I open the nightstand again and give it a more thorough look. Still nothing.

I drop to my knees beside the bed, breathing in dust and body odor. Seconds pass as I run my hands over piles of shorts and t-shirts and boxer briefs, then tug at the safe. It's locked and, no, Vic was not so considerate as to leave the key under it. I crawl toward the dresser, patting hoodies and jeans and more underwear. Then my hand brushes against something solid and bulky.

I claw at the clothes pile, stuffing my hands inside the pockets of a pair of Diesel jeans.

A key chain with a single key.

I lunge toward the safe. My hands shake so violently it takes a few tries, but the key slides in.

I open it, half expecting to find a note saying "Smile, you're on *Candid Camera*." But, no. The safe is empty except for a picture of a girl, maybe sixteen or seventeen, with blonde hair pulled back in a high pony, laughing as an insanely adorable Manx kitten tries to squirm out of her hands. I'm staring at the photo longer than I should be when I hear footsteps on the stairs. I slide the safe back under the bed, forgetting to remove the key. Oh well.

I had counted eighteen stairs. He's on number three. That gives me about twenty seconds if I'm lucky. And let's face it. If I was lucky, I wouldn't be here.

I jump to my feet and dash to the dresser. There are too many drawers to search. I try the top left drawer, pulling slowly in case it squeaks. The good news is it's silent. The bad news is there's nothing inside but jeans, and Ron Michaels is now coming down the hall.

Last shot. I open the top right drawer.

It's there.

Sitting on top of a pile of t-shirts is a TracFone, one of those prepaid cell phones broke college students use. I pocket it and slide the drawer shut just as Ron Michaels walks into the room.

"You shouldn't be here." His voice is stern, but there's no real anger in it.

"I'm sorry. I just wanted to take a look. You know, to feel close to him." The lie makes me sick to my stomach.

"The cops say I'm not supposed to touch anything. They're going to be by here to take a look this morning."

"I should leave."

Before I can make a move, Ron Michaels says: "You religious, Justice?"

The question seems sinister, though I can't be sure if that's just my bias slipping through. I step back and look for any sign of tension in his body. But he's standing there on his heels, still lost in some world I can't imagine.

"No," I say, relaxing a bit.

"Oh, that's too bad. You can't go through life not believing in something. I guess some people, they have the wrong idea about religion. They imagine it's about showing up to church each Sunday and saying ten Hail Marys. I think you'd be surprised, if you gave it a chance."

"I have," I say. "I just can't find much comfort in a book that says men should have authority over women or that, hey, you know that quirky girl next door? She's a witch, go kill her."

I instantly regret my rant, but he just nods. "I'm willing to bet no one is going to try burning you at the stake. Look, sweetie, you can find pretty much anything in that book if you go looking for it. That don't mean that's what it's about."

I don't know what to say, so I turn back to the dresser, inspecting a framed photo I had noticed when I was scanning the room. It's four boys in basketball uniforms. Vic is second from the left, his arms around the two black guys I recognize from the club. They're all giving that "I'm too cool to smile" look.

"Vic was good," Ron says as he moves up behind me, close enough I can smell the Old Spice. "I coached him myself when he was at Lower Merion. Helped us win a state championship. Villanova was even scouting him his senior year."

"I didn't know that. What happened?" I wince, the question sounding way harsher than I intended. But let's get real. Villanova is probably the best basketball college in the country. And Haverford? We're Division III, and as far as I know, Vic wasn't even on the team.

"I guess he didn't like talking about it. He was in an accident. On prom night, if you'd believe it. Should've killed him. We can thank the Lord it didn't, but it ended his basketball career. That's for sure."

"I see."

"You know, when Terrance and Warren made it to Villanova, I was worried. I figured that might tear the boys apart. That Vic would get jealous. He never did, though. If those boys ever fought, I never saw it. What's that saying from *The Three Musketeers?* All for one and one for all? That was them." There's life in his voice for the first time since I arrived.

"What about him?" I say, pointing to the boy on the far right, who could almost pass for Vic's brother except for the red hair.

"Him? No one that mattered. Not one of my stars. My God, I can't believe they're gone."

I spin around to face him.

"What do you mean?" I can barely get the words out.

Ron Michaels looks at me uncomprehendingly. "What do you mean, what do I mean?"

"You said *they're* gone."

"Heavens, girl, didn't you know? It wasn't just Vic. Terrance, Warren… all three of the boys were killed last night."

CHAPTER FIVE

I WALK SOUTH ALONG CHURCH ROAD, my coat pulled tight around my body, wind scraping down my neck. The sky is a swirling mixture of whites and grays, and the air smells like snow. My body's numb, and the only thing I'm aware of is distance. The distance between Ron Michaels' house and my own. The distance between my childhood home and Pennsylvania. The distance between me and every passerby, which feels like infinity packed into inches.

For a moment I forget where I came from and where I'm going, until I remember Vic's phone tucked in my back pocket. I consider chucking it into the sewer or smashing it on the pavement, but Pop taught me better than that. There's a word for hastily disposed-of evidence—*evidence*. I pocket the phone and keep walking.

Soon my mind is twisting and wrestling with questions I don't know how to answer and images I don't want to see. I try to focus on the motion of my feet and the sound of my heels against the pavement.

Then I realize my feet have stopped moving and I'm standing on Lancaster Avenue, outside the Lower Merion Police

Department. Just a few more steps and I'm inside and I tell them everything.

Like what? Like how I killed a guy—but, pinky promise, I had nothing to do with the two other dead guys? Oh, and by the way, I just stole evidence from one of their houses?

I'm tempted to do it. But after what the cops did to me in Michigan? And even if I go to Cadence's dad, the one cop I do trust, there's the media. What if I turn myself in and the story makes the news? Somehow, Pop will see it. Somehow, even though he's hundreds of miles away, he will see it and *he will find me.*

After what seems like hours, but which turns out to have been only forty minutes, I reach Bryn Mawr. Less than three percent of students at Haverford live off campus. Heck, I think most of the professors live on campus. Anyway, I'm in the three percent. I have been since my freshman year. Technically, all freshmen are required to live on campus and, technically, I had a dorm room. But no way was I going to subject myself to full-time supervision. Besides, I already had a place to live.

I arrived in town a year before I started at Haverford. I had a single suitcase and was down to my last forty bucks, which would have been fine except I knew exactly no one in the area. I remember sitting in Rosie's Coffee down by Villanova and posting a Craig's List ad that said something like: "New arrival needs place to stay starting tonight. Can't pay yet. Will pay someday."

I got two responses. One guy wrote that he had a detached room with its own kitchen, and he didn't need me to pay until I got on my feet. Andy's email came a few seconds later. She had a small attic space I'd have to clean out, and I'd have to come up with rent by the end of the week.

I've lived with Andy ever since.

Our duplex opens into a small foyer leading to the living room. Andy's there on the couch with two bearded guys sporting black hoodies. As I walk in, Andy looks up, sort of startled and says in a lifeless voice, "Oh, hi, Justice."

Andy's everything I'm not: tall, blonde, voluptuous, rich. Her dad runs a wealth management firm out of Conshohocken and sends her five grand a month, even though Andy tells him she works. I guess he's worried she'll have to wear the same designer jeans twice in one month.

Andy doesn't introduce the guys but instead leans down to the coffee table and snorts God knows what up her nose. "Jesus Christ, Andy," I say, hanging up my coat. I walk over to the three of them. Two blue lines of powder are left on the table.

"It's just Adderall," Andy says. Her pug, Winston, jumps up on the couch and buries his head in her lap.

"Hey, Cheech and Chong," I say. "Time to go."

Cheech stands up in front of me, his six-plus feet towering over my five-foot-nothing frame. "She cool?" he asks Andy.

"Oh my God. She is so not cool. She's won't say anything, though. Right, Justice?"

Before I can answer, Cheech tries to poke my chest with his finger: "Better not—"

Big mistake. I twist his arm counter-clockwise, spinning him around, then trap his leg with mine, and send my full weight into his waist. He slams into the floor nose first, and I'm instantly mounted on his back, yanking his arm as hard as I can toward the opposite shoulder blade. I lean down and put my lips next to his ear as spit flies from his mouth onto the hardwood floor. "You picked the wrong day."

I get to my feet and head for the stairs. I stop there and turn back to them. Chong begins helping Cheech up while Andy just stares at me, dumbfounded.

"I want them out by the time I'm finished," I say.

I enter my room, lock the door behind me, and sit on the floor beside my bed. The bed is my one real indulgence—one of those high-end mattresses by a company called Purple. Maybe I should make that my motto: live hard, sleep soft.

As I stretch out my arms, my fingers brush the strap of my duffel bag. I think of the sealed Ziplock hidden inside and the bloody clothes that still need to be disposed of. I'll torch them along with the cell phones, but I haven't figured out where to do that without drawing attention.

But one thought keeps coming back to me. The voice of a girl telling me to run.

Before I know what's happening, I'm on the floor, sobbing. A torrent of thoughts and emotions that must've been muted by adrenaline come rushing in, and I'm overwhelmed by terror and guilt and the look on Vic's face as he tries to stop the blood gushing from his neck. And not just that, either. I think of Michigan and the Heiden and the sisters I left behind. All of it comes pouring out in salty tears and snot and self-hatred.

By the time I calm down, I realize I have to make a decision. For five years, I've made safety my god. My only goal was to hide and to survive. But all the while, I was building a life for myself—a real life, with passions and flaws and friends and a vision of the future that belongs to me, not to Pop. A life I love.

Can I throw that all away just so I can have more days on the Earth? Would those days mean anything to me? Leaving the Main Line, leaving Haverford, leaving Cadence—how is abandoning everything I've built any different from having Pop track me down and take me back to Michigan against my will?

So I'll stay. For now. I'll stay so long as there's any hope of salvaging the life of Justice Winters.

But the first sign of trouble and Justice Winters will have to die.

I fish the duffel bag from under my bed. I throw in Vic's phone, two days of clothes, and five days of underwear. The two stacks of cash totaling somewhere in the neighborhood of seven grand are already in there.

If I do have to run, I'm going to need more money.

I head to the closet. Down on my knees, I carefully pull up the carpet. I feel around until I find the edge of the hardwood and pull up the false floor I crafted when I moved in. I grab my pistol, a SIG P365 compact I barely know how to use, along with a concealed carry corset and place them into the duffel bag. Then I throw in a manila envelope I haven't opened since I left Michigan.

I replace the false floor, zip up the bag, and shove it back under my bed.

Then I get a text.

CHAPTER SIX

THE TEXT IS FROM MY Abnormal Psych professor. The school is canceling classes for the day, but he's going to have an optional class for students who want to talk about the murders.

If I'm going to get through this, I'm going to have to ignore my instincts and go on with my day the way I normally would. Or, I guess, the way any normal student would on a really, really abnormal day. Although sitting in a classroom is the last thing I want to do, it's the most normal thing for me to do.

I reach Haverford, a tiny blip in the two hundred square miles that make up the Main Line. I guess when the railroads became a thing, rich people realized Philly was a dirty-ass city and moved their families out this way. Technically, the Main Line stretches out from Merion to Malvern; but my life has mostly been confined to the three-mile stretch of Lancaster Avenue that somehow contains five freaking colleges—Villanova, Rosemont, Bryn Mawr, Harcum, and Haverford.

Everyone knows Villanova. You can't avoid it. Its buildings loom over Lancaster, along with this bizarre graveyard in front of the admissions office, I guess for people who take "school spirit" literally. Haverford, though, is a different animal. You can drive by our campus every day and not notice it. Tucked away down a long road that runs past Duck Pond, the campus consists mostly of a central hub of stone buildings surrounded by a two-mile nature trail.

I amble through campus trying not to make eye contact with anyone before finally reaching Sharpless Hall. As I enter my classroom, Dr. Harper is seated facing us on a tall stool.

He's always been something of an enigma. This is a pretty liberal campus, but Dr. Harper is a popular teacher despite rumors he's a closet conservative. He leans forward, elbows on his knees, hands pressed together as if he's praying. His chin rests on the tips of his fingers and his eyes meet mine before moving on to the next student who arrives. I grab my usual seat in the back of the room, folding my coat over the backrest.

The class is generally about thirty strong, but only a dozen or so of us are here. The room is silent and tense, and I stare straight ahead thinking maybe we'll just sit here like this for an hour, sharing our terror. I wonder for a moment if the other students are looking at me, if they can see through me.

I hear familiar voices behind me, and when I look, I see Cadence and Izaak stopped at the entrance whispering to each other. After a moment, Izaak nods solemnly, then takes his customary seat a few rows in front of me. Cadence sits next to me. We glance at each other and both turn away without a word. I'm so caught in my head I know not to trust my feelings. But my feelings are telling me that something has changed. There's a distance between us and I have no idea why.

Finally, Dr. Harper sits back, loosens his tie, and lets out a deep breath. "Well," he says, and lets the word linger. His voice sounds tired and thoughtful and it almost seems like he's going to cry. But he goes on. "I've thought a lot about what I wanted to say. And I guess one thing that's worth doing is just starting with some basic facts because we don't know much and a lot of rumors are going around. But this is from this morning's press conference. Okay?"

I wrap my coat around my shoulders and consider walking out now. It won't be a big deal. People will just think I'm overcome with grief, if they even notice. But I can't make my body move. At first I think it's fear. Then I realize it's curiosity.

Dr. Harper starts reading from a steno pad, dryly and impersonally. "The bodies of three young men were found this morning on the property of the Merion Golf Club. Warren Armstrong, twenty-one, was a student at Villanova. Terrance Down, twenty-one, was a student at Villanova. Vic Michaels, twenty-one, was a student at Haverford. Armstrong and Down were both African American, and police are working with the FBI to determine whether this may have been a hate crime. Right now they are looking into several persons of interest but have no suspects."

"I'm sorry, but this is bullshit," Cadence yells out. "*May have been a hate crime.* They lynched them. Hanged them from a tree. What else could it be? The black guys killed the white boy and committed suicide?"

A lynching? *What the hell happened out there?*

Another girl says, "Actually, I heard they wrote the n-word on a tree."

"It wasn't a tree," Cadence says. "They carved it right into Vic's chest. 'Death to niggers and nigger lovers.'" Her words take the air out of the room.

I try to catch her attention, but her eyes are fixed on Dr. Harper, who listens intently but reacts to none of it.

"Is anyone actually surprised this happened?" says Cody, a junior who always sits in the front row and takes notes like he's keeping a court transcript. He doesn't have his laptop out today. Instead, he's reading something off his cell. "Haverford is sixty percent white, seven percent African American, eight percent Latinx. So, like, how are you going to have a system of institutionalized racism and not have it lead to violence?"

"Look," says Cadence, "we all know who did this. Every minute we wait to arrest them, we're just asking for this to happen again."

"Who did it?" I say, the words barely escaping my parched mouth.

She looks at me like I'm new. "The Exiles."

The Exiles are a group of anonymous trolls who post online about how colleges like Haverford are social justice enclaves and there need to be safe spaces for straight white males. Annoying. Disgusting. But before now they've never done anything in the real world, at least not publicly. Hell, no one even paid attention to them until Izaak started writing about them last year.

The class erupts into half a dozen different conversations, and you can feel the fear turning to anger, and now I understand how mobs form.

Then Dr. Harper stands, and it's like a volume knob just got turned down.

"Cody," Dr. Harper says, "what's the white population of Pennsylvania?"

"I don't know."

"It's something like eighty percent. So white students are arguably underrepresented on campus. And what about the faculty? We're rated 'highly diverse.' I don't remember the exact numbers, but people of color are overrepresented on our faculty compared with the general population."

"So, you're saying there's no racism here?"

"That's not what I'm saying. I'm saying these things are complicated and we should approach them thoughtfully. Facts matter."

A girl seated next to Cody says, "I just don't see why we're talking about statistics when three people died. We feel unsafe, and no one is doing anything about it."

"What do you think should be done that isn't being done?" Dr. Harper says.

"I don't know. But at least we could start with people being honest about what happened last night, instead of pretending it's some big mystery."

Harper shakes his head like he's trying to hold something back. Finally he says, "You don't get it, folks. These murders are not what you think."

Shock swallows the room. The class starts trading glances. I see Izaak turn around and think for a moment he's looking at me. Then I realize, he's watching Cadence. After what feels like minutes, Cadence breaks the silence.

"Oh, hell no. You just said this isn't about race."

"No, he didn't," says Cody. "He's saying it's more complex. Right, Dr. Harper?"

"Actually, Cadence has it right." Dr. Harper's voice sounds defeated, like he's been compelled to admit something he would have preferred to keep private. "I think when the truth comes out, we're going to find out that this has nothing to do with race."

The class erupts, and I can't make out particular words, just sounds of disbelief and rage. Then I hear the door burst open.

I jump but then see that no one is entering the class. Students are exiting. One by one they file out, some in red-faced anger, others following tentatively, as if they think they're supposed to.

Cadence waits for the room to empty, icy eyes aimed at Dr. Harper the entire time. Then she stands, grabs her coat, and looks at me. But I can't leave. Not without knowing more.

"You coming?" she says, and it doesn't feel like a question. It feels like a test.

"I'm sorry," I whisper.

"Mmm." She says it like I've confirmed something for her and she flounces out of the room. What have I just done?

When we're alone, I ask, "Why did you say that?"

Dr. Harper stands slowly, his tall frame moving gracefully toward me, but with a clear sense of purpose. He sits where Cadence had been and removes his glasses, concentrating on my face.

Dr. Harper has been my advisor for a while, and though he has never been anything but kind, professional, and helpful, the same thought runs through my head that has run through my head every time we've been alone. He's a loaded gun.

"Why don't you think the killings were about race?" I say.

His lips soften and there's something deeply warm about the way he looks at me—and something deeply penetrating. I shift uneasily in my seat.

"I could be wrong, you know," he says.

"That's not an answer."

He seems to be considering something, then nods. "How are *you*, Justice?"

"Me?"

"You."

"I don't want to talk about me."

"I do. Why are you here?"

"I told you. I want to know why you said what you said about the murders."

"That's not what I mean. I mean, why are you in college? What is it you're after?"

He's being evasive. Then again, so am I.

"If I tell you, will you answer my question?"

"I'll answer any question you have."

He damn well better.

"Okay, then the truth is, I'm after nothing."

"Nothing."

"Anonymity. Safety. Peace and quiet. You know, nothing. I just want to be left alone."

"You don't need a degree for that."

"*I* do."

I mean to be enigmatic, but he nods like I just read him my bio. "You know why most students major in psychology, don't you?"

"To fix their own crazy."

"But for you it's self-protection." I don't react, which is as good as a confession. "You've never said much about how you grew up."

Silence.

"No?" He twirls his glasses in his fingers. "You said you're after safety and anonymity. But you just defied a dozen other students who marched out of this classroom in protest. I expect they noticed."

"Yeah, well, it's not like my reputation can get any worse."

"Oh. Right. Nevertheless, you stayed. That tells me it might not be anonymity you're seeking, after all. There's something more important to you."

"I still don't know why we're talking about me."

He crosses his arms. "I like puzzles."

"Well, I don't. I answered your questions. Answer mine."

He replaces his glasses and takes in a deep breath. "Fair enough. Did your parents ever tell you why they named you Justice?"

I swallow hard but keep my voice even. "No."

"Well, the story we tell ourselves is that justice is blind to prejudice and passion. But sometimes it's blind to facts. Then it becomes vengeance. I fear that's where we're headed. These killings? Everyone is talking about them and demanding blood. But no one is really looking at them. What would you see if you looked—I mean, really *looked?*"

I don't trust myself to thread this needle. "I don't know. What would I see?"

"Everyone is blaming the Exiles. And, my God, it's not like they haven't asked for it with the filth they've posted online. But that's just it, isn't it? Whoever committed this crime clearly wanted to get away with it. Ideologues don't do that. They go down with the ship."

"Usually. Not always."

"No, not always. But it's a clue. Now, add to that this idea that they wrote something bigoted at the scene. That's too much. Too in-your-face. The killers lynched two African Americans. Did they honestly think we wouldn't get the message?"

"So that's it? This isn't about race because it looks so racist?"

"Yes. Not by itself. But look at the whole picture. It just doesn't fit. Two kids stabbed and lynched. And the other?

According to the news, his neck was torn to shreds by a broken bottle. Just wait. If I were a betting man, and I am, I would bet those kids are found without their wallets, their cell phones, jewelry."

"Robbery?"

"Maybe. Maybe something else. But the truth will come out, and when it does, it will not be what people expect."

Well, that much is true.

I've been fooling myself. If a humanities professor can see through the crime this easily, how long until the police—or, worse, the media—come for me?

It's not that I want to throw away the life Justice Winters built. It's that I already have. If I stay, I lose. If I leave, I lose. But at least if I leave, I'll have the chance to try again. And maybe, possibly, someday I'll find a way to reconnect with Cadence.

But I can't worry about that now. All that's left to do is get my hands on some more cash and then get the hell off the Main Line.

CHAPTER SEVEN

"YO, FANTINE." BOBBY'S WATCHING the back entrance of Night Shade tonight and gives me a fist bump. "Abe's looking for you."

I swallow hard. "He still here?"

"I don't know. Was earlier. I hear you stirred up some shit last night."

How would a girl who wasn't worried about being hunted down by the police respond? "Wasn't the first time. Won't be the last."

"Okay, girl. Go make that money."

When I enter the dressing room, five girls are scurrying around in various stages of undress, fixing their hair, caking on eye makeup, and dousing themselves in cheap perfume. We always use cheap perfume because if we didn't, half our GDP would end up in the pockets of Gucci and Chanel.

Scarlett is the one person I was hoping not to see tonight. But there she is, staring into the wall-length Hollywood mirror and fixing her lip gloss. Part of me wants to ignore her. What she has to say doesn't matter to me anymore. But I can't help myself.

"You have a minute?" I hop up on the counter beside her.

"They're calling me up soon," she says coldly.

"The three guys you were with last night."

"Wasn't me."

"I'm not the cops."

She gives me a crooked smile. "Wasn't me."

"Scarlett. They were with you all night. I just need to know. Did they say anything to you? Anything they were involved in?"

"Theoretically?"

"I think you mean hypothetically." Goddamnit, Justice.

"*Hypothetically*, I didn't take notes."

"I'll tell you what. You don't have to talk to me, but I'm pretty sure Abe wants the details."

"Whatever. It was just typical college guy talk."

"Details," I say.

"Hell, I don't remember. 'Nice this.' 'Can I touch that?' 'Do you have a boyfriend?' Like I said, typical. They were spending way more than most college guys, though. They kept bragging about playing in the NBA someday, which was cute. I didn't have the heart to tell them we get real ballplayers in here every week."

"Anything else?"

I hear the DJ call Scarlett to the stage, and she starts walking out. "Gotta go."

I block her path.

"Jesus Christ, Fantine."

"What did they say?"

Scarlett shakes her head like she's resigned herself to humoring me. "They kept trying to get me to go to some party out in Phoenixville. That's how I got their number. Kept saying I'd want to meet their friend—Spike or Pike or something—but I was like, thanks but no. Then the white boy recognized you and said he was going to try to get you to go."

"That's it?"

"Pretty much." She's trying to push her way past me, and I can hear the DJ call her name again, which is definitely not something you want to have happen. "Now move your tiny ass or this is going to get messy."

"Why would they think you wanted to meet their friend?" I say. But she's past me now and doesn't hear or doesn't want to answer.

I peek down the hall that leads to Abe's office, but I'm afraid to go back. Instead, I undress and slip into a red strapless chemise. They call it a chemise, but it's specially made for dancers and has lots of slits along the sides and back to show off maximum skin. Honestly, it's a horror show, but it does the job.

I'm about to start putting on makeup when Jewel whispers into my ear, "Abe knows you're here. Better go see him."

Here we go. I toss my things onto the counter and walk as slowly as I can manage in the direction of Abe's office.

Abe Shariff is my favorite criminal and the only man I trust. When I first moved out here, he was the one who set me up with a new identity, and I'm pretty sure he cheats on his taxes. But that aside, he plays fair when it comes to our pay, and he never tries to sleep with the girls. I asked him once how he got into this racket. His story was that he used to run a car service downtown and would hear stories from dancers constantly getting ripped off. So he decided to start a joint that treated us with respect. If I heard it from anyone else, I'd call BS. But knowing Abe? It's the God's honest truth.

"Fanny, Fanny, Fanny," Abe says as I enter. I close his office door behind me and sit on the couch across from his desk. Abe's in his early sixties, with just the right amount of heft around the middle, and a mane of hair the color of rain clouds. "What's the matter? You look like shit. You need a masseuse? I know a guy. He'll take good care of you."

"Nothing six inches of makeup can't cure."

He waves his hand, then checks his cell, his thumbs tapping away as he continues. "It's fine, babe. It's fine. Truth is, he's a crap masseuse, anyway."

"Jewel said you wanted to talk to me."

"That's just like you. Always down to business. You know, in Japan they wouldn't tolerate that. They'd want to spend time together, get to know you." Abe has always thought of himself as a legitimate businessman, on the verge of running some billion-dollar multinational. Behind his desk there's a bookshelf with titles like *Good to Great*, *The 7 Habits of Highly Successful People*, and—my personal favorite—*The Innovator's Dilemma*. Seriously, Abe, what's your big innovation going to be? Give the customers binoculars?

"I'll keep that in mind," I say.

Abe pounds his desk, still looking at his phone. "Who's a guy gotta blow to get some gluten-free rugelach? Okay, okay. Listen, Fanny. I don't intrude upon your personal life, do I? When's the last time I showed up at Thanksgiving or Arbor Day and asked you to shake your ass for a twenty?"

"Not recently."

"Right? And so I tell myself, Fanny would never bring her personal business to work. But then, why do I hear that last night you get into a wrestling match in the parking lot of my club?"

"I'm sorry, Abe. It won't happen again."

"Won't happen again? Of course it won't happen again. The poor son of a bitch you're tussling with went and had his neck ripped open by a soda bottle." Abe pulls a newspaper out of a drawer and tosses it across the desk. I can't help but think he saw the story on TV and had someone run out and grab him a paper, just so he could do that.

"Would it help if I said he started it?"

"Fanny, I don't think you understand. The police were here. They were asking about those boys."

I feel my skin go flush. "What'd you say?"

"Turns out our cameras weren't working last night, and no one remembers anything. You know how it is. But one of the boys bought drinks on a credit card, so they must've been here. But other than that?" Abe shrugs.

"Thanks, Abe," I whisper.

"You going to work tonight?"

"I'm going to work."

"And tomorrow?"

I say nothing.

"You know, Fan... you don't have to run. Whatever it is, I've got friends, which means you've got friends. But if you do decide you need to go, you tell me, okay? I've got people up in New York who are real good with that sort of thing."

I consider it, but as much as I trust Abe, it still leaves a loose end. "I'll be fine."

"You need money?"

"I'll be fine."

"*Justice,*" he says, and I can see he said it deliberately, the way a father might say his daughter's name. "You don't have to do everything on your own."

I know if I try to speak I'm going to bawl, so I just shake my head and rush out of the office.

I more or less wander out onto the floor, feeling the opposite of talkative, let alone sexy. But I've never needed money more than I need it now.

"Hey, honey, you mind if I sit down?" I say to a Korean guy in his late fifties who's sitting at the bar and pretending to watch TV. One thing I don't understand is guys who come to strip clubs and pretend not to care about seeing naked girls. The usual line is, "I'm just here for a drink," which is like going to the movie theater for the popcorn.

But this guy doesn't make excuses. He sort of smiles and looks me over, his eyes stopping on my chest. "Don't take this the wrong way, but I was hoping to meet a girl who was, um…" he holds his hands out a foot from his chest, "healthier."

I smile the best smile I can muster. "Good luck."

I turn around in my barstool and motion to Brenda, Abe's wife and the house mom. She also doubles as bartender most weeknights. She's forty but looks thirty, with bleach-blonde hair that reaches to the small of her back.

"What'll it be?"

"Shirley Temple."

She returns a minute later with my drink and leans over the bar. "You sure pissed off Scarlett something good."

"She'll get over it."

"Yeah, well you better watch yourself with that one. You remember Jade?"

"Which Jade?"

"The black girl. From Allentown."

I nod.

"You know why she left, don't you? Scarlett caught her talking to one of her regulars. The next day, Jade storms in and says someone sent her parents photos of her dancing."

"And Abe didn't fire Scarlett over that?"

"Oh, don't believe he didn't lay into her. But she denied it, and you know Abe. He's all about second chances."

"I'll be okay."

"All I'm saying is be careful. Some types'll stab you in the back. Others won't wait for you to turn around."

I finish my Shirley Temple and get back to work.

I end up making nine hundred dollars before my shift is over—seven hundred after I pay out my tips and house fees. Way less than I want but enough that I can make it down to Miami, find a place to live, and put a down payment on a new identity.

But as three a.m. nears and I stumble into my house, my heart drops to my stomach and I realize none of that matters. Someone was here.

Drawers are open, and the floors are littered with clothes and silverware and celebrity magazines. Our couch is turned on its side, and the TV stand is at a ninety-degree angle. I call for Andy, but as far as I can tell she's still out clubbing.

I race to my room. The lock has been torn out, probably with a crowbar, but otherwise nothing has been moved. Nothing is out of place. Which means they instantly found what they were looking for.

There's nothing under my bed, which is bad, because when I left the house there was definitely something under my bed. My duffel bag with my gun and my money and my bloodstained clothes and two incriminating cell phones and an envelope that matters to me more than anything on this Earth.

My mind races through the possibilities. But before I can put the pieces together I hear a noise coming from downstairs and I realize—someone is here.

CHAPTER EIGHT

I'M HALFWAY OUT THE WINDOW when I hear a familiar voice calling my name from downstairs. It's Izaak.

"Yo, Justice! Hey, whoever the hell is in here, I'm calling the police."

Can't have that. I race down and find Izaak in the mudroom, the front door wide open, his cell phone in his hand. I smack it to the floor before he can react.

"J, what the fuck?"

"What are you doing here?"

"You okay?" he says. "Your door was open. What happened in here?"

"I was looking for something. Why are *you* here?"

"I tried calling."

"I was at work."

He bends down to retrieve his phone, moving slower than he needs to, and I get the impression he's stalling. When I see his lips start to move and then hesitate, I know he's stalling.

"What is it?" I say, my mind all cobwebs.

"It's Cadence. She… we need to get to the hospital."

The ride to Bryn Mawr hospital is short but tense. I press Izaak for details but he just shakes his head, as if speaking the words will make something real that he's not ready to face. Any other night, I'd be screaming and pleading at him to tell me what's going on. But the truth is, right now? Right now I'm not sure I'm ready to face the truth either.

We pull into the parking lot, which is pretty full even though it's late. I guess a hospital never sleeps. The car stops but Izaak leaves the engine running and closes his eyes, leaning back in his seat.

"What happened?" I say, the words so quiet I'm not sure he even hears them above the roar of the BMW's heater.

"The Exiles," he says. He opens his eyes and without thinking about it places a hand on my knee. "She texted me about an hour ago."

"Is she okay?"

"She will be."

I automatically reach for my phone and pull it up to check my texts and missed calls. Nothing except for three calls from Izaak. Cadence didn't even try to contact me. I ask him: "Why you? Why didn't she call me?"

"I don't know. I mean… we used to be… I don't know."

"Well, what are we waiting for? Let's go in there."

"We can't. Not yet. She said the cops were talking to her, and my guess is the FBI will too at some point. She said she'd let us know when we can come up."

"Both of us?"

He nods. "Look, all I know at this point is she said two white guys jumped her and claimed to be Exiles."

"But Dr. Harper…" My voice trails off. Nothing makes any sense. So how was this supposed to have worked? A bunch of white supremacists stumble on a dead white guy, happen to track down his two black friends, kill them, make it look like a hate crime so obviously they'll be targeted… then go after the brand new president of the Black Students' League, just in case the FBI wasn't already itching to track them down and throw them in prison?

I watch the clock on Izaak's car tick forward, minute by minute. After a long stretch of silence he says, "There was a witness you know. Not for Cadence. But the murders? Some old lady says she saw a skinhead-looking guy with a neck tattoo walking with two black dudes past her house in the direction of the golf course around two in the morning."

"How do you know this?"

He says, not cocky, but unable to hide the pride in his voice: "I have my ways."

"Your ways." A stray thought passes and I perk up in my seat. "Were there any signs of robbery?"

"Robbery?"

"Like, was anything missing? You know, their phones, maybe?"

"Why would you ask me that?" It's the first time I've shocked him, probably in my life.

"Just a hunch."

Izaak nods slowly, though I can't tell why. "Well, that's the funny thing. The guys had everything on them. IDs, cash, jewelry. But no cell phones. Fact is, the police can't even find records of any of them owning a phone."

The silence returns and though I don't remember falling asleep, I find myself opening my eyes and seeing hints of yellow and pink above the tops of trees. I hear the sound of Izaak's phone and then his voice say to me: "She's ready."

I step out of the car and into the winter morning and allow Izaak to guide me into the building. We're stopped at a security desk, where they print out visitor badges for us and send us on our way.

As we approach Cadence's recovery room, I stop cold as a police officer slips out of the room and closes the door behind him. Then a wave of relief washes over me as I realize it's Cadence's dad, Ty Jenkins. Ty's a lieutenant with the Haverford Township Police and runs the Detective Division. Cadence never knew her mom. Maybe that's why we bonded.

Ty waves us over and gives me a big hug, his massive arms pulling me tight against his chest.

"She's been asking about you," he says, his voice weary. He probably hasn't slept since the murders. Still hugging me, he reaches out to shake Izaak's hand. "Hey, boss. Thanks for bringing her down."

"We won't be long," Izaak says.

"The girl needs to sleep, but you can imagine how much my advice is worth. Just know we're going to find those bastards." He raises my chin so I'm looking into his eyes. "That's a promise, babe. I don't want you to worry. Just keep your head down. Life will be back to normal in no time."

"Thank you, Ty," I whisper.

He checks his watch. "Duty calls. Stay safe, you two."

My first thought when I enter Cadence's room is *That's not Cadence.* It's a girl who used to be Cadence. Only now she's a mass of swelling and bruising and bandages. Her face, once the most shockingly beautiful face I'd ever seen, is an ode to violence.

"It's not as bad as it looks," Cadence says, her voice slightly hoarse but alert and coherent.

"What's happening?" I say. "This isn't Mississippi. It's the goddamn Main Line."

"It's America," Cadence says.

Izaak walks around to the other side of the hospital bed and I see him eying the tubes and the room.

I don't know what to do or say and finally blurt out the last thing I want to say. "Why him?" I nod toward Izaak. "Why didn't you call me?"

Cadence smiles, or maybe winces. I can't tell. "I didn't want you to be alone when you heard it."

Izaak seems to be stuck in his own struggle for what to say. He cups Cadence's left hand in his and asks, his voice gentle: "I'm sure you don't want to talk about it, but I've got to ask. What happened out there?"

Cadence pulls herself up as if she's been waiting for this moment. "You're right. I don't want to say." Then she looks at me: "But you need to hear. I was walking down Haverford Road, I guess around two. You know the nature trail down that way? Two white guys pulled me down there and started pounding on me."

"Why do you think they were with the Exiles?" I say.

"I guess because while they were punching me in the mouth, they kept saying, 'Don't fuck with the Exiles.'" She gives her best attempt at a playful smile. All I can manage is a blank stare that hides a feeling I haven't felt in seven years—not anger or hatred but wrath.

Then her face grows serious. "There's something else I need to tell you." She glances at Izaak and for a moment I think she's going to tell him to leave us alone. She doesn't. "I managed to get to one of the security alerts." Our campus has a bunch of these boxes you can use to call for help in an emergency. "That's when they ran off. But before that… Justice…" She's searching for the words, simple words to state a simple fact, but words so powerful that you can't bring yourself to say them, and so you struggle for an approximation and you sound like someone trying to weasel out of a lie. I know. I've been there myself.

"They tried to rape you," I say.

Her eyes squeeze shut and tears form at the edges as she nods and says, "I sat with the cops and the FBI all last night. And even though my father is who he is, and even though I came in looking like this, I could feel it. I could feel the way they looked at me like I was the suspect. They questioned me like I was telling lies, like any minute they were going to slap the bracelets on me and haul me off. I get why you took back your story. What they would have put you through… I think you did the right thing."

Did I? I bet at least one innocent victim out there is certain I didn't.

Innocence.

"They said they'd be back. They said they'd come for me and everyone I care about. That's why I needed to tell you. I need you to stay off the radar until my dad figures this all out. Can you do that for me?"

It feels as if all the threads of my life, all of the tragedies and bad choices, the lies and the loyalties, have now tied themselves together into a knot I can't untangle. Yet, for the first time since I watched a boy take his last breath, it's as if I know exactly what I need to do.

"Of course I will," I say. And I wonder if Cadence knows it's a lie.

CHAPTER NINE

IZAAK TAKES ME BACK TO my place so I can clean up before Andy stumbles home.

"Need some help?" he asks, following me inside.

The words barely register. I start to shake my head, but then I'm jolted by a thought. "Yes. I do."

As we re-stack bookshelves and turn over chairs, I try to figure out how to explain my plan to Izaak in a way that doesn't sound insane. Soon, the downstairs is back to its normal state of disarray, and I still haven't made any progress, so I just blurt out: "I'm going to take down the Exiles."

I expect Izaak to burst out laughing. Instead, he studies my face, and I can see concern in his eyes, with just a hint of skepticism. Finally, he says, "Yeah?"

I hesitate to say the words. I don't want to say them for so many reasons, but I think of Cadence and let them pour out. "And you're going to help me."

This time the laugh comes, but when he stops, he isn't smiling. "How's that going to work, J? Going to run some Facebook ads asking white supremacists if they want to confess to a hate crime?"

It's a fair question.

"Listen," he continues. "The cops? They got this."

"Do they, though? You know how these things work. We play to win the game that pays us. The cops have no reason to get to the truth. Their job is to make the headlines go away. They make an arrest, they get the stat."

"Even for you, that's pretty cynical. You think Ty doesn't want to get to the truth?"

"I think he'll hit a wall. If it really is the Exiles who murdered those guys and attacked Cadence, the cops'll maybe track down the henchmen. But what about whoever's giving the orders? The guys at the top, they never…"

"What?"

"They never go down—unless one of their own turns on them. That's it, Izaak. If I'm going to take down the Exiles, I have to join them."

"That's the plan? To throw in with a gang of killers?" Izaak checks his phone. "We need to think this over. Come on. Let's grab some breakfast."

As we make our way toward campus, I can sense Izaak struggling to break the silence. Finally, he says, "I get why you want to do it. What I don't get is why you want me to be any part of it."

"Do I have a choice?" The words are sharper than I intend. "Look, let's put our cards on the table. You and Cadence broke up… when?"

He's watching the road but the muscles in his neck twitch like he's struggling to keep himself from doing a double take. "What? High school."

"Uh huh. And when's the last time you hung out with her dad?"

His face relaxes and he's unable to suppress a wide grin. "You're smarter than you look, J."

"So he's feeding you information about the case. But there's something else. You've been writing about the Exiles for the last year."

"So? It's news."

"Not really. Not until now. And you're always telling Cadence that it's a mistake to obsess about race. You know something about these guys. Something about them makes you afraid."

"Hmmm." He says nothing else as we turn into a Haverford parking lot. We hit up the Dining Center. He grabs a breakfast burrito, I grab a cup of coffee, and as I start to sit down at a table he tugs gently at my arm and says, "Not here. Let's hit the basement."

We enter a brightly lit meeting room filled with ten square tables and four times as many orange plastic roller chairs. We're the only ones here. I take a gulp of my coffee. Izaak sits down across from me, takes a huge bite of the burrito, and offers me some.

"I'm vegan," I say, unbuttoning my coat and hanging it on the chair. He stares at me for a moment like I've just told him I'm a Celtics fan. "I just… I like animals."

Izaak chuckles. "So do I." He wipes his face with a napkin and leans back, the faint scent of his cologne reminding me I haven't showered. "So here's the deal. Last year the Exiles reached out to *The Clerk*. They sent us this insane letter to the editor we never published. Here." He holds out his cell phone, which has an email pulled up. He scrolls down so I can see that the screed goes on for over a dozen paragraphs. "There." Izaak points to the screen.

I read the text silently.

How do you spell minority? W-H-I-T-E M-A-L-E. Everyone knows it. No one admits it. Professor Rhinehart teaches a whole semester about slavery and it's supposed to be an American History intro class? Says that when we cover the CONSTITUTIONAL DEBATES it's all just old white men protecting their PROPERTY and when a white student objects and Rhinehart says, "Maybe the white students should listen instead of lecture," the whole class cheers? How is that judging people by the CONTENT OF THEIR CHARACTER instead of the colour of their skin?

"Jesus Christ," I say when I finish.

"You see it, right?"

"One of them was in that class."

"Odds are," he says.

"And is British?"

"Probably not. But listen to this. Last year Rhinehart has one history one-hundred-level course. The course was *called* History of American Slavery, by the way."

"Dear Lord. Did you show this to anyone? Does Ty know about this?"

He shakes his head with a guilty frown. "Didn't see any reason to before now. Anyway, look. The class roster shows thirty-eight students. But thirty-one of them are either girls, LGBT, or non-white."

"So that leaves us with seven. What do you know?"

"I was able to track down some writing samples from each of them—blog posts and shit like that. My mom connected me with some experts her law firm works with. Basically, they said based on word choice and sentence structure, we could pretty confidently count out two of the guys."

Two girls wander in and sit across the room at the table by the door. They're talking about the murders. One of the girls, heavyset but all confidence and sparkle, says, "I'm just saying, isn't there a thing where you get automatic A's if your roommate dies? I think they should do that for the whole school."

Izaak catches my eye and shakes his head.

"Anything else?" I say, dropping my voice just above a whisper.

"You heard of Matt Hyatt?"

"Vaguely."

"He plays lacrosse. Turns out he has two arrests. One for harassment, one for simple assault. Both ended up getting dropped, though."

"Seems promising."

"Could be. Aside from that?" Izaak shakes his head. "It's pretty thin. You'd think: Hey, they're just posting stupid memes and complaining about progressives. Not exactly a sophisticated criminal operation. But as far as I can tell, that email is the only clue to who they are." He wraps up the remains of his burrito and tosses them halfway across the room into the garbage.

"Can't the FBI just trace their posts or something?"

"'Trace their posts'? Girl, you watch too much TV. Yeah, for your average user that's easy. Like, your accounts? I could have a guy track you down in half a heartbeat. But for someone who's trying to stay anonymous? They don't have to be some master hacker. Just takes some cheap equipment and half an hour on YouTube."

That's terrifying. And not because of how much of my life is online. The thing that dawns on me is how much of my life isn't online. If someone goes digging, and I'm a blank slate before a few years ago? I make a mental note to talk to Abe about finding someone who can create a fake online past for me.

"Hey, you guys talking about the murders?"

It's Miss Sparkle. I send a pleading look Izaak's way.

He leans over the table like a starving dog smelling food. "You guys hear anything?" Not exactly the reaction I was hoping for. But, hey, a reporter's gonna report.

Miss Sparkle shines brighter. "We heard that Vic was connected, and that actually it was a mob hit."

The friend, a mousy girl dressed to the twos in worn jeans and an oversized sweater, swats Miss Sparkle's hand. "Stop telling people that." She purses her lips and says to Izaak, "We saw Vic. You know, earlier that day?"

"Yeah," says Miss Sparkle. "We were grabbing some coffee at Green Engine. He rolled in there with the two basketball players. What was it? Around four? Yeah, around four."

"He say anything?" Izaak asks.

The friend says, "He was teasing Lizzy for getting her coffee with sugar and milk."

"It's crazy. To think we were talking to a dead guy."

Izaak flinches, and it's as if an invisible force grabbed him by the collar and pulled his body erect in his chair. For a while he doesn't say anything, just nods a bunch.

"How well you know Vic?" he asks, rising to his feet.

"We had some classes together," Lizzy says, her voice tense and low.

Izaak stalks around the room, his hands clasped behind his back. "Describe him."

She looks dumbfounded.

"If someone said, 'What was he like?' What would you tell them?"

Lizzy squirms in her seat. "I don't know. I guess… he was just a normal college guy."

Izaak stops next to a support column that stretches from floor to ceiling a few feet from the girls and leans his shoulder against it. He looks relaxed, but it's a studied relaxation, and it feels like at any moment he might seize the girls and shake them until their bones crumble.

"What do you want to be when you grow up?" he says.

"Huh?"

"What do you want to be?"

Lizzy is staring helplessly at her friend who is staring helplessly at me. Finally, Lizzy says, "I don't know. Maybe something in finance. Or a consultant."

"That's the dream? Little Lizzy, she wanted to grow up someday and be an accountant?"

"Not accounting. Like, an options trader."

Izaak pulls out an empty chair from their table and straddles it backward, his face a few inches from Lizzy. "People say these murders were a tragedy. But death isn't a tragedy. We die every day. Every time you change. Every time you say the wrong thing, or get wasted, or fuck the wrong guy? That's death, right there. It ain't death that's tragic. It's dying and not having your life mean anything. It's dying and all that anyone remembers is that you died. Vic? His life is going to be this big blank canvas with 'victim' written across it. That? That's worse than never living. But you know who I blame for that? Not his killer. I blame Vic."

"Izaak—" I say, but he holds up his hand without looking at me.

"You've got to justify your life. You've got to leave the world a little different than it was, or else why the fuck are you here? But that? That ain't easy. It means standing tall. Only standing tall means making enemies. And sometimes you stand so tall you don't notice when you're stepping on people—even your closest friends."

He doesn't look my way, but I know who he's really talking to, and what he's trying to say.

"Vic? He shouldn't have died. And the piece of shit that killed him? He has to live with that. And eventually he'll get caught, and he'll have to live with that, too. But none of that matters. What matters is the lesson that you," he points at Lizzy, "and you," he points at her friend, "and she," he points at me, "and I take away from this. So, you can look at this all and see it as some 'TMZ comes to Haverford' thing. Just some crazy shit that went down when you were in college. But me? It's a warning that screams, 'Make your mark. And do it quick because the clock is running out faster than you think.'"

I snatch up my things and bolt past them through the door, running up the stairs and out of the Dining Center. I stop a few feet away in front of Lloyd Hall, trying to catch my breath. A group of students shuffles past and I can feel them watching me with trepidation.

I have no clue what I'm feeling or why, but my hands are trembling and my thoughts are coming in half-formed images of Vic's eyes and Izaak's hands and my father's grin.

A minute later, Izaak catches up to me and puts his arm around my shoulder.

"You okay?" he says.

I slap his chest with both hands but don't pull away. "What the hell was that?"

"Just something that needed to be said."

"You terrified those girls."

"Good. They should be scared. This shit is real, J. You want to do this, you're risking everything."

He's right. More right than he knows.

CHAPTER TEN

WE SIT ON THE CURB out front of Lloyd, Izaak propping his elbows on his knees and letting his head slink down between his legs.

"You don't think I should do this," I say.

"Of course you shouldn't. But, no, that's not what I'm saying. It's just…"

"I get it, Izaak. You want me to do this because it means you get yourself a story that maybe brings you fortune and fame. Only you feel guilty about it. Like you're using me again. Well, don't. I'm doing this with or without you, for my own reasons. It's not on you."

He winces at the "using me" line, and I can see him struggling to decide whether it's worth it. I keep asking myself the same thing.

"So, what now?" he says. "We could hire a private investigator to maybe look into these guys."

That's the last thing I want. Another professional poking around.

"No way," I say. "Are you willing to risk him finding something and selling it to some national outlet?"

"You got a better idea?"

I think of Dr. Harper, and how he was able to see past the surface of the crime—and of me.

"I know what we need to do."

We cross the street and enter Sharpless Hall.

Dr. Harper's office is on the second floor, and though the building was completely renovated a few years ago, his office is right out of the nineteenth century with an ancient oak desk surrounded by dark wood chairs. The walls are bare, and the only hint of modernity is an outdated Dell laptop closed on the corner of his desk. Harper is scrawling notes onto a yellow legal pad, and I knock on the open door to get his attention.

"Izaak. Justice." He motions to two ladderback chairs across from him and goes back to his scrawling. We sit and wait for him to finish. A few moments pass, and he crumbles up the top sheet in frustration and tosses it in a wastebasket. Then he bites his pen and stares at us, waiting for one of us to speak.

"You said you like puzzles," I say. "We need your help with one." I elbow Izaak. "Show him the email."

Izaak retrieves his cell phone from his pocket and lets Harper see it. "That was sent to the student paper last year from an untraceable email address," Izaak says. "Signed 'the Exiles.'"

"We need to find out who that student is," I say. "We've got it narrowed down to five possibilities. But I think you can help us do better than that."

Dr. Harper's eyes don't leave the phone, and I get the sense he's reading it for the third or fourth time.

Finally, he says, "I can't help you."

"You don't understand," I say. "This is totally off the record. We're just—"

He holds up both his hands, palms out. "I can't help you.

Not with this. Someone reported my comments from yesterday's class to the administration. There's going to be an inquiry."

Izaak gives a silent chuckle. "Who?"

"That doesn't matter. What matters is that I not double down and turn a tempest in a teapot into an actual storm."

"I get it," I say. "You need to protect yourself. But I'm trying to protect myself, too. Izaak's going to expose them in *The Clerk*. After we figure out who they are, and I convince them to make me part of their club and get them to talk. I don't want to go in blind."

Dr. Harper's eyes widen. "My God, Justice. That's incredibly dangerous."

"I thought you said they didn't do it."

"Who knows what else they've done—or what they could do if they felt backed into a corner?"

"Then I'd better be convincing."

Izaak pats my knee as Dr. Harper closes his eyes. Part of me feels guilty for manipulating him, and part of me feels scared because I know that he knows I'm manipulating him.

"What do you want to know?"

I fold my arms on Dr. Harper's desk and lean towards him. "For starters, how can they believe this stuff? It just seems so obviously wrong. I'm supposed to go in there and pretend to be all racist, but it's like if you asked me to pretend that Zeus was real, I wouldn't know how to do it. Maybe they don't really believe it. They just say it because it gets a reaction."

Dr. Harper jerks his head and looks at me with dread and urgency. "*That* is the worst mistake you can possibly make. It's the mistake good people have always made in the face of evil ideologies. You have to take seriously that people are moved by

71

ideas. The only reason you can't believe they accept these ideas is because they are unusual. But they haven't always been."

"Okay, but what attracts them to these ideas? Why don't they pick something respectable, like Mormonism or something?"

"Hah." He doesn't laugh. He just says the word *hah*. "That's a good question. What do you think?"

I look to Izaak, but he waves me on as if to say, "Hey, this is your dance."

"It's easier, right?" I say. "You have automatic status just because you're white."

"Right. Every form of tribalism, I would say, has its roots in fear. The world is hellish. It's filled with sickness, loss, pain, malevolence. You need something to orient yourself in reality so you can cope with the suffering, or else you'll be paralyzed by fear. A healthy person aims for something high. But that's demanding. It's so much easier just to cling to the group in self-protection. And the most obvious, easiest group to cling to is one that you don't have to choose. It's one that chooses you. Your nation, your sex, your skin color. You're good not because of your choices but because you're a man or a woman or white or black. Group identity is all about thinking that obedience is easier than knowledge, that loyalty is safer than responsibility."

"But now I feel like you're equating things. Like feminists and the Manosphere, or the Black Students' League and the Exiles."

He points out the window. "Is that what you think, or is that what they think?"

"It's what I think."

"Well, I would say this. It's not a *moral* equivalence necessarily, but there is a similarity. If you play the group identity game, you're by necessity fueling the other side. Look, I understand why the Exiles exist. It's tempting, isn't it? To fight fire with fire?"

Izaak leans forward, attentive. I'm growing uneasy but say nothing.

"They're not completely wrong," Dr. Harper continues. "What they're saying about the universities is true in important ways. The universities haven't opposed tribal politics. They've merely sided with the tribe that seems oppressed. But unless one side is powerful enough to eliminate the other, all you do is manufacture resentments. I hate to think it, but it's possible these murders will do some good. If people see the danger of tribalism and identity politics, if they decide to stop playing this horrible game altogether..."

He doesn't finish, and I'm happy he doesn't.

"So how should I approach them?"

A long exhale, and Dr. Harper says, "The temptation will be to come on too strong, mouthing a bunch of racist slogans you read online. Don't do that. You have to remember these are people, not cartoon villains. That's not a moral judgment. It's a psychological fact."

"That's what I'm worried about. I feel like every time I try to say something I've heard them say, I sound like a D-list actor."

"They will not be judging you by what you say. They'll be judging you by how you react to what *they* say. Play the role of a student. Let them give you the words. People want to be listened to. They want to feel visible. Give them that. Let them give you 'ah-ha' moments."

Izaak reaches for his phone. "Like she said, we have it narrowed down to five. We're thinking it's this one. Matt Hyatt. Got arrested for smacking around his girlfriend."

Dr. Harper shakes his head. "No. You're looking for a loner. Someone who feels incredibly alienated. He probably doesn't have a girlfriend, and if he does, he wouldn't hit her. That would take too much courage. No. If he's violent it will only be in a group setting, where he feels as if he's not responsible for his actions. What do you know about the others?"

"Alex MacArthur," Izaak says. "He's on the lacrosse team."

"You're looking for someone who considers himself an intellectual. Extremely pretentious but extremely shallow. He'll be widely read, but only sources that support his views."

"Well," Izaak says, "there's this guy. Dax Morrison? His freshman year he tried to start some libertarian club, but it never went anywhere. He considers himself an anarcho-capitalist, which I guess is someone who hates government but loves Walmart."

Dr. Harper leans back in his chair and locks his fingers behind his head. He doesn't say it, but I know what he's thinking. Dax Morrison is our man. "Look, guys. I can't help you. I can't condone what you're doing, and I can't be in the position of accusing students of being genocidal murderers. What I recommend is that you take that email and you pass it on to the authorities." He looks knowingly into my eyes. "But if you do go ahead, be sure to keep me in the loop."

CHAPTER ELEVEN

I FOLLOW IZAAK UP THE stairs of Barclay Hall to his dorm room. The place is pretty spotless, considering two guys live here. Two beds. Two desks. A bookshelf filled with more packs of Ramen noodles than books. Amazingly, no posters. How are people supposed to know what music they like?

"You ready for this?" he says, retrieving his laptop.

No. Not at all. "Just find out where he is."

It's amazing that my entire generation isn't dead yet. In the old days, you had to have some advanced spy gear to locate someone or at least the connections to track credit card payments. Now? Now people can't eat a cream cheese bagel without posting it to social media.

"What do you think about what Dr. Harper was saying?" I ask while Izaak scours Instagram and Snapchat.

"What? You mean why are people racist?"

"I guess."

He shrugs. "Never given it much thought."

"Really? Never?"

Izaak keeps typing, not looking up from the screen. "Who knows why people believe the shit they believe?"

"Seems like it would be relevant. I mean, you're not going to tell me you've never encountered this stuff."

He stops typing and stares at me, a hint of condescension in his eyes. "Sure. But the way I see it, people are going to hate you for all sorts of reasons. Because you're smart or because you're dumb. Or because you got too much money or not enough. My grandparents? Now that's a different story. But truth be told, J, I've got privilege coming out my ass. For me, it's more like white people being weirdly friendly and trying to prove how down they are. We'd have these law partners come over to the house, and I'd have some fifty-year-old white dude saying, 'I'm a huge fan of Kanye.' And I would just be like, 'Yeah, I'm going to go listen to some Nirvana.'"

"I think you're being naive."

"Yeah. Kanye's dope."

"You know what I mean."

"I just don't worry about stuff like that. It's there. I see it. It's bullshit. But I've got things I want to do, and anything that can't help me is noise." He looks back at his computer and grimaces. "I guess it's a good sign, but looks like Dax plays it pretty close to the chest. No recent photos or updates. Not publicly available, anyway."

"So?"

"He got an underage drinking citation last year, which God only knows how he got that at this school. I can check if there's an address listed."

I wander over to the bookshelf and run my hand across the titles. "So, why journalism? Not exactly a growth industry."

"You sound like my mom."

"Is she wrong?"

He turns around in his chair. "I think she's short-sighted. If

I was trying to maximize my chances for making mid-six figures, then, yeah, I'd be all for working eighty-hour weeks tweaking Excel sheets for an investment bank. But that's not the game I'm playing."

"So what game are you playing?" I pull a copy of Frederick Douglass's *My Bondage and My Freedom* off the shelf. "I thought you didn't think about this stuff."

He walks over, takes the book from me, flips through the pages, and returns it to the shelf. "I said I don't think about why insecure assholes are obsessed with skin color. That don't mean I don't know where I came from."

"Must be nice." He waits for me to elaborate, but I wander over to the other side of the room and change the topic. "Who's your roommate?"

"Aaron McAfee."

"Izaak, no!" I nearly leap back to Izaak's side of the room. "What?"

"Aaron? Lorelei said he threatened to post a video of her going down on him after they broke up."

"So she says."

"Christ, Izaak. Is the girl always lying?"

"You don't know what you're talking about, J."

I start to say something, but Izaak thrusts his finger toward the window. "You see that?" he says. "How high are we?"

I peer out the window. "Four stories?"

"Right. Four stories. And you know what I did when Lorelei told me? I took Aaron and I told him if that video ever came out, he was going to feel every inch of those four stories."

I turn away from Izaak, not quite ready to stop feeling indignant. "Just the fact that he threatened her, though."

"He didn't. He has texts from her. She was pissed because she saw him dancing with some girl from Bryn Mawr College. He was so drunk he doesn't even remember, but I know for a fact nothing happened because I'm the one who carried him out of that party. But she didn't care. She said she was going to release the video herself and blame him, just to make him pay for embarrassing her. And you know what Aaron said to me? He said not to tell anyone about the texts because he didn't want Lorelei to get in trouble. You see, J. For me, it ain't about believing women or not believing women. It's about getting to the truth."

Maybe. But isn't that what people always say? I'm not racist, I'm just looking at the data. I'm not sexist, I'm just ignoring the eyewitness testimony of a woman until the DNA evidence comes in. How do you know when someone really cares about the truth and when they're pretending to in order to hide their real motives?

Izaak turns his back on me and leans over his desk. "Okay, the police report lists an address around the way. You heard of The Loft apartments?"

"Just off of Lancaster?"

"I don't know if it's still good, though."

"You let me know if you have a better plan." I start for the door.

"Hold up," Izaak says. "What *is* the plan?"

That's a good question. My spy skills are nonexistent. I haven't even seen a James Bond film. But there is one thing I'm good at. "I think our friend Dax is going on a date tonight."

Izaak shakes his head but can't keep himself from smiling. "Yeah? And what if you're not his type?"

I throw one end of my scarf over my shoulder. "I can be anybody's type for a night."

Twenty minutes later I'm in front of Dax's apartment building. The building looks new with large glass windows, freshly painted walls, and balconies lined with steel balustrades. My plan had been to knock on Dax's door looking for so-and-so and somehow turn my mistake into a serendipitous meeting of star-crossed racists. But the main entrance is locked and the security desk is unmanned. I settle onto a bench outside the main exit with no choice but to wait.

But wait for what? Because as I work through different scenarios it dawns on me that very little can go right. On the one hand, the Exiles could buy my ruse and invite me into their slice of hell, which would mean they didn't steal my bag and probably didn't kill Terrance and Warren. Result? I get nowhere.

On the other hand, maybe the Exiles did kill Terrance and Warren and did steal my bag and have every reason to suspect I'm playing them. In which case they either tell me to get lost, or they let me into their circle—only it's a trap. So really, what I'm doing makes absolutely no sense.

On the other, *other* hand, what's the alternative? For the first few weeks I lived with Andy, she would take me out every night to this bar that didn't ID, and she'd drink while the two of us played pool. Neither of us were very good, and unless I had an easy shot, my strategy consisted of smashing the cue into the largest group of balls on the table and hoping for the best. So, it's Exiles or bust. Worst case, I'll keep Izaak happy while he continues to feed me information and maybe find the thugs who attacked Cadence. And if it is a trap? Well, then I guess I'll just have to outsmart them.

Two hours pass, and I'm about ready to give up when a door swings open and out comes a white French bulldog followed by a pale, rail-thin guy in track pants and a t-shirt—never mind that it's in the low forties. Dax lights a cigarette and we make eye contact.

"You go to my school," I say.

"Justice Winters," he says, which is pretty much the most disturbing thing he could say. Dax strides over with his dog and stretches out beside me, and now I'm pretty sure I'm going to die.

"You're that chick who lied about almost getting banged by the NBA's next all-star." Yep, I'm definitely going to die—of embarrassment.

"You live here?" I say.

"How'd you guess? Hurry it up, Al."

"You named your dog Al?"

"Had to name him something."

"Dear lord."

Al sniffs around, finds a good spot, squats, then reconsiders. Dax is staring off into the distance, not particularly aware of Al's existence or mine.

"My roommate has a pug," I say, mostly to keep the conversation going.

"What are the odds?"

"He's cool. But he lost all his teeth, so now his tongue hangs out of his mouth and he has to eat mush. I don't have a dog, myself. Why bother, right? Now I get all the benefits with none of the responsibility. Though, actually, I end up walking him half the time." I'm talking way too fast, and it's like my words are just bouncing off of him. It occurs to me that stripper magic works in part because you're dealing with a self-selected group—guys desperate to talk to pretty girls.

The conversation dies, and now I'm starting to worry that Al's going to do his business before I can charm his owner.

I've never really figured out small talk. In the club, it's different. Something about the atmosphere allows you to comfortably jump from "where are you from?" to "what are your deepest, darkest desires?" in a span of five minutes. I guess because there's no pretense and nothing at stake. You start out half-naked, you're going to get full naked, and at the end of the night both of you are going to go home alone.

But in the real world, conversation feels like climbing Mount Everest. You have to struggle just to get to basecamp, and once you're there you push and push and push, and at the end of the day, where do you end up? Freaking forward basecamp. Certain people make that look easy. I am not certain people.

"You wanna have sex?"

Dax chokes on cigarette smoke and Al's ears perk up. "Are you serious?"

"Just feeling ignored, and I wanted to see if you were still listening."

"You really are crazy." Dax checks his phone and stretches out his legs.

"What about you?" I say.

"What about me?"

"Are you crazy?" I have no clue what I'm talking about anymore.

"Why do you care what I am?"

"I'm just curious."

"Curious enough to spend two hours sitting outside my apartment?" He snickers and tosses his cigarette into the grass. He starts to get up, like he's ready to head inside, but instead pulls a pack of American Spirits from his pocket and lights another one.

I shrug. "I wanted to meet you."

"Yeah? Why's that?"

My initial plan was to come on to him real strong, but something inside me screams that's the wrong move. I dig in my purse for some lip balm, and while I'm applying it say, matter of factly, "People say you're in the Exiles."

I'm expecting protests. He barely reacts. "Why would they say that?"

"Well, are you?"

"Al, just shit!" He takes a drag and blows a long cloud of smoke into the air. "I didn't have anything to do with those murders, if that's what you're asking."

"But you know who did?"

"There's a lot you don't understand, Justice."

"Educate me."

He examines his cigarette like it has the meaning of life inscribed on it. Then another long drag, and I can't help but mourn for the state of his lungs.

"It doesn't matter who killed those guys. The media has its narrative, and now it's all about furthering the narrative. Read the stories. It's like they're happy this went down, because it gives them an excuse to do what they wanted to do anyway."

"Which is what?"

"Isn't it obvious? They're the ones who want to start a race war. No one was talking about race before that black kid got killed down in Florida a while back. And who was it who killed him? A freaking Mexican. But all of a sudden it's 'Black Lives Matter' and white privilege and deplatforming and cancel culture. The Exiles? Who the hell knows who they are? But they're just doing what everyone else is doing. Everyone says have pride in your ethnicity, and the Exiles are saying, okay, we're white, so we have pride in being white. How is it okay for blacks to do that, but not for us?"

I kind of want to vomit, but I press on. "Yeah, that makes total sense."

"Just watch. They're having some memorial at the school soon for those guys who died, right?"

"I guess."

"You should go. Just go there and listen, and tell me if it wasn't an excuse to push their agenda."

I nod. "I'll do that. But, look, those guys they killed? I'm not saying I support it, but I get it. You know what's going to happen next, though. There's going to be a backlash. Maybe an all-out war, like you said. And I feel like all of us, we're going to need protection, and I thought you might be the person to talk to."

"Good boy, Al. Good boy." Dax stands up and flicks his cigarette at my feet. "You're used to getting your way. Aren't you?"

"Not really."

"Girls think they can go around flashing T and A, and guys will just give them whatever they want."

I pull my coat tight around my body. "I don't recall showing you either my T or my A."

"It's an expression."

"I'm serious, Dax. I can be an ally."

"Yeah? Swing by tomorrow night around nine. We'll see how serious you are." Al scampers beside him as Dax disappears into the building.

Mission accomplished. But what bothers me is that it all feels too easy.

CHAPTER TWELVE

"SO, YOU'RE SURE IT'S HIM?"

"He all but admitted it," I say.

Izaak and I are walking along the slate sidewalk that runs past Duck Pond, and I swerve right to avoid a streetlamp, my coat catching against the wood post from the fence that surrounds the pond.

I fill Izaak in on the conversation with Dax. He listens, asking a few follow-up questions, but otherwise stays silent, his eyes locked on some distant point. Then he says, "So when do you think we'll have something we can publish?"

"I don't know. Izaak… he scares me. I mean, I guess I should've expected it. But you know how sometimes you picture something in your mind, and it seems so easy, and then, when reality hits, you just fall to pieces?"

Izaak veers right onto the long stretch of grass behind the pond, and I struggle to keep up with his long strides. "Maybe there's another way," he says.

"What?"

"Ty says the police have a new lead."

"Wait, did you tell him what we're doing?"

"Course not."

"I don't want anyone else to know," I say. "Not him. Not even Cadence."

"I got you. Anyway, Ty says someone saw the guys arguing with some white chick in the parking lot of a strip club the night before."

Right. Because everything has been going far too swimmingly. "Who?"

"One of the dancers I guess."

"No, I mean who was the witness?"

"Anonymous tip."

"A guy? A girl?"

"Damn, J. Does it matter? Whoever it was, it's legit. Cell phone records and receipts put them there. And that's not public."

"Do the cops know who she was? The dancer?"

"I don't think so. I've got some things I've got to do this evening, but I'm going down there tomorrow night to try to find out more."

"No!" He shoots me a quizzical look. "Let me do it."

"You?"

"It's just they're more likely to open up to a girl."

I see him thinking it over. "Makes sense. Why don't we do this? Let's meet up tomorrow night and head there together. Double our chances."

I struggle to think of a reason why that's a bad plan and come up empty.

"We should split up now," he says as we approach campus. "In case we do decide to chase down Dax at some point. Though depending on how much the Exiles know about Cadence, you might already be on their radar."

"I thought about that," I say.

"And?"

"That would be bad."

Izaak chuckles, then heads right as I make my way back to College Lane. As I near Barclay I'm about to turn left in the direction of the Alumni Field House, where the memorial is taking place. But I hear echoes of someone speaking through a bullhorn, and before I can turn, I see a large crowd formed on the field across from Sharpless Hall.

The air is swarming with fists and protest signs, and between roars of approval I can make out slices of the speaker's rant: "administration," "safety," "violence," "color." I try to make sense of the signs, but they all have these vague slogans, like "Fascist Speech ≠ Free Speech."

I ask one of the students watching from the fringes what's going on.

"You know that psych professor, Harper?"

"Yeah," I say.

"They're saying the school needs to fire him."

"Because of what he said yesterday?"

"I don't know. The Black Students' League says he's making the school unsafe."

The next thing I notice are a couple of guys with news cameras milling about and taking shots of the crowd. Not just local media. National media's here, too. I guess I shouldn't be surprised. Murder only matters anymore if someone can make a political point out of it. In any case, the last thing on earth I want is to end up on the news, so I dart in the direction of the Field House.

The Alumni Field House is an indoor athletic center that also houses commencement ceremonies and other special events.

Today, metal folding chairs are arranged in long lines with a single aisle running down the center. At the front of the room is a riser and a podium. I see a few members of the administration and faculty up there along with someone dressed in religious garb.

I take a seat in the back, a few empty chairs separating me from the nearest students. I fold my hands and bow my head against the chair in front of me. As I close my eyes, it's like the rows of chairs become walls and I can feel them moving slowly toward me, pressing in, and squeezing the breath out of me.

Dr. Harper once gave a lecture on lying. He said whenever you lie, you create invisible demons that will haunt you. Serial liars don't experience guilt, but they do experience fear because they know the facts they're trying to cover up are still out there, waiting to be discovered, including the fact that they lied. And so every time they see people whispering, every time they get an unexpected phone call, every time they walk into a room and people glance at them with indecipherable expressions, they wonder: *Does someone know the truth? Are the demons here to claim me?*

I nearly broke down in tears when he said it. That's been my life for five years. Only now it's worse. Now the demons have multiplied, like Gremlins in a swimming pool, and I'm suffocating from the sense that threats are closing in on me from all sides. What does Dax know? What do the Exiles know? What do the police know? Where is my bag? How does this thing end?

There is a way out. I can go hat-in-hand to Abe and ask for help getting off the Main Line. I can write a letter to the police and tell them about Dax and the Exiles and about what really happened to Vic. I can save myself and still do my part to bring down Cadence's attackers.

Only I've been down that road before.

The summer after I lost Innocence, I decided to play message in a bottle. I left a note for the cops folded in the pages of a Bible and tossed it on the side of the road. The only question was who would find it first—one of the joggers who occasionally pass down our street or Pop.

I couldn't sleep that night and when I heard a knock on my bedroom door the next morning, I sat paralyzed on my bed, expecting SWAT officers to storm inside and pull me into their arms, taking me and my sisters to safety—or for Pop to walk through and end my life.

Instead, two uniformed sheriff's deputies sauntered in, Pop behind them. One of the deputies held up my note. "You write this?"

I glanced at Pop, but his face was implacable.

I nodded.

"It true?"

I started to deny it but then I thought of Innocence, and, holding my father's glance, I said: "Every word of it."

I waited to see if Pop would react, maybe make a run for it before the deputy could whip out his cuffs. For a moment, nobody moved. Finally, the deputy looked over his shoulder at Pop. "This going to be a problem?"

Pop grinned. "No problem, Charlie."

The deputy crumpled up my note and pressed it into Pop's palm. He took a few steps in my direction, stopping in front of me, his crotch eye level. I closed my eyes and felt his sticky hand grab my jaw and tilt my face back. When I opened my eyes, his face was close to mine, so close I could see the beads of sweat caught in his mustache and smell the coffee breath steaming, not from his mouth, but from his nostrils.

"Your daddy loves you a lot. You should show him some respect." Then he squeezed my jaw so tightly I thought it would crumble and pulled me so close his whiskers touched my nose. "No one is coming to save you."

Sometimes, when the walls are closing in and the demons are out in full force, the solution isn't to run away. It's to run forward, toward danger and through it, as fast as humanly possible.

The Field House grows silent and when I open my eyes, I see the dean standing behind a podium, adjusting his glasses as he prepares to speak. "We've all seen the legacy of slavery. We've seen it in our police, in our neighbors, in our own souls. We cannot erase the past. We cannot undo what has been done. But we can, if we're brave, open our eyes and our hearts to the stories of every man and every woman." He's going to catch hell for that from the gender activists. "We cannot step beyond the boundary of our lived experience, but we can cultivate a deep empathy. Not the empathy of one who says, 'I get it. I know,' but the empathy of one who says, 'I will never know. Tell me more.'"

Every word of the dean's speech is banal, and I wonder how Dax would see it. What political message would he read between the lines? I've heard Dr. Harper criticize the notion of "lived experience." He says those are code words meant to reject the idea of universal truths accessible to reason. Seems a bit too philosophical for Dax; but then again, the only thing I really know about Dax is that he has absolutely no respect for this country's Surgeon General.

Next, the religious guy comes up and starts talking about how we are all God's children, and how our skin isn't the same color as our souls. Then he tells a story that involves some guy named Bill putting his hand on his shoulder and saying something profound. Why does that only happen to preachers? You'd think they constantly have people coming up and hitting them with deep one-liners. The most insightful thing anyone's ever said to me, they stole from Norm Macdonald.

When it's over, I watch as hundreds of legs march past me. The torrent of people turns to a trickle, and after a quick pep talk, I pull myself to my feet.

"Good morning, Justice."

At first I can't place the face, but when I do, I almost fall back into my chair. It's Ron Michaels—Vic's dad.

"Oh, hi, Coach."

"Thank you for coming."

I force a smile and stand there awkwardly.

"I've been meaning to talk to you," he says.

"Me?"

"The police came by after you left. I showed them Vic's room. You don't remember seeing Vic's phone there, do you?"

"His phone?"

"I wouldn't ask, except that it was there in his dresser that morning, and when the cops came, it wasn't."

"I'm sorry, I need to sit down." I collapse back into my seat, my head in my hands. When I look back up at him, what I see isn't anger, but fatherly disappointment. "It's just that, well, there were some embarrassing texts."

"Some embarrassing texts." Someone comes by and gently slaps Ron Michaels on his shoulder, wishing him well as he passes. "That hurts. You know why? Because if you really cared about my son, that would've been the last thing on your mind."

"Did you tell the cops?"

"There you go again. I considered it. I did. But I gave you the benefit of the doubt. If you were important to him, well, that's something I'd like to honor. Honor means a lot to me, Justice." I can't help but notice he hasn't called me sweetie. "I do need you to return it, though."

"The phone?"

"The phone you took."

"I… it was stolen."

He shakes his head, and I have never felt more pathetic.

"I know what that sounds like," I whisper. "But it's the truth."

"Well, I'll tell you what. I know you don't believe in the Lord. But I do. I want you to get your life together and start thinking about your choices. Start thinking about how they affect other people. You hear?"

"Thank you."

"No, Justice, don't thank me. Truth be told, if it were up to me, I would be calling the police. You thank God for this one. He's watching out for you."

I nod and watch him leave. Then I lean against the seat in front of me, wishing I could cry and vomit and disappear.

CHAPTER THIRTEEN

DAX'S F-150 RAPTOR SPEEDS UP 95 North, and I'm watching the exit signs and billboards, trying to get my bearings. No one knows where I am or where I'm going. And all *I* know so far is that Dax likes Cliff Burton-era Metallica, wears too much Drakkar Noir, and can repeat long stand-up comedy routines from memory. Seriously, if it weren't for the fact he's probably a genocidal maniac who made me leave my cell phone at his apartment, this would be pretty much like every date I've ever been on.

"I saw this wino eating grapes, and I was like, 'Dude, you have to wait.' No? You don't know Mitch Hedberg? You had a deprived childhood, Justice."

He's not wrong.

"So, what do you do for fun?" he says.

It's been like this the entire time. I'm waiting for Dax to pontificate on the future of the white race, and he's making small talk. If he's trying to make me feel at ease, it's not working.

"I don't know. I mostly just study."

"Come on. Movies? Sports? Concerts? What are you into?"

"I like basketball," I say in the hopes that he follows up with, "What a coincidence, I just murdered a couple of basketball players." Instead, he goes on this riff about the UFC and why mixed martial arts is superior to boxing.

"I train MMA," I say, eager for him to know I'm not an easy mark.

"Really? No way. I wouldn't have guessed. Have you ever fought somebody for real?"

I could tell him the truth, but he would never believe me, so I just shake my head. "Just sparring and grappling."

"Cool. Cool. I took Tae Kwon Do when I was younger, but my dad lost his job in 2008, so we had to stop doing extracurriculars after that."

Just past Fishtown, Dax veers across two lanes and exits at Girard/Delaware Avenue. I usually stay on the south end of Philly near Night Shade, so I don't know this part of the city.

"You from around here?" he says.

"Orange County, originally."

"Oh, really, what part?"

If I had to do it over again, I would have come up with a better backstory. But when I moved to Philly, the only place I had been other than Michigan was the Laguna Beach area for eight months. The trouble is, half of everyone has spent time in Orange County. Since then I've spent hours studying Wikipedia and Google Maps to make sure I don't blow my cover. I probably would have been better off taking my chances and saying I'm from some no-name town in Wisconsin. Yeah, if I ever ran into someone from that town, I'd be dead to rights, but chances of that would be slim. And it would explain the damn accent.

"Southern part mostly. We moved around a bit."

"I have a cousin in Pasadena. Is that close?"

It sounds ridiculous but this is not the first time someone has asked me literally that same question. Most recently it was an Uber driver and I was like, "Oh, yeah, just down the road from me." Turns out "down the road" was sixty miles.

"Nope. That's north of L.A. I rarely ventured past Long Beach."

We've been heading up York for a few minutes, and the city is going from bad to worse.

I've never made my peace with cities. At their best, you get to walk down the street and breathe in sewage and sidewalk hot dogs while you pass luxurious stores selling two-thousand-dollar handbags. At their worst, they eat your soul.

I've spent hours wandering the streets of Philly. I've seen the shined shoes of hedge fund managers winning at life and the torn faces of old ladies who long for death.

What I see now is worse than death. It is life robbed of hope. Nothing is more haunting than an abandoned building—stories buried in burned-out rubble. As we drive, each block takes us further and further into despondency. Soon Gucci and Dolce corrode into "We Buy Gold" and Chinese food joints that make you order fried rice through bulletproof glass.

But now, I see that something else happens, too. The corners *breathe*. Communities form. Instead of strangers marching here and there to their own little islands of humanity, people congregate. They gossip and chatter and commune. There is darkness, there are drugs, and every corner has seen blood fall. But there is also laughter and joy.

Dax pulls the Raptor into an alleyway along a main street, just across from a laundromat and one of those places that will cash your check for a ten million percent APR. He puts the truck into idle. Four black guys in their early twenties are standing on the corner, chatting casually.

"Where are we?" I say.

"Kensington."

"Why?"

"It's good you came to see me, Justice. You were right, you know? We do need to band together for protection. Look at that." Dax motions across the street as two white kids in a Toyota Corolla pull up to the curb, and one of the black guys leans into the vehicle. "You see what they're doing to us? It's not bad enough they're living in hell. They want to drag us down there, too."

"I don't understand," I say, even though I understand just fine. Like Dr. Harper said, be a student.

"That was a drug deal that just went down. What, you think those guys were stopping to ask for directions?"

Dax rolls down his window and lights a cigarette, the icy air mixing with a heater on full blast. I hold out my hand, and he places an American Spirit between my fingers. I don't smoke, but it just seems like the thing to do at the moment. Dax lights his Zippo, and I lean down toward him, my hair almost catching the flame. I inhale and my virgin lungs can't handle it. I go into a coughing fit.

"You all right?"

I nod and take another drag. This one goes better, and I feel a rush of energized dizziness. "So, what do we do about all this? That's what I don't get. What's the solution?"

"That's the question, isn't it? But it's like any other social movement, right? See, with the blacks, they had Martin Luther King, Jr., and they had Malcolm X, and they had Huey Newton."

"Who?"

"Started the Black Panthers. Violent sonofabitch. My point is that we all have our own views about the solution."

"What's your view?"

"Here's the thing, Justice. I meant what I said. I'm glad you came to see me. But it's the timing that worries me." I start to answer but he interrupts. "No, I get it. You always had these ideas but were too scared to explore them until the killings pushed you over the edge. But how did you know to come to *me*?"

I shiver but hold his stare as my mind tumbles through possibilities. Then I take an extra-long drag and blow the smoke out my window. "The Black Students' League. They were saying you were involved with the Exiles. I don't know how they know it."

"Really? Good friends of yours?"

"Cadence Jenkins is in my class." I instantly regret it. Yeah, a fine cover story, but what if it makes her more of a target?

Dax rubs his chin. "I mean, it all makes sense. But you can see why I would be concerned?"

"You shouldn't trust me, Dax. You shouldn't trust anyone right now."

"Right. But on the other hand, our movement needs to grow. Especially now. We have this once-in-a-lifetime opportunity. People are questioning. We have leaders who support us, even if they can't say it openly. Now's not the time to close ourselves off. Now's the time to build an army. So, you tell me: What should I do?"

I look out on the street and say, "A test."

"You read my mind."

Dax reaches into the back and pulls out a ream of paper and tosses it onto my lap. Flyers printed on bright orange paper. I read the headline: "Save our race: everything we cherish is under assault by ZOG and the darkies and mud people they protect." Subtle.

"What's ZOG?" I say.

"It's an acronym."

"I gathered. What's it stand for?"

"Zionist Occupation Government."

"That's one thing I've never understood. Why the Jews? They're white, aren't they?"

He snickers. "If a terrorist unleashed smallpox and wiped out half the country, who would you blame? The terrorist or the smallpox? Them—" He points out the window. "They can't help what they are. But the Jews? They're the ones trying to take away our rights and contaminate our culture."

My deepest hope is that Dax is guilty because every fiber of my body wants to tear him to pieces. My other deepest hope is that I'm wrong about what Dax is going to ask me to do.

"And so you want me to walk down this street handing out those flyers?" I say.

"That was the plan."

"Was?"

"I've got a better idea." Dax pumps the volume of his speakers up to eleven, and we speed back toward the highway, the opening bars of Metallica's "Disposable Heroes" rattling the city air.

We're halfway through "Damage, Inc." when we pull onto campus, just down the block from Barclay Hall.

"There," Dax says.

My stomach falls. What does he know?

"Why there?"

"Like you said, Cadence Jenkins is going around mouthing off about me. She needs a wake-up call."

I want to scream, *you gave her a fucking wake-up call.* Instead I say, "She lives in Barclay?"

Dax nods. They've been watching her. But apparently not closely enough to notice me. At least, I hope.

"Someone is going to see me," I say.

"Not if you're fast."

"Someone is going to *see* me."

"We all have to pay our dues."

I can't do it. I don't want to do it. I will never forgive myself for doing it. But I see my legs moving as I hop down to the pavement and move slowly in the direction of Barclay, a hundred orange flyers tucked under my arm. An occasional snowflake brushes against my nose as I walk, and I fight to remind myself that if I don't infiltrate the Exiles, they might not only get away with murder. They might add a few names to their roster.

I stand in front of the archway that marks Barclay's main entrance. I can hear the sounds of cars moving in the distance. Everything else is still except the beating of my heart, which fights against my rib cage. A voice seems to whisper in my ear that no cause, no matter how noble, justifies atrocities. And God knows whether my cause even qualifies as noble.

I breathe deeply and in one motion toss the entire pile onto the steps. They spill out face up.

I hurry back in the direction of Dax's truck, my eyes on my feet, and it's not until I nearly run into her that I notice Cadence standing in front of me. I freeze. Her face is shrouded by the dark, but I can make out the two bandages and swelling around her left eye and jaw.

"Hey, Justice. You okay?"

I say nothing but start running. I keep running until I'm at

Dax's truck, my heels burning from the bite of the pavement. As I reach the door, I force myself to look back.

Cadence is too far away for me to see her face, but I can make out her figure in the distance silhouetted against Barclay. She is looking my way and holding something small and orange.

CHAPTER FOURTEEN

I'M PACING AROUND MY HOUSE, checking my phone every three seconds to make sure a text didn't come through without me hearing. I've been trying to get hold of Cadence, but she hasn't responded. I send another text and run to the cupboard to dip into my stash of sea salt chocolate.

That's when I hear voices, and then someone playing with the doorknob of the front door.

I rush to the door and swing it open. It's Andy and some guy I don't recognize. He's puffing on a vape mod and rubbing his other hand under Andy's coat.

"Hey, Justice," Andy says. Her words aren't slurred, and she's standing of her own volition, but something is off about her voice, and despite the brightness of the door lamp, her pupils are the size of frisbees.

"What's his name?" I say.

"Josh?"

I lock eyes with him. "What's your name?"

"Wyatt."

"Goodnight, Wyatt." I yank Andy harder than necessary and haul her toward the living room sofa. "What are you on?"

"Nothing."

"Okay, great. Now, what are you on?" My phone starts ringing but I send it to voicemail.

"I told you, Justice. Nothing. God, you're freaking me out."

Usually, I leave Andy to her own devices, but I can't do that anymore. I've failed too many people already. I prop her legs up on the couch and run to the kitchen for a glass of water.

When I come back, she's on her knees in front of the couch, digging through her purse.

"I just have to find something," she says.

I grab the purse, and she tries to protest but collapses onto the floor.

"Is this what you're looking for?" It's a baggy the size of my thumbnail, empty except for some crystalline residue. I'm pretty sure it's meth. "When's the last time you slept?"

"I don't know. A couple days, maybe."

"Did Wyatt give it to you?" I hear murder in my voice.

"No, no, it wasn't like that."

"Oh God, you didn't go into the city to get this?" I think of Andy stumbling around Kensington, and for the first time I understand what it must feel like to be a parent.

She shakes her head. "I ordered it off the internet," she says.

"I guess Amazon really is the everything store."

"No. You have to go on some special websites. They call it the Dark Web. It's real safe. They have ratings and everything. So you don't get ripped off. It's actually crazy. You know Bitcoin, right? My dad bought some for me years ago, and now it's worth like thirty thousand dollars. And you can just send it, and then they FedEx you whatever you want. Glass. Molly. Pot. You can even put a hit out on someone." She's talking insanely fast, and I'm getting palpitations just listening.

"I don't need a how-to guide. Is that all you have?"

She nods, but I keep searching her purse just in case. When I'm convinced she's clean, I sit down beside her. "You need to sleep."

"They were following me," she says.

"Who?"

"I could hear them, but they must be professionals because whenever I turned around, they would just jump into the bushes and hide."

I assume she's paranoid, but you know the old saying. I check the windows. It's dark in front of our home, except a streetlight about fifteen yards down the road. My heart skips three beats as my phone goes off again. It's Izaak. I send it to voicemail and lock the door, just in case.

When I turn around, Andy's gone.

I scream her name and get no answer. I race upstairs and see her bedroom door slam shut just as I turn into the hall. She's screaming something I can't make out, and by the time I get there, the door is locked.

"There's no one out there," I say.

"You're one of them. I just know. I just know it. You're one of them."

Sometimes the girls at work share drug stories. I remember one of them talking about how she smoked so much glass that she thought her boyfriend was secretly working with ICE to deport her mom.

"I get it, Andy. I get it. I can totally understand where you're coming from. But think this through. You've known me more than five years. I've seen you do drugs, how many times? If I was going to rat you out, wouldn't I have done it by now?"

She's not talking anymore, so I keep going.

"So, I'm not going to tell you to trust me. It's okay not to trust me." My phone goes off again, but I ignore it. "I just want to make sure you're okay. So why don't we do this? Let's go back downstairs. You stay on the couch, and I'll just sit there with you. Okay? I won't touch you or talk to you, but if you need something, I'll get it. That's it. I just want to know that you're okay."

I hear the door creak open, and I take a step back. My shoe catches on the rug and I stumble, just as the door flies open and Andy comes running at me with a pair of scissors. As I fall backward, I swing my heel into her knees, which was dumb because she instantly collapses on top of me, scissors aimed at my face. I thrust my shoulders forward and hips back just in time to hear the metal dig into the floor, inches from my nose.

Andy's screaming again and I roll on top of her, pinning her wrists above her head. She squirms, but I bear down hard on her hips so she can't gain any leverage.

"Here's what we're going to do," I say through gritted teeth. "You're going to knock this shit off. Then we're going to sit on your bed and do shots until we pass out. Got it?" I know it's not standard operating procedure, but it's all I can come up with. And I guess it was the right move because the one thing you can say about Andy is the girl will never turn down an opportunity to drink.

I pocket the scissors and drag her into her room. She's mumbling something apologetic, and I wonder what sort of trauma could bring a person to this. Then I think about my own past, and part of me resents Andy. Why can't she be stronger? We all have pain. But we face life and try to build something. Why does she have to be so weak?

Then I think. Come on, Justice… are you really any better than her? Didn't you run when you should have fought? And Andy, she's just betraying her own life. How many lives have *you* betrayed?

I hunt around the room for anything else that could stab or bludgeon me. I toss the scissors and an iron into the hall, then walk over to the wood-grain dresser Andy bought from Wayfair, which doubles as a dry bar.

I don't always pound liquor, but when I do, I pound Jameson. Andy has a bottle of Limited Reserve that's twice as expensive as anything I've ever imbibed. I pull open the cap and take a swig. It's smooth, as far as booze goes, so I don't feel like a total amateur. Then I hand Andy the bottle and order her to drink.

Half an hour later, she's not quite passed out, but she's calmed down enough that I'm no longer worried she's going to stab me with office supplies.

"You know what you are, Justice?" she says as I run my hand through her hair, trying to calm her. "You're good people."

"Yeah? Tell me more about me."

"I mean, you can be a total bitch sometimes, and I'm pretty sure you're a virgin. But you're still good people." Her words are slow and honest, and at moments she reminds me of Laudie Mae.

"I'm a stripper," I say.

She bursts out laughing. "What?"

"I'm serious. You wondered where I work? I'm a stripper."

She can't catch her breath. "Oh my God. I would pay to see that."

"Glad I could amuse you."

"I bet you don't even masturbate."

"Dear lord."

"You do have nice boobs, though. Like, I know mine are killer. But in twenty years? Yours will still be pointing due north, and I'm going to be swaying in the wind."

"Thanks?"

We chat about nothing for what seems like hours, the space between her words stretching out like bubblegum. Occasionally, one of us hits the Jameson.

"Andy, can I ask you something?"

She flings her arm in the air as if waving me on.

"Why do you mess with that stuff?"

Her eyes are heavy, and the words just sort of drip out. "Don't be a prude, *Mom*."

"I'm not judging. It's just I don't understand."

I have her head cradled in my lap and she closes her eyes and smiles. "Have you ever been happy, Justice? Like, in the moment? Have you ever thought, oh, that's good? That's enough?"

"No."

"Well. Now you know."

I climb off the bed and start rummaging through her DVD collection. "Jesus, Andy, what is this garbage? It's like you raided the discount rack at Walmart." I settle for *Three Men and a Little Lady*. It's not Hitchcock, but then again this hardly seems like the time for Hitchcock.

I start the DVD and by the time Donna De Lory is finished singing "Always Thinking of You," Andy has drifted off with the hint of a smile still on her lips.

I slip out of the room and crouch down against the hallway wall, checking my messages. Four missed calls, all from Izaak. Three voicemails. I polish off the Jameson before hitting play.

"J. Checking in to make sure you're okay. Cadence found

those flyers you left. You were damn lucky I was the first person she ran into because it took me two hours to convince her not to tell her dad. Call me back, girl."

"Yo, J. I haven't heard from you. Hit me up and let me know you got home okay."

"*Justice*. I'm serious. Where are you?"

I start to hit the call button but the room is spinning and I rest my head on the floor and let the world disappear.

CHAPTER FIFTEEN

I'M STILL IN THE HALLWAY when something jolts me awake, and I realize that it's not the pounding in my head but the pounding of our front door. I stumble down the stairs still half asleep, and before I have a chance to second-guess myself, I open the door.

It's a uniformed patrol officer, his face drawn in that determined seriousness they must teach in the academy. "Sergeant David, Lower Merion Police. Justice Winters?"

"Yes."

"Do you mind if I step inside? It's a little cold out here." He doesn't wait for my answer before entering. He's trim and clean shaven with eyes so light they must constantly appear to be on the verge of tears. Pop used to call them Cal Ripken eyes.

Even though my brain is moving at the pace of a taco, I think of this rant Abe will go on occasionally, about how we should never talk to the police, never let them in our homes, never consent to them searching us. It all made perfect sense, yet in the moment it feels impossible to do anything but follow orders.

"Nice place," he says looking around, and I hope to God Andy didn't leave anything in plain sight. "Just you?"

"I have a roommate. She's upstairs."

"And what's her name?"

"Andy."

He's writing everything down. "Andy what?"

"Simmons, I think. What's this about?"

"Where were you last night?"

"Here." Stop talking, Justice. But part of me still feels like if I play innocent, I'll come out of this unscathed.

"All night?"

"Yes."

"From what time to what time?" This is why Abe says never talk to the police. He's trying to pin me down on details. And one provable lie—or even one mistake—can then be used twist my arm until I tell the truth, the whole truth, and nothing but the truth. But what Sergeant David doesn't know is that I've watched an embarrassing number of *Law and Order* marathons.

"I'm not sure."

"Ballpark it for me."

"I honestly don't know. I wouldn't want to lie to you."

"I appreciate that," he says. "Did you go anywhere yesterday?"

I guess I should've seen that coming. "I'm sorry, what's this about?"

"We'll get to that. I just need to check a few details first. Let's start in the morning. Where's the first place you went?"

"Around campus."

"You talk to anyone?"

"Lots of people."

"Anyone specific?"

"I'm not sure. Lots of people. Everything's been kind of a blur since those boys were killed."

"I see." I don't like how he says it. "Did you leave campus at any point yesterday?"

I can feel the vise tightening. There's no good way to admit I went to Philly without admitting I was in Philly with Dax. And even though I'm confident there's no evidence I was in Philly, I can't know that for sure. Success isn't the only thing that leaves clues.

"I'll be honest with you. I was pretty drunk yesterday." True that. "I could've taken the train into Philly to see *Hamilton* and wouldn't remember."

He shakes his head in disapproval or frustration. I can't tell which. "So, you wouldn't remember, for example, driving around with some guy in a blue truck?"

"No." The vise tightens.

The first thing that occurs to me is that he's by himself. Is that right?

"And if someone said they saw you passing out flyers on campus, you wouldn't remember that, either?"

I can't get the words out but manage to shake my head.

A Lower Merion sergeant? It's possible, but...

"Look, Miss Winters. I've been honest with you, haven't I? And I expect the same from you. But right now, we both know you're not telling me the truth. We both know you were out last night, passing out flyers. And we both know what was written on those flyers. Who were you with?"

In my house? Not the station?

"I don't feel comfortable right now," I say. "Can you have a female officer come?"

"What?"

"I don't like being alone with men. Could you just have someone else come here? I'll tell you whatever you want then."

"It doesn't work like that, Miss Winters. We don't take requests."

How much do you trust your instincts, Justice?

"I want to talk to my lawyer," I say, taking a step back and pulling out my phone.

He moves toward me. "Put that away. You can talk to your lawyer when I'm done with my investigation."

I take another step back. "You're done. I want my lawyer."

He takes another step forward and I reverse directions and lunge at him. I have one hand wrapped desperately around the grip of his Glock while I throw my other arm around his neck. I'm scrambling to take his back without letting go of the gun, but the physics just aren't working. His hand is squeezing mine, trying to keep the gun holstered while the other hand starts yanking at my hair.

Then he lets go and I feel him start to tumble backward under my weight. We crash into the door and I'm about to sink my teeth into the skin of his neck when a crushing blow hits my temple.

I'm on the floor and through blurry vision I see him going for his pepper spray. I swing my open hand into his wrist and the can goes tumbling across the room.

He tries to throw his arm around my neck but I keep my chin down and slide out easily, only to feel his knee drive directly into my solar plexus. By the time I can even begin to catch my breath, there's a Glock pointed at my face.

I brace myself for the impact of the bullets. But he doesn't shoot—and he doesn't call for backup.

"Justice! Justice!" It takes me a second to realize it's not coming from the officer but from someone who has just run through the front door.

"Dax?"

He's kneeling beside me and laughing. "What the shit happened in here?" He looks up at Sergeant David, who is breathing heavily, his gun still aimed at my face. "Jesus, Chuck, you were just supposed to talk to her."

"The bitch went for my gun."

"You did *what?*" Sergeant David holsters his Glock as Dax pulls me to my feet.

"He's not a real cop," I say.

"Fuck you," Sergeant David says.

"Oh, he's a legit cop." Dax looks me up and down. "But what the hell are you?"

"Confused."

Dax laughs again. "How'd she do, Chuck?"

"You mean besides nearly getting her brains splattered all over the floor? She kept her mouth shut."

"Well, Justice. Go get yourself ready. We're going out."

CHAPTER SIXTEEN

DAX TURNS OFF THE RAPTOR'S ignition, and even though we've been driving for forty minutes, my adrenaline is still off the charts. We're in the parking lot of something called the Airport Bar & Grill, just down the street from the Pottstown-Limerick Airport. The parking lot is empty, except for a few beat-up trucks, an old-school Harley-Davidson, and a Tesla Model S with a license plate that reads HVYDUTY.

I haven't talked the entire ride, and when Dax sees my face, he reaches out and touches my thigh. I bite my lip and fight the urge to pull away. "Hey, you okay? You're not still pissed about Chuck?"

What, the cop who almost de-brained me an hour ago? Haven't thought about it once. "What is this place? It looks like a junkyard threw a barbecue."

"It's not much to look at."

"But…"

"But this is where we're eating."

We head inside. A bored-looking waiter with a gut spilling over his jeans and a stained shirt half untucked ushers us into a back room of the restaurant. Dax walks ahead of me, and we enter something called the A-6 room, which is decorated with photos of old Navy jets and aircraft carriers and smells like fried everything.

The room is empty, except for two men seated across from each other at a table set for six. The older one looks like a bulldog with thinning hair, a jet-black goatee, and a couple of spare chins. Think Rip Torn but after a bender. He's holding court, and his gravelly voice echoes against the walls.

"...and I say to him, 'Never bluff a sober Scotsman.'"

He roars with laughter and, noticing us, waves us over. "Dax!"

Dax pulls out a chair next to the younger guy and motions for me to sit before plopping down across from me. "Chuck had to bail, guys. Justice, this is Arnold Lyons." He motions to the guy beside me, who nods but doesn't look my way. Lyons is dressed in a tailored suit and looks like an undertaker, with heavy bags under his eyes that give him the appearance of eternal weariness. His pallid skin is dry and lifeless, and it looks as if it would feel cold to the touch.

Dax continues. "And this—"

"Jack Jackson." The bulldog sticks a meaty fist across the table, and it swallows my hand. "You didn't say she was beautiful, Dax."

"You all ready to order?" the sloppy waiter interrupts.

"Just bring out a few of your appetizers and a round of Manhattans." Jack Jackson leans toward me. "They make great Manhattans here. The best I've ever had."

"I'm on the mend," I say.

"Even better. Hair of the dog, am I right?"

The waiter looks at me and I shake my head. Once he leaves, Dax spreads out in his chair, stretching out his hands like he's unveiling a work of art. "Meet the Exiles."

"Some of us," Arnold says, cracking his knuckles.

"There are local chapters everywhere," Dax says. "But we were the first. Thanks to Jack."

Jack nods like he's accepting an award. "Oh, I can't take all the credit. I'm just the money man. These boys do all the work."

"He's modest," Dax says. "Jack's the one with the vision. There's a lot of people who think like we do, Justice, but no one has come up with a strategy to move the ball forward."

"We'll get to that. We'll get to that," Jack says. "But first… tell me about yourself, Justice."

"I'm just happy to be here."

"Don't you be modest, girl," Jack says. "Brag a little."

"Be careful, Jack," Dax says. "She almost took out Chuck with his own gun."

"I didn't know he was with you at the time," I say.

"With *us*," Jack says. "Now, Dax says you're a student. What are you studying?"

"Pysch."

"What are your plans after school?"

"I'm not sure. Maybe law school."

"I love it. I'm in business, myself. The leading supplier of low-emissions, heavy-duty vehicles. Mostly natural gas so far, but we're coming out with a fully electric line. Maybe you saw me on CNBC last week?"

"Sorry," I say.

"Well, no, I guess I'd be surprised if you had. So a lawyer, eh? Not bad. Not bad. That's useful. We've got a good group here. Dax with his computer skills, Chuck with his law enforcement connections, and now a lawyer? What kind of law you plan to practice?"

"Criminal."

"Well hell, girl, you're like manna from Heaven." He laughs long and hard.

"What about him?" I say, nodding toward Arnold.

"Oh, Arnold? He's… let's just say he's a jack of all trades."

Arnold scoffs, still playing with his hands.

The waiter drops off a few dishes, none vegan. "I'll be back with the drinks," he says.

"You wanted to know the solution to white genocide, Justice?" Dax says. "Well, it isn't kicking the shit out of random wetbacks. And it isn't walking down the street screaming protest slogans."

"Justice, you ever see the movie *Independence Day*?" Jack says.

"No."

"I guess it was a bit before your time. But you have a bunch of aliens attacking planet Earth. And what we figure out is that these aliens, you see, they're all just drones run by a central brain. You take out the central brain, the drones are powerless."

"That's not what happened in *Independence Day*," Dax says.

"Whatever. The analogy holds."

"What Jack's trying to say," Dax says, "is that we've identified the real root of all evil—the source of white genocide—and we've figured out a way to fight it."

"Okay," I say tentatively.

"The universities." Jack slams his fist against the table. "Isn't it obvious? The universities are the problem. That's where we mass-produce Progressives. In these indoctrination factories."

"You know how many conservatives are in the social sciences?" Dax says. "Less than five percent. You know how many self-described Marxists there are? Eighteen percent."

Jack Jackson nods enthusiastically. "You ever heard how

116

Progressivism got its start in America? The universities. Hundred fifty years ago or thereabouts, you wanted to be an academic, you went and you studied in Germany. So kids would go over, they'd study Kant, they'd study Hegel, they'd study Fichte, they'd study Marx. They'd imbibe Bismarck's new welfare state. Then they'd come home and pass on that poison to Americans."

"I'm confused. Aren't we pro-Germany? I mean, didn't they get it right... you know, before the war?" I can barely get out the words, but no one seems to notice.

"Some of us think so. Some of us are," Jack looks at Dax, "a little squishy."

"I just don't think that violence was necessary. I don't see why it can't just be whites with whites, blacks with blacks, Jews with Jews. If we just stick with our own kind, there's room for everyone."

"You're a utopian. That's why I love you, boy. Anyway, that's not what she was asking. Justice, the point is that the Germans, they got half the story right and half the story wrong. Their mistake was thinking you needed big government to have good government. That you needed an all-powerful state to organize people and tell them what to do. But you go down that route, you end up somewhere you don't want to be. For the Germans, that led to fascism—not just for Jews but for all of them. Then for the Russians, the same ideas led to Communism. You know what the Communists said, right? They said race doesn't matter. Black, white, yellow... it didn't matter. What mattered was you were part of the same class."

"Okay."

"Well, in America, that becomes modern Progressivism.

Take away our rights, grow the government, and use it to create Communism-lite. Fascism, Communism, Progressivism, even Libertarianism… none of them gets to the root of what's good."

"What's that?"

"Patriotism. That's what we're missing. The big government folks think strength comes from government. Then you've got the small government folks who go and pretend we're all isolated individuals. But we're not. You can't live unless you live for something greater than yourself. That's what patriotism means. It means sticking by your people because they're your people. That's true strength."

"So, what's the strategy?" I mutter, just wanting to get the whole thing over with.

The waiter returns, and I wonder if he knows what kind of men these are. And if he does know, what must he be thinking of me?

"Ready to order?"

Everyone orders, and even though I'm not hungry, I'm desperate for something to calm my nausea. "Do you have any vegan options?"

I can feel the table look at me suspiciously. "Health reasons. It's not a political thing."

"I don't know. We got a tomato and spinach omelet."

"Never mind. Just bread."

He leaves and Jack polishes off his Manhattan.

"So, you were saying?" I nudge. I have to be careful, though. There's a fine line between normal curiosity and the over-eagerness of a snitch.

"Right, the strategy. Well, really, it's simple. Sunlight is the best disinfectant. Once people know about how corrupt the universities are, they'll lose their influence. It's really that simple. Once they know it's a guild system designed to protect radical lefties who want to indoctrinate children, what parent is going to spend a hundred thousand dollars a year on that? More importantly, what alumnus is going to pour millions into that?"

"And people are already starting to realize it," Dax says. "They see mainstream conservatives getting attacked by social justice mobs. They see liberal professors getting fired for not being left-wing enough. They read a bunch of academics in *The New York Times* saying America is an evil country because we had slaves—never mind everyone else had slaves, too, and that ours were sold into slavery by other Africans."

"Frankly, the universities have been headed for extinction for a long time," says Jack Jackson. "We're just speeding things up a bit."

"How?"

"That's the easy part. We just find allies on the inside and we throw money at them. Money to tell the world the truth about our colleges. Money to start alternatives. Money to hire more allies so we have more insiders to expose the system."

"But how many allies could there be?"

"Oh, you'd be surprised."

The waiter returns. "These are biscuits," I say.

He stares at me blankly.

"They're made with butter. Milk."

"We use grass-fed, I think."

I consider ordering fruit, but reconsider. "I'll take that Manhattan."

Dax leans forward and, with his eyes on me, says to Jack, "Can I tell her?"

"Tell away."

"We've got someone at Haverford."

I know what he's going to say before the name spills from his lips, but I ask anyway. "Who?"

"Peter Harper."

Part of me wants to argue. Didn't Dr. Harper say he was hoping the killings would end identity politics? Didn't he dismiss the Exiles' rantings as garbage? But I decide to let it go.

"Well, look. Everything you're talking about? It sounds great. But I'm not a patient person." I plant my eyes squarely on Dax. "When I said to you I wasn't sure I agreed with what happened to those basketball players? That wasn't true. I think that's exactly what has to be done."

Dax starts to speak, but Arnold Lyons holds a finger to his lips and lets out a long, "*Shhhh.*" He places his hands on my shoulders, and his black eyes look unflinchingly into mine. Then he runs his hands slowly over my arms, then up my sides, then over my breasts and my belly. When he reaches my lap he whispers, "Take it out."

I pull out my phone and toss it onto the table.

"Unlock it," he says.

He examines it for a moment before dropping it into my lap. Without another word, he turns back around and returns to cracking his knuckles.

"You can never be too careful," Jack says. "Look, girl. Right or wrong, what you're talking about is unavoidable. But it's all about being strategic. There's a time and place for everything. What we've got at your school right now is a lot of scared people thinking we're the enemy. That won't do. What we need is a cauldron. And for that to happen, we need our own victims.

We need the other side to overreact and to overreach so everyone is outraged and afraid. The world needs to see us, not as a rogue gang attacking the blacks, but as agents of justice standing between decent society and chaos."

I see Dax eying Jack. He hasn't heard this part before.

"Dax tells me you had your own run-in with their kind. Last year. A boy named Kareem Hanley."

My stomach sinks. I look at Dax but he's deliberately not looking my way.

"Oh, don't go getting bashful, my dear," Jack says. "That's why I wanted to meet you. It's perfect. Damn perfect. You come out and you tell them—everything you said was true. But you tell them how you were pressured not to say it."

"I *was* pressured. His dad—"

"Not just his lawyer dad," Jack continues, as if we were writing partners collaborating on a screenplay. "The Black Students' League, too. They came to you and said: 'You drop this thing or we're going to scream racism.' You see it, don't you? You see how perfect it is? Now we've got victims on all sides. A cauldron, girl. You're going to help us build our cauldron."

I feel completely boxed in and have no clue how to wiggle my way out. "If I do that, Kareem Hanley's dad is going to come after me."

Jack's grin turns into a full-blown smile. "You'll have the best lawyers money can buy."

"I'm shy. I don't think I could take having the whole world knowing my name, looking into every piece of my life."

The smile disappears. Jack picks up his napkin and twists it around his thumb. "What I'm hearing is a girl searching for excuses. Now, I need to know. Are you a team player?"

Dax's eyes dart from Jack to Lyons to me. He gives me a subtle nod, and I'm not sure whether he's encouraging me or warning me.

I try to run the calculations. If I say no, maybe they don't let me walk out of here. If I say yes, the clock is ticking. With a little luck, I can string them along for a week or two.

"Of course I'm a team player, Jack. I just need a couple of weeks to get my affairs in order." Whatever that means.

"You've got two days," Jack says. "And I'm being generous."

So much for luck. "Fine. But if I do this, I need something from you."

The grin returns. He expects people to follow orders, but apparently appreciates moxie. "What else is family for?"

"I need to know. The murders… was that us? The BSL president… was that us?" It's reckless. I'm pushing way too hard and I can feel the tension level at the table rise. But this may be my only chance to find out the truth.

Lyons snaps, "Why do you care?"

"Oh, come now, Arnold," Jack says. "No need to scare the girl. But my friend makes a good point. Why do you care?"

I hold Jack's stare: "I need to know if you're the real deal."

"You need to know that, huh?"

"I do."

"Yes, Justice. It was us. We're the real fucking deal."

CHAPTER SEVENTEEN

POP NEVER TALKED MUCH ABOUT the killings. It was just something we did, the way other families attended church or vacationed in the Poconos. When I was thirteen, though, I worked up the courage to ask him how it all started. He was scraping mud off a four-wheeler and didn't stop to look at me.

But he answered, the way he always did, with the words flowing like poetry in his thick, guttural voice. His captivating voice suggested refinement, and I've always suspected his own childhood was spent in boarding school manor houses.

What surprised me about the first killing was how accidental it was. Pop was nothing if not deliberate. Laudie Mae used to joke that he would draw up plans to take a shit. But that first time? It was October, and we were hit with an early snow. A Heiden had stopped her car at the end of our road to take pictures. Pop said she had some fancy camera, back in the day when they still used real film, and waved him down as he was driving past to ask if he'd take a few photos of her dancing in the flurries.

When people ask if I believe in fate, that's what I think of. Had the snow not fallen, had her car stopped a mile further down the road, had she not waved down Pop, she'd still have her life.

I guess you could say it's so random only fate can explain it.

But me? I see it the other way. Our lives are ruled by the blind forces of accident.

That's why, crazy as it sounds, I believe the Exiles killed Terrance and Warren. Maybe they were waiting for the opportunity and it fell into their laps. Maybe they needed me to shed first blood so they could work up the courage. Maybe they were hoping the cops would find Vic's killer's DNA at the scene.

Or maybe I'm just haunted by all the other possibilities.

I arrive on campus just after nine and meet up with Izaak at Barclay.

"I've got them," I say.

"Yeah?"

I tell him about Jack Jackson, about the Exiles' vision and their strategy. I don't mention the thing about Kareem. "They say Dr. Harper's involved."

"Harper?"

"I don't see it. But that's what they said."

"Anything else?"

"There was this one guy. Arnold Lyons. He didn't say much, but he gave me the creeps."

"So, you're sure it was them?"

"Jack told me straight out."

Izaak nods and seems to be contemplating something.

"Well?" I say, "When are you going to write on it?"

The question knocks him out of his trance. "What? J, what you got is great, but it's only a start. We got a lot more work to do, starting with this stripper."

"But… I mean, isn't that beside the point now? We know it was the Exiles."

"That's not how this works. If I'm going to put my name

on something, I need to be able to look myself in the mirror and know I played the game the right way. That I chased down every lead. Once we go public, the whole country is going to be asking questions. We take shortcuts, that's going to come back on us. So, what I'm going to do is I'm going to head to the club and find out what there is to find out. You in?"

Good question. Going to Night Shade with Izaak is very high on my list of potentially dumbest things I could possibly do. But at the same time, the idea of him in there alone, hearing God knows what from God knows who? At least this way, if someone tells him about me, I'll know. I can't imagine a worse nightmare than pacing around my house all night anxiously wondering.

"I'm in," I say.

Izaak offers to drive, but I tell him he's going to need to drink if he doesn't want to come off as sketchy. That's not technically true. Plenty of guys come to the club and don't drink. But my hope is a few cocktails will throw Izaak just enough off his game that I can avoid this turning into a literal farce.

We ride in silence, too nervous to make small talk and too paranoid to discuss the case in front of the driver. I spend the drive thinking about how I'm going to get Izaak to go to press before Jack's forty-eight-hour deadline. When I ask myself why I didn't just tell Izaak the truth, I'm shocked by the answer. I didn't want to hurt Izaak's feelings by mentioning Kareem. Why Izaak's feelings should matter to me is a question I'm too afraid to ask.

I have the Uber drop us off down the block from Night Shade. "We shouldn't go in there together," I say. "We should play it like we're strangers. Let me go in first, and then you swing by in, like, five or ten minutes."

I'm counting on a couple of things to make this work. The first is that none of the girls are going to talk anyway. Izaak is smooth, but like all customers, he's an outsider. And even if you don't like the girls on your team, when it comes to outsiders, you protect your own. It's like the military. But with nudity.

The other thing I'm counting on is that I won't run into any regulars. My main plan is to get lucky. My backup plan is to come up with something brilliant on the fly. My tertiary plan is to slip Izaak a Mickey and hope he forgets the whole thing.

I walk in the front entrance. Bobby's checking IDs and collecting the cover.

"Didn't know you were working tonight," he says.

"Just stopping by for a bit."

He doesn't ask questions, so I don't elaborate.

Inside, it's unusually busy, which I count as a mixed blessing. More opportunities for the wrong person to say the wrong thing but also more likely I'll get lost in the shuffle.

The first girl I see is Jewel, fresh off the stage.

"So… really weird favor to ask," I say.

"Oooh. I'm in. What is it?"

"A guy I know is coming by in about five minutes. He doesn't know I work here, and I don't want him to know."

"Fanny, you minx. Taking your man to a strip club. Right on."

"Not quite. Here's the other thing. We're pretending not to know each other."

Jewel adjusts her bra. "And I thought *my* love life was twisted."

"Will you spread the word?"

"Like VD in a brothel."

She races off, and I make a beeline for the bar. This just might work.

"Next to the stage, give it up for Scarlett!" the DJ announces.

Looks like I might actually have to track down that Mickey.

I take a seat at the bar. Brenda's off tonight. It's Wendy and Gus. Wendy used to dance, but quit after she had a baby and became self-conscious about her belly. But she liked working for Abe, so he made her a bartender, even though she's so klutzy I have to think replacing all of those glasses is going to drive Abe into the red someday. Still, she's sweet as honey, and despite what she thinks, has the kind of body I'd go to town on if I was into that sort of thing.

"Fantine, what'll it be?"

"It's Justice tonight," I say as loudly as I dare.

"If you say so." She pours Absolut Vodka and Midori into a shot glass. "I just learned this one. Gus calls it an Absolut Legspreader."

I'd usually pass, but something this classy? I down it just as Izaak walks in. He somehow manages to find me immediately without making eye contact, then heads right over to the main stage. Part of me wishes he seemed awkward here, but he's as smooth as ever.

Someone taps me on the shoulder. "That him?" Jewel says, nodding in Izaak's direction.

"That's him."

"Yummy."

"He's all yours."

"He have money?"

"More than we ever will."

"Double yum."

"You talk to the girls?" I say.

"Not Scarlett. She was already on the stage. You need me to?"

"No. It's better if she doesn't know."

Jewel takes off for Izaak. I'm taking a gamble with Scarlett. But my hope is that the issue doesn't come up. By my count nineteen dancers are on tonight, and there's every reason to think Scarlett will end up in the VIP area with someone before Izaak gets to her.

"Hey, seat taken?" A guy rounding sixty, wearing sweats and a hunting hat, sits down next to me before I can answer. "Now what's a pretty girl like you doing in a place like this? Bartender," he calls to Wendy. "Bartender, get this girl another of whatever she's drinking. And, aw well, go ahead and make one for me, too."

"Best not be hitting on my girl," Wendy says. "She's all mine."

"You don't say."

I shrug, and as hunting hat gets up and wanders away, I fold my hands in prayer in Wendy's direction.

When I turn back around, I don't see Izaak by the stage. At first, I think he's gone to the back with Jewel, but then I see three other girls with him at a half-moon booth in the corner of the main room. Efficient.

The evening passes like that. Guys stop by and try to pick me up, Wendy shoos them away and feeds me drinks, and Izaak makes the rounds like he's a man on a mission. Which of course he is. Once eleven hits, I'm plenty tipsy and don't even notice him lean over the bar right next to me.

He signals for the bartender and orders a glass of Patrón.

"How you doing?" I say.

"Time of my life," he says, and I can't tell whether he's still in character.

An arm slips around his shoulder and now I'm staring at

Scarlett. Izaak turns to look at her, and I'm really hoping Scarlett can read lips.

I don't work here. We don't know each other. PLEASE.

She sees me but pretends not to, and I breathe a sigh of relief as she starts running her game. After a few minutes she's ready to go in for the kill.

"How about a dance, honey?"

"Nah, I'm good."

"You can bring your girl."

Izaak glances at me over his shoulder. "Her? We just met."

"No better way to get to know each other."

"Sorry, you're not my type," I say to Scarlett.

"That's not what your pimp says," Scarlett snaps.

"Girls, girls, let's take it down a notch. Man, this place really is crazy. I heard one of the girls here went to town on some kid a few days back."

My God. So. Fucking. Smooth.

Scarlett winks at me, and I brace myself for what's coming.

"It was something else," Scarlett says.

"Which one was it?"

"She's not… working tonight."

"I'm just asking 'cause I'm all for a little crazy. What's her name?"

"Ask around for Fantine. You won't be able to miss her. She's tiny…" Scarlett points at me. "About your height. She has short, dark hair…" More pointing. "About like yours. She's smart, too. I think she studies psychology somewhere on the Main Line."

"Wow," I say, "just like me."

"What a coincidence," Scarlett says. "Well, you change your mind about that dance, you let me know."

She struts away, and I'm searching Izaak's face without looking like I have a care in the world. I can't read him at all. "You ready to get out of there?" I say.

He finishes his Patrón and tosses a healthy tip on the bar. "Yeah. Yeah. Let's get out of here."

The ride home is as silent as the ride uptown, only this time the silence is tense and uncomfortable. We're dropped off just after midnight and walk down to Duck Pond, where we lean against the wooden fence posts and look out at the still, dark water. The sky is black and traces of white and red from the cars driving along Lancaster flicker in the darkness. Izaak keeps sneaking peeks at me like he's going to say something. I decide to break the ice, terrified of why the ice is there.

"What did you find out?" I begin.

"Just what you heard."

"So, what do you think?"

"Forget it, J. It's a dead end."

"Why do I feel like you're not telling me something?"

"You really want to go down that road?"

He's right. I don't.

"You don't think we have enough to find that dancer?"

He rubs the back of his neck. "Has to be dozens of girls meet that description. Of course, she shows up at *Night Shade* again…"

"So, what do we do? We include that in the story?"

"Justice, we don't have a story. We don't have anyone willing to go on the record. We don't have any hard evidence of anything. Not unless you recorded that dinner of yours."

I quake just thinking about those hands on my body. "No."

"We need more."

"I can't go back there, Izaak. With the Exiles? I almost

snapped last time. When they were talking about a race war like it was an aspiration? I wanted to kill them. Every one of them. And what would I even say? 'Hey, guys, I wasn't paying attention last time. Can you repeat your grand master plan?' Jesus, *what do you want from me?*" I'm screaming at him now. "I'm telling you what I heard. Heard with my own ears. But that's not enough for you. *What I say is never enough for you.*"

There's hurt and indignance on his face. I don't care. All the anger and hatred I've bottled up is pouring out like acid and I want every word of it to burn. To make him feel for one moment the way he's made me feel every day of the last a year.

"That's not fair," he says. "This wasn't my idea. You asked *me* to help *you.*"

"You owe it to me. What you put me through? The shame? The humiliation? That's a debt you can never repay. You're so worried about your name and your reputation. What about mine? If you had one ounce of integrity, you'd print any damn thing I told you to."

My face is a mess of tears, and I can't stop my shoulders from convulsing.

"Jesus Christ," I say. "You can't even look at me. Look at me, Izaak. Take it in because you did this."

"You think I don't know that!" He grabs a fence post and slams his foot against it, the crack of old wood echoing in the campus air. He leans against the broken post, head on his arms like he's gathering his strength. When he looks up at me, tears are in his eyes. "I knew this would happen. When Cadence told me to publish the story, I warned her that this is how it would play out."

"What are you talking about?"

"After shit went down with Kareem, Cadence came to me. She said you wanted to speak out, to make sure he didn't hurt anyone else the way he hurt you. Only you were scared. She said if I ran the story, it would give you the courage to tell the truth."

"You're lying."

"Am I?"

"Why wouldn't she tell me? Why wouldn't *you* tell me?"

"Because I knew what it would do to you. She was the only person who stood by you. You think I wanted to take that away from you, too?"

I'm lost, trying to reconstruct the entire narrative of my life post-Kareem, but I can't put the pieces back together. "What, so I'm supposed to forgive you now? You had no right. Neither of you. Speaking out was my choice." It's all true, but there's no conviction in the words. They tumble out like cans from an overfilled recycling bin.

"I'm not asking for forgiveness," he says, his voice quiet. "I'm not asking for anything. I just thought I owed you the truth."

The truth.

I don't want to say it, but I realize I have no choice. He has to know. I take a deep breath and then force out the words: "There's something I didn't tell you about my meeting with Jack Jackson. We have a deadline."

I tell Izaak about the Kareem thing. He listens quietly, then says, "So basically what you're saying is we've got about two days until the Exiles start thinking maybe you're not an ally but a threat." He buries his face in his hands. "Shit, J. This is what I was afraid of."

I turn around to look at our campus, the lighted buildings like an oasis in the dark. Someday maybe I'll be able to stand here and figure out what it all means. To sort out my feelings for Izaak and Cadence, to experience my life not as a desperate quest for safety or vengeance, but as a peaceful struggle for joy. But that's a luxury I don't have. My time and my thoughts don't belong to me. They belong to Jack Jackson.

After a long silence, I say, "There is a way we might be able to verify this story."

"Yeah?" Izaak says.

"But trust me when I say it's better if you don't know."

"So. More secrets."

"Yeah," I say. "More secrets."

CHAPTER EIGHTEEN

"HOW DO YOU PICK A LOCK?"

I press the phone to my ear with my shoulder as I struggle to clean up Winston's mess while Winston struggles to chase after another dog. It suddenly dawns on me that any self-respecting person would've demanded a discount on the rent for walking their landlord's pet.

"So, you're going to start robbing houses now?" Abe says.

I need to get into Dax's apartment, and contrary to every eighties movie ever, you can't actually break into buildings with just a credit card or a paper clip.

"Sort of."

"There are easier ways to make money, babe."

"I'm not after money."

"Well, then, it's pretty simple. You smash a window or break down a door. That's all there is to it."

"No, this is an apartment building. I can't be making a bunch of noise. Can't I just jimmy the lock somehow?"

"Oh sure. First thing you do, you get yourself a drill…"

"Bye, Abe." I hang up, drag Winston back in the direction of our house, and settle in for a bit of research.

My initial plan had been to follow Dax until he went

somewhere incriminating. But that could easily take days. And what exactly would I be looking for? Some nefarious headquarters with an Exiles sign out front? Besides, if Dax is who I think he is, he just might have my bag. No question, I need to get inside that apartment. Alone.

The one thing I have going for me is I've been inside the apartment before. At the start of our "date," Dax made me leave my phone in his kitchen, so I know a few things. First, I know there's a security guard who isn't likely to let me up to snoop around. Second, I know that even if he did, Dax deadbolts the lock when he leaves. But, third, I know it's a second-floor apartment with a sliding-glass door that leads to a balcony. Maybe he leaves it unlocked. And if he doesn't? Well, five minutes on YouTube and I'm pretty sure I'll be able to get in anyway.

I grab a screwdriver from our shed and head out in the direction of The Loft.

I've been at the Starbucks across from The Loft for close to three hours when I see Dax's Raptor exit the parking garage. I start the timer on my phone. I figure I'll have at least twenty minutes, which should be plenty of time. Unless he's buying cigarettes, in which case I'm screwed.

I dash across the street. Dax's balcony is half covered by trees and hard to see from the sidewalk. Still, I'm pretty sure someone would notice a girl acting out her Spiderman fantasies. So I pick my moment, and when the coast looks as clear as it's ever going to be, I jump onto the downstairs neighbor's railing and I leap up, managing to get one hand on the top railing, another on one of the balustrades. And I hate to say, but I've climbed enough poles in my day that scaling the rest of the way onto the balcony is a piece of shoofly pie.

I try the door and of course it's locked. Time to see just how reliable the internet is. I shove the screwdriver between the bottom of the door and the doorframe. Then some downward pressure and I push up on the latch. It pops open.

Easy as can be. The hard part is pulling the door open once it's unlocked. It's old and it takes all my strength just to slide the damn thing the six inches or so I need to be able to slip inside. I start to shut it behind me but reconsider. If I need to make a hasty retreat, I don't want to be stuck wrestling with this aluminum and glass beast.

I step into the living room and the search is on. The one thing I'll say about Dax is that he's fastidious. The place is immaculate. Even the books piled neatly on a large bookshelf in the living room are in alphabetical order by author.

I scurry down the hallway to the back room. There's a queen-size bed with red sheets pulled tight over the mattress and four oversized pillows propped up by the headboard. A nightstand with three books and a black moleskin journal. That should be interesting.

Near the other side of the bed is a walk-in closet. Inside, I find the first chink in his armor of neatness. Dirty clothes are piled in one corner, but otherwise everything is tidy and organized. I can't reach the shelves, but as best I can tell they're uninteresting. Just an iron, extra deodorants and hair-product containers along with a few shoe boxes. The shoe boxes could be worth going through, if I have time.

I peek under the bed, and for a split second I think I see my bag. In reality, it's just a backpack that is definitely not mine. I rummage through it, but it's empty, except for two packs of cigarettes and a lighter.

Eleven minutes left.

I head for the second bedroom, set up as an office. Dax has three large computer monitors hooked up to a PC. He has a MacBook Pro opened beside them. I move the mouse on the PCs and a password screen comes up. No way I'm going to get through that. I try the Mac.

The good news is that the screen saver vanishes and no password is needed.

The bad news is I'm looking at a live feed of six cameras. One shows a view of the front of the building and appears to be coming from a camera on Dax's balcony. The other five show the inside of the apartment. I see myself leaning over the desk, watching myself watch myself.

My first thought is to swipe the laptop, but it's pointless. The video has to be backed up to the cloud. The one thing I have going for me is that it's unlikely Dax sits around watching old footage of his apartment. Unless there's some motion-detection feature that alerts him if someone enters. Guess I'll find out sooner or later.

I rifle through the office a bit, but anything interesting is probably on the computers. I give a quick check of the laundry nook. Next to the washer and dryer is floor-to-ceiling plastic shelving. On the bottom are some packing materials and folded cardboard boxes. Above that, laundry detergent, bleach, and stain remover. Above that are stacks of DVDs, mostly slasher films, sci-fi, and old British comedies. Weird place to keep your DVDs. I grab a copy of *Monty Python's Life of Brian* and open it. But, no, just a DVD that says *Life of Brian*.

I'm about to leave, but just in case, I open the washer and the dryer. They're empty. I'm sort of tempted to leave the washer door open, since you're supposed to do that with front loads, but I guess the upside of helping prevent mildew is outweighed by the downside of making it obvious someone broke into the apartment.

Three minutes left.

I rush to the bedroom and swipe the journal. I thumb through it. Nearly the entire thing is filled with tiny, flawless lettering. I'm about to start reading when I pause. Which way was it facing before I picked it up? I can't remember, and I decide that next time I do a B and E, I'll take pictures before I touch anything.

Every page is dated and I flip around until I find January 17. Unfortunately, it does not say, "Brutally murdered two basketball players last night." In fact, I can't make heads or tails of it. It's strings of numbers and a few seemingly random words—Irving, Blackwell, Stone, Bluestill—followed by addresses. About a quarter of the pages are like this. The others are filled with random thoughts, inspirational quotes, and a few sex fantasies that are surprisingly tame.

I'm now two minutes in the hole, but I keep reading. Finally, I hit pay dirt.

For Exiles: take over existing groups? Turning Point? Students for Liberty?

I snap a picture of the page and keep scanning. A few more pages have notes about the Exiles and I photograph those without reading them. Then I hit an entry from July and see something that shouldn't be there.

My address. My address written down months before I had ever heard Dax's name. *How long has he been watching me? And why?*

That's when I hear voices and the sound of keys turning the

front door lock. I place the journal back as close as I can to how I found it and consider making for the closet. That seems more like a death trap than a hideout, so I bound toward the utility room and close myself in just as the front door opens. I hear the pitter-patter of dog paws followed by Dax's voice.

"Let me grab my backpack." Footsteps, and then I see movement through the door slats as Dax walks by.

Then quiet.

Then Dax's voice again. "Yo, Pike. Al wants some water. Let him out on the patio."

Pike? I remember Scarlett telling me about the guys trying to lure her to a party. I struggle to recall… didn't she say the guy's name was Pike?

The pitter patter of dog toenails clicks across the hardwood. Shit. The door. Dax passes by again, and I'm holding my breath, trying to hear the conversation and hoping Pike doesn't mention the door was already open.

I need to see Pike's face. The witness said the man with Terrance and Warren was tall and had a shaved head with a neck tattoo. I try to see out the doors, but at best I'll catch a glimpse of his shoes.

"So, what'd the big man say?" Dax asks.

A gruff voice with a faint Philly accent answers. "There's a lot of heat right now because of the killings. He wants everyone to lay low."

"For how long?"

"Until some loose ends get tied up."

"Okay, so what does that mean? Everything stops?" Dax says.

"Our thing is fine. But what's this I hear about you bringing some new girl around?"

"She's cool. I made sure of it."

"You made sure of it, huh? You can't trust anyone right now. Give me her information. I'll check her out."

"Like I said, I made sure of it."

"Her name."

Everything inside me freezes and I wonder if I'm getting a backstage pass to my own execution. In a moment, my name will touch the ears of a hunter, and I'll be at the mercy of a phantom, a question mark with the name "Pike."

But what if it doesn't have to be that way? What if he's at my mercy? Yes, I'm tempting fate, but at least it's a fate I can control.

I throw the door open and step into the kitchen. "My name is Justice Winters."

Two faces twist in surprise. But before they can move, I dash toward the patio and throw myself off the balcony.

Falling never feels like you think it's going to. It's fast and violent and the thoughts come, not in words, but in sensations. I expect to feel my legs crack as I land, but my knees are able to absorb most of the fall. Only I tumble forward and have to reach out my arms to keep my face from smashing into the grass. I feel something in my wrist snap.

The pain sears my body and I want to cry. But as I pull myself to my feet and start running, I'm laughing.

Because Pike was tall, his head was clean shaven, and on his neck was a tattoo of the talons of a hawk.

CHAPTER NINETEEN

IZAAK PULLS ME CLOSE as we step out of health services, and both of us scan the landscape for trouble.

"You should stay with me," he says.

I rub my wrist, which is wrapped tightly in black athletic tape. "Jesus, it's a sprain, not a limb-ectomy."

"They might come after you."

"I hope they do." Who do you think you're fooling, Justice?

"Stay with me until the story comes out."

I argue but only halfheartedly. The truth is I've had the same fear. And even if I don't need Izaak to keep me safe, nothing wrong with a good hideout.

We sequester ourselves in his dorm and turn to the next item of business—to confirm as much of the story as possible.

Some information comes easily. Jack Jackson's foundation has thrown millions at academics writing about liberal bias in academia, including a few people already on the Southern Poverty Law Center's Hatewatch list.

But the big win was the witness who saw Terrance Down and Warren Armstrong just before they died. Izaak calls her, and she doesn't want to talk at first, but he somehow manages to work his magic. Finally, he asks if the neck tattoo she saw could have been a hawk's talons. "Yes, yes, that's exactly what it was."

We spend a few hours trying to hunt down information on Pike but come up empty. No Pikes on social media. Or with a billboard that says, "For all your murderin' needs, call 1-800…" Must be a nickname.

"Look," I say, "we've got Jack's confession, we've got Dax's journal entries tying him to the Exiles," I haven't told him about my address showing up in the journal, "and we've got a witness who puts one of them at the scene. We're good, right?"

Izaak is hesitant. "The journal stuff is cryptic, never mind how we got it. The witness has one foot in the grave and didn't say anything about a hawk until we asked her about it. And that confession was to a source whose name we can't use."

"I can't get dragged into this, Izaak."

"You think I want you to be more of a target than you already are? But what I'm saying is this is weak, J. If we had more time, we could turn this into something."

"But we don't."

"But we don't," he says. "What we need to do is hand this over to the cops. Maybe it's enough for them to get warrants. At least put the spotlight on these guys and force them to lay low."

"We can't go to the cops," I say. "We know Jack has connections in law enforcement."

"So we go to Cadence's dad."

"And if it takes them a month to follow up? Izaak, the Exiles are looking for me *now*. We've got to go public. At that point I become irrelevant and the cops will be forced to follow up."

Izaak stretches out on his bed and turns to look out the

window. After a few minutes he says, "We downplay the murder angle. Focus on Jack's connection to the Exiles, on their strategy to discredit the universities. We can hint at the rest, enough that people will put the dots together, but we can't come right out and accuse them of anything."

My eyes are suddenly teary and I'm not sure why. I try to keep my voice even as I say, "Thank you."

He rolls over and faces me as I finish wiping my eyes dry. "But you got to sit down with Harper. He's the key. We confirm someone from this school is on the Exiles' payroll? That's the story."

"I… okay. Tomorrow." It's a conversation I'm dreading and after a little pushback, Izaak gives in and lets me procrastinate.

We spend the evening on Izaak's floor, watching Bruce Lee movies on his laptop.

"So, what's this one?"

"*Fists of Fury*," Izaak says as we go on to movie two.

"Wait, I thought the other one was *Fists of Fury*."

"No. They called it *Fists of Fury* in the US, but the real title is *The Big Boss*."

"Okay," I say, "so we've got *The Big Boss*, *Fists of Fury*. So next it's *Enter the Dragon* and then *Return of the Dragon*."

"No. *Return of the Dragon* comes before *Enter the Dragon*."

"I'm so confused."

We've just finished the scene where Bruce Lee Bruce Lees an entire karate studio when Izaak's roommate, Aaron McAfee, comes in carrying a grocery bag in both hands. He dumps the bag on his desk and turns ladybug red when he notices me. "Sorry, guys. Izaak, you didn't do the thing." He whispers the last part like I won't hear him.

"Nah, it ain't like that. Justice, Aaron. Aaron, Justice. Justice is just a friend."

"What's the thing?" I ask. "Oh God. Not the old sock on the doorknob."

Izaak shakes his head.

"He's supposed to write 'Come Back later' on the whiteboard," Aaron says. "Get it?"

"Dear lord."

"Don't worry about me," Aaron says. "I'm not going to be here anyway."

"Back with Lorelei?" Izaak says.

"Until she changes her mind."

He throws some items in the fridge, grabs a backpack, and heads out the door.

I jump to my feet and start throwing my best Bruce Lee punches and kicks. "I wish we could've seen him fight in the UFC," I say. "Though maybe that ruins the legend. He gets taken down by a GSP or Khabib and that's the end of that."

I throw a kick over Izaak's head and feel him sweep my other leg out from under me. I land on top of him and instantly I'm in his guard. I push myself up and squeeze my right leg out so my knee is wedged near his groin, but before I can escape he brute forces me back down and rolls me onto my back, my face now smothered in his chest. He shoves his forearm under my neck for a moment but then rolls off of me.

"Hey," I say, "I almost had you."

"Right," he says. His voice is mocking but his face looks troubled.

"What's wrong?"

At first he shakes his head like he doesn't want to speak but then says, "You got will. And you got skills." He's not looking at me anymore but at his own forearms and hands. "But at the end of the day, it's not going to be enough to save you."

"Screw you. I've tapped out guys your size before."

"Yeah? Ever do that while one of them was pounding on your skull? Look, J. You ever end up in a situation where you've got some guy coming at you and you can't run, fuck Jiu Jitsu. Do damage. Find a weapon. And if you can't find a weapon, squeeze his trachea, dig your thumb into his eye. Don't go for the victory. Go for the kill."

I almost say it. I almost tell him about Vic, and Pop, and the Heiden. It almost comes spilling out of me like water bursting from a broken dam. But I freeze, paralyzed by the question: what will he think of me?

"I'm going to get ready for bed," I say, walking over to his desk and grabbing my bag. "Mind if I change here?"

"Yeah. Sure, J. No problem."

Izaak turns back to the movie and I stand behind him undressing. For a moment I'm fully naked, just watching him watch Bruce Lee, and I'm torn by so many emotions I can't move. But after a deep breath I slip on my gym shorts and a black t-shirt and dive back to the floor. A moment later, I hit pause on the laptop and roll onto my side.

"Can I ask you something?" I say.

"Depends on the something."

"You remember our date ten forevers ago?"

"What date? Who dates?" he says.

"Don't even pretend that wasn't a date."

He chuckles. "Okay. What about it?"

"What *happened?*"

His brow wrinkles. "Shouldn't I be the one asking you that?"

"What are you talking about?"

"J, every time I asked you a question, you would just give these one-word answers and then just sit there staring at your drink. It wasn't pulling teeth. It was pulling Thor's hammer."

I drop my head in my hands and can't stop from smiling. "Was I really that bad?"

"You were the worst." He smacks the space bar on the computer and Bruce Lee comes back to life. I roll onto my belly and wait for Izaak to steal a glance at me or my body, but his eyes don't leave the screen.

It's dark when I open my eyes, and for a moment I can't remember where I am. The pieces come flooding back, and I realize I'm still on the floor of Izaak's dorm, only now I have a pillow and Izaak's comforter is spread over my body.

"You okay?" Izaak whispers from his bed.

The soft light of a clock that reads 3:30 highlights his face, but I can only make out its shape, not its features.

"Fine. Were you sleeping?" I say.

"I can't. It's really going to happen, J. We're close."

"Well, rest up. Tomorrow's a big day."

"Hey. Justice," he says. "I'm glad we did this together."

"Me too," I whisper.

The next morning, I work up the courage to text Dr. Harper. He says to meet him at Lutnick Library at eleven. When Izaak and I get there, I stop him at the door.

"You sure you want to go in there alone?" he says.

I nod.

"This is it. After this, we go to press."

Dr. Harper was placed on leave while the administration

reviews the complaints about his comments. I find him on the upper balcony of Lutnick, seated in a small gray sofa chair. I take the seat across from him.

I hardly recognize the man. He looks haggard and aged, his hair unkempt and his face infested with patchy stubble. He takes a sip from a large coffee, and even that seems to be a struggle.

"You look awful." It's not what I meant to say.

"Yeah. Well, it's been a hell of a week, I suppose."

"What do you think's going to happen? You have tenure, don't you?"

"I have tenure, not immunity. But it will be a process. I suspect they'll wait to see how things go. The firestorm dies down, I may keep my job." He juts his chin out, as if pointing to my wrist. "What about you? Staying safe?"

I cover my wrist with my other arm. "Just took a spill."

"So, why did you want to see me, Justice?"

I'm too uncomfortable to answer and avoid the question. "Do you regret it? Speaking up?"

"I wish I could answer that. Sometimes I do regret it. Other times I think... Academia isn't very friendly to conservatives. When I went to grad school, I made a decision that I would keep my ideas to myself. I told myself: It's hard enough to get your PhD. Why risk making enemies? Then once I got my degree, I told myself: It's a tough job market out there. Wait until you have a full-time teaching position. Then it was: Wait until you have tenure."

"And then?"

"A thousand other excuses. You live in a closet because you think it's keeping you safe. By the time you realize it's become a coffin, it's too late."

"But maybe you were right. Maybe the mistake was speaking out this time. You had what you wanted. Didn't you? You got to teach. People left you alone."

"It's funny. Bacon said that knowledge is power. But he was wrong. It's knowledge plus courage. I've written entire books on the human soul's need for truth. On how we fool ourselves when we think money or fame or status or sex will fulfill us. We need to live for something—for truth, for an ideal, for… justice. I knew all of that. I believed it, believed it down to the marrow of my bones. But I just never had the courage to act on it."

"Until now."

"No, Justice, what you saw wasn't courage. What you saw was the desperate scream of a betrayed soul."

I believe him. But on the other hand, there's something incongruous about it, like a four-year-old solving calculus problems. Can you really see so much—and still betray it?

"You were wrong," I say. "About the Exiles. You heard about Cadence, right? And it turns out a witness saw one of their associates with two of the boys just before they died."

Dr. Harper closes his eyes and I feel like I just passed a death sentence. "I suppose it doesn't change anything." He sees my face. "Oh, I see. There's something else."

"I have to ask."

"Go ahead."

"What is your relationship with the Exiles?"

"Justice…" It's a plea, and I have to force myself to keep talking.

"Have you ever taken money from them?"

"Of course not."

I want to believe him. I want him to deny everything and

convince me it's all a big lie. That the Exiles are trying to take down a good man.

"Have you ever heard of Jack Jackson?"

"Yes." Bafflement.

"Have you ever taken money from him?"

"He sponsored some of my work."

"What kind of work?"

"Some papers I've drafted. On the state of the humanities. What are you saying?"

"And you never knew anything about his relationship to the Exiles?"

"God, no." His head is in his hands, and when he looks at me again his eyes are wet and red. "You're making a mistake."

We sit there together as he sobs quietly.

CHAPTER TWENTY

"YOU NERVOUS?" I SAY.

"Hell no," Izaak says with conviction, then gives me a wide smile and nods yes.

"It's what you wanted."

"I *wanted* to get on Fox News."

At noon, we sat in front of Izaak's laptop and together pressed the enter key and published the story to *The Clerk*'s website. I had wanted to tell Cadence first, but after how we left things the other night, I couldn't bring myself to just text her. I told myself it would be better if the story came out, the cops start making arrests, and then we can be reunited in sisterly bliss. Even then I knew I was full of shit and that really I was just scared and ashamed.

Izaak spent the next hour sending around the link and a press release to major media outlets while I sat on his bed and contemplated my next move. Within an hour he received a call from the people at *The Evermen Report*, a national news show, asking him to record a segment at five.

"How do I look?" Izaak asks me, checking himself in the mirror. He's wearing an impeccable dark suit with a charcoal-gray vest over a fern-green shirt and tie. I walk over and straighten his tie.

"Dashing." I've never said that about a guy, but it fits.

He places his hands on my shoulders and looks straight at me. "I owe you, J. It should be both of us doing this."

"You really hate me, don't you?"

"From here to the moon and back. You sure you don't want to come?"

I shake my head. "If it were up to me, neither of us would leave this room until they arrest those guys."

"Destiny calls."

"Good luck," I say. "Break a leg."

"You can't... thanks."

After he leaves, I open the window and stretch out on the bed, a frosty breeze purifying the air and leaving me relaxed and refreshed. I feel like I can finally see the finish line.

Then I bolt upright in horror. The moment the cops go to arrest these guys, they'll find my bag.

My pulse starts to calm as I think it through. No, the Exiles are evil, not stupid. The moment they hear the news, they'll dump anything incriminating. I know I would.

Still, I find myself pacing the room, sweating through my t-shirt despite the cold.

I try to distract myself by stress eating, and when that runs its course, some mindless internet browsing on Izaak's laptop. For a moment, I'm tempted to check out his web history but manage to resist. Lord knows I would die if anyone looked at mine. Instead, I go down a YouTube hole and, thirty MrBeast videos later, it's almost time for his appearance.

I pull up the show. *The Evermen Report* is apparently recorded in New York, but Izaak is doing a satellite linkup from ABC 6. The first segment has to do with Social Security yadda-yadda-yadda. When the second segment starts, I see Izaak on the TV, split-screened alongside Michelle Evermen, host of the show. Seeing his face, I actually squeak.

"We've all been following the story of the Haverford massacre. Our next guest is a reporter for the Haverford College student paper, *The Clerk*. Izaak Lane, welcome to the show."

There must be a delay because he pauses unnaturally before saying, "Thanks, Michelle."

"Now, Izaak. You published a piece earlier today claiming to identify the suspect spotted with two of the victims around the time of the murder, a man who goes by the name Pike."

I cringe for a moment. Izaak buried the line about Pike deep in the story, but I guess we were naïve to think the media would focus on anything else.

"That's right. We were able to confirm that this person, Pike, was the one seen by the witness, and we were also able to confirm that Pike is tied to the Exiles." *We.* It's as if he's winking at me on national television.

"You actually claim that the Exiles aren't just an informal network of alt-right online commentators but a formal organization."

"We discovered that the Exiles were founded by the truck tycoon Jack Jackson to discredit the higher education system."

"You say that's because it's hostile to white nationalism."

"Exactly."

"You go on to say that the Exiles have allies from within the university system, including a professor at your very own college."

"That's right. Peter Harper is a psychology professor recently placed on leave for making racially insensitive comments in class."

"Your story has created quite the sensation," Michelle says. "This is something the police missed, the major media outlets missed. Tell me, how did you figure all this out?"

"As we mention in the article, we had an unnamed source from inside the Exiles."

"Now, Izaak, we had some information come in just before we went on air. I was hoping you could help me make sense of it."

"Sure," Izaak says, and even though he tries to sound confident, I can hear the hesitancy in his voice.

A picture flashes on the screen along with a name that rocks me to the core. "We're being told that Pyke refers to Mathis Pyke, a decorated veteran from Montgomery County." It's him. The same cold eyes. The same shaved head. The same tattoo. *Mathis* Pyke?

"We weren't able to confirm his full name."

"Well, what we're being told is that Mathis Pyke was in Haverford Township on the evening of the murders but has an alibi for the time period in question."

"Like I said, Michelle. I don't know if it's the same person, but if it is, we're confident in our reporting. He's associated with the Exiles, and a witness puts him with the victims. I'm sure the alibi won't stand up. Again, if it's even the same person."

"What I'm hearing is that Cadence Jenkins, head of Haverford's Black Students' League, and a leading critic of the Exiles on your campus, says she was with Mr. Pyke that entire evening."

"I… we'll certainly look into it."

What is happening? I leap to my feet, and again I'm pacing the room. Only now what I feel isn't fear. It's confusion and rage.

"Now let me ask you about your source. Is it true that she is a student named Justice Winters?"

Oh God.

"What?" Izaak says.

"And is this the same Justice Winters you yourself accused last year of leveling a false allegation of attempted sexual assault against Villanova's star basketball player, Kareem Hanley?"

"I… no. I mean, I can't speak to that at this time."

"I'd like to welcome another guest to the show. Jack Jackson, president and CEO of Jackson Trucks. Jack, thanks for coming on."

I'm screaming now, and it takes every ounce of strength I have not to pick up the laptop and hurl it at the wall.

"Great to be here, Michelle. Love your show."

"Now, Jack, you don't deny you've given money to support criticism of academia."

"Deny it? I'm as proud of it as I am of my own children. The universities today are teaching Marxist propaganda, which is why we have a country where more young people today call themselves socialists than capitalists."

"But you do deny Mr. Lane's claim that you are the head of the Exiles."

"A total fabrication."

"So, you're not involved with the Exiles at all?"

"Not at all."

"You're not a white nationalist?"

"I am not a white nationalist."

People talk about watching a slow-motion car accident. This is like watching a slow-motion massacre.

"Mr. Lane? How do you respond?"

My phone has been going off and I've been sending it to voicemail. But when it rings for the third time, I take it, desperate for an escape.

"Dax?"

"What did you do, Justice?"

"I told the truth."

"You have no idea of the truth. The people you're messing with… they're dangerous. They're going to come after you, and they're going to come after me."

"You mean Jack?"

"I can't talk over the phone. I'm leaving my apartment now. You need to meet me somewhere."

"Hell no am I meeting you. Say what you have to say."

Silence.

"Why did you have my address in your journal?"

Silence.

"Dax? Are you there?"

"I thought I heard something. Look, Justice, I don't know why you did what you did. But you really fucked things up and now my life is over."

"Right, so you figure you bring me to Jack and maybe he'll forgive you for leading me to him in the first place."

"Forgiveness doesn't exist in my world." He hesitates. "Shit. I can't do this."

"Do what?"

"I'm ready to go to the cops, but I need you to vouch for me. I'll tell them everything I was involved with, but you need to let them know I was never violent. I never hurt anyone."

"I don't know that. How am I supposed to know that?"

"Because I'm telling you—"

He doesn't finish his sentence and I know he'll never finish his sentence. Because the last sound I hear is the blast of a gunshot.

CHAPTER TWENTY-ONE

WE'VE BEEN WALKING for what seems like hours through patches of leftover snow and mud. My feet are wet and frozen, but I know not to complain. Mist seems to rise from the ground, and I sing quietly, so quietly that no one else can hear.

"When peace like a river, attendeth my way,
When sorrows like sea billows roll
Whatever my lot, thou hast taught me to say
It is well, it is well, with my soul."

As the sun begins to ebb, we reach the edge of a gully and stop. The roaring wind numbs my body and whips strands of hair across my face, stinging my skin.

"Now, girl, you go untie her," Pop commands.

I look to Anna Claire, and she nods. Anna has made the journey, which we call the Reise, many times before. She was the one who woke me early in the morning and told me to dress.

"It's time." She said nothing else. She didn't have to. We've both known this day was coming for weeks. On every new moon, Pop and Anna Claire would vanish, along with one of the Heiden. Now that I'm nine, it's my turn. In a couple more years, I suppose I'll be preparing Laudie Mae.

I untie the Heiden. She looks a little bit older than Anna Claire, but not by much. Her thin body shivers in the cold, and her sunken eyes seem lifeless and sad. "It will be okay," I whisper. "Soon you'll be saved." Pop has spent the last six months purifying her. Now is the final step.

I take her hand and we step into the stream. The icy water bites at my ankles but I ignore it.

"You got to kneel," I say.

She obeys.

Pop steps into the water, his boots inches from my face. Then he speaks, his voice gentile and quiet.

"Almighty and ever-living God, you sent your only Son into the world to cast out the power of Satan, spirit of evil, to rescue man from the kingdom of darkness and bring him into the splendor of your kingdom of light. We pray for this child. Set her free from original sin, make her a temple of your glory, and send your Holy Spirit to dwell with her. We ask this through Christ our Lord."

"Amen," we all say. I tug on the Heiden's arm. "You got to say, 'Amen.'"

She says it.

"Up, girl," Pop says, pulling me to my feet. Then he hands me something. It takes me a moment to realize that it's a hunting knife with a black blade, about the length of my forearm.

I don't understand. This wasn't supposed to happen. I look to Anna Claire and she's laughing at me and Pop is laughing and the Heiden is laughing. Laughter echoes loudly through the woods and I feel a lonely kind of terror that becomes my entire universe.

I swing the knife and it breaks through the skin of my thigh.

I keep swinging, digging gashes into my belly and my chest and my eyes and all I can do is scream…

When I awake I'm alone, but I hear a gentle tap coming from my bedroom door.

"Go away," I muster.

The door opens and I see Andy peek her head through. "There's someone here to see you."

I turn, blurry-eyed, and see the clock. It's just after 1 p.m. "Not interested."

"It's a cop."

I throw off the covers and scramble for my jeans. "You didn't let him in, did you?"

"Who'd be dumb enough to let a cop in their house if they didn't have to? Anyway, he says he knows you. Jenson or something."

I feel a wave of relief as I realize it's Ty. "Okay. Tell him I'll be right down."

Andy hesitates, then says with a big smile, "I got a job!"

"What?"

"I'm waitressing at The Grog." The Grog is a popular Irish tavern on Lancaster.

"Um. Okay." I slip on my jeans, trying to make space in my mind for the trivia of normal life. "You think that's a good idea?"

Her smile vanishes. "I thought you'd be proud of me."

"It's just that… I am proud, Andy." And I am. After her freak-out, she vowed that she would never drink or get high again. Only at the moment I couldn't give a damn if she started snorting lines of Ketamine off my nightstand.

"I know. It's a bar. But I'll be fine. I told you. I'm done with all that. Promise. Anyway…"

"Like I said, I'll be right down."

I stand there for a moment trying to recapture my sense of reality. After the call from Dax, I ran to the train station thinking I would just skip town right then. But as I stood in the SEPTA parking lot, I realized I didn't care anymore. I didn't care if the Exiles found me or the police arrested me or even if Pop tracked me down. I was done running, done fighting. I was done. So I called an Uber, stumbled to my room, and fell asleep.

I should've gotten on the train.

When I step out onto the patio, I see Ty sipping coffee from a Dunkin Donuts cup. He hands me an identical one. "I always forget if you take sugar."

"Black's fine," I say. It's warmer than usual outside but still chilly in the shade, so I walk down and sit on the bottom porch step. The sun warms my neck as I take a sip of the coffee, which isn't smooth so much as watery.

Ty sits down next to me and holds his cup to his lips but doesn't drink. "We used to live down this way. Back when Cadence was a toddler. You know that?"

"No," I say.

"Oh yeah. Just past Conestoga. Where that renovated duplex is? It was a single family back in the day. Cadence's mom, she sold life insurance. Did pretty well for us. But, funny thing. We never did buy any for ourselves. Just kept putting it off. There's always tomorrow. Until there isn't."

Tell me about it.

"Havertown isn't so bad," I say.

"No. Not anymore. Was when we moved there, though. Took the Millennials moving in and... what's it called?"

"Gentrifying?"

"Yeah, that's right. Gentrifying it." He finally sips the coffee, then carefully sets it down between his feet. "Look, Justice. You know why I'm here. I told you to keep your head down. Now you see why."

I nod and try to look embarrassed, which honestly isn't hard. "I was just trying to help."

"Cadence says you went and started looking into things, and now I got people saying we got to look into you."

"I don't want to get in trouble."

"That's why I'm here, Justice. I know your heart was in the right place. But I got to be able to go to my people and tell them, hey, nothing to see here, folks. And I can't do that unless you tell me why exactly you're tossing around the names you named."

I'm at a loss. I fumble around for a few seconds, and when I can't form a coherent sentence, I just shrug.

"I see. Seems to me what must've happened is you found out Jack Jackson funded research from that racist teacher of yours, and you just jumped to conclusions. Who wouldn't? And then you go to Cadence and you tell her about it, and her friend Mathis, maybe he says: 'Hey, you're being ridiculous.' And now you're angry and maybe a tad paranoid. You think: What if he's involved, too? You're young. It's been a hard week. Who could blame you?"

"But that's not—"

"It's not an easy thing to admit. I get that. But I'm trying to protect you, Justice. To keep you safe. And I need you to forget about your ego for a minute and trust me on this. You let me tell it like it is, and all of this? It's over. No more cops knocking on your door. No one snooping into your business."

I bow my head. "Don't make promises you can't keep, Ty. Even if you guys are finished with me, the press isn't."

"Oh, I'd say they got bigger things to talk about."

"You lost me."

"That's the other reason I wanted to come down here. See, because we found the killer. What's left of him, anyway."

"You found him?"

"A kid named Dax Morrison. You know him? Went to your school."

I shrug.

"He must've known we were closing in on him, because he went and shot himself yesterday. Left a note confessing to everything."

I want to jump to my feet and scream that it's bullshit. To tell him that everything I said was true and Dax is being made to take the fall for Pyke and Jack Jackson. But I'm stuck between an exhausted kind of apathy and the knowledge that believing me means doubting his own daughter. So I don't move. I just ask, my voice limp, "But what about the others? Cadence was attacked by two guys."

"Don't worry. We'll find them. It's going to take some time. The Dax kid cleared out his apartment before he offed himself, so there's not much to go on. But that's what we do. We find a thread and keep pulling at it 'til the whole thing comes unraveled."

"So, what now?" I say.

Ty stands and adjusts his uniform. "Now we go on with our lives. What else can anyone do? That's one thing I've learned. Things throw you off course from time to time, and all you can do is deal with them the best you can and keep moving forward. And if you can't, if it's too much, you just head home, and you sit down next to the people you love and who love you, and then, when you're ready, you try again."

"But what if you can't go home?"

"You can always go home, Justice. Even when you think you can't, you can."

I sit on the porch for a long time after Ty leaves, and I'm so lost in thought that it's not until I hear a car door slam shut that I realize Izaak has driven up. His face is solemn, and I can't tell if he's waiting for me to come over to him or gathering up the courage to come to me.

Finally, he walks up the driveway and I stand, my hands gripping the handrail behind my back.

"I'm fine," I say abruptly.

"I'm not."

"Look. I'm sorry I left you hanging." Not one of my more sincere-sounding apologies.

"No, I don't mean that," Izaak says. "Yeah, at first I was furious with you, like you put me in this situation. But that wasn't fair. We did this together. Anyway, like I said, that's not why I'm here. I'm here because I've been worried about you."

"We're not doing that."

"You weren't there when I got back to the dorms."

"What's it to you?"

"I get it. You think I didn't want to disappear? But this isn't over. You and I both know they got it wrong. All of them."

"So what? It doesn't matter what we know. What matters is what the Exiles know, which is that we're after them. What matters is Ty just made it abundantly clear that if I don't sit down and shut up, I'm going to have every cop on the Main Line knocking on my door. I'm out, Izaak. It's game over."

I rush up the steps and start to open the front door.

"It's game on," Izaak says. "I mean, facts are facts. You can cover them up. You can't erase them. The cops? Like you said, they'll be happy to take the W and pin the whole thing on Dax. So it's on us. We've got to keep pushing. We let them get away, then what the hell did we do all this for?"

"Stop with this 'we' bullshit, Izaak. I'm not part of your stupid fucking student paper. This has nothing to do with me. I wish you would just go away and let me go back to my life."

"I can't, J. I care about you." He tries to step toward me, but I hold out my hand and back up.

"That's not fair," I say. "Izaak, you don't know me. You think you do. But you have no idea."

"You're wrong."

"Please, just leave. I've got someplace I need to be."

"Where?" he says.

I hold his gaze and say, deliberately and pitilessly: "Night Shade. I have to work."

CHAPTER TWENTY-TWO

THE CLUB IS DEAD, and Jewel and I sit at the bar watching a poker tournament with the sound off.

"He should've bet out at the turn," she says. "Watch. Now the girl knows he doesn't have the nuts, so she's going to go all in on the river, unless an ace falls. He'll have to fold." Sure enough…

"What the hell are you doing dancing? Go out to Vegas and make some real money," I say.

"Nah, I just watch it on TV. I'm no good unless I can see everyone's cards."

Six guys pour in the front door and linger for a moment in the entryway. I can't make out what they're saying, but the tallest one is shouting and pointing like he's just found the promised land. The others are taking quick peeks, but mostly looking at their shoes.

"Bachelor party," I say.

"Yep," Jewel says.

Before we can move, the tall one struts over. He has a Van Dyke beard, a North Face jacket, and a shit-eating grin. "How we doing tonight, girls?"

"Who's the lucky man?" Jewel says.

Van Dyke points to a stocky guy with dark curls. "I'm Eric. That's my boy, Zach. He's getting married next week."

"Bring him over," I say.

Eric pulls out a thick stack of bills. "We're doing this right tonight, girls. You got a private room?"

"Follow me," I say as Jewel heads back for the others. "Brenda, get these boys some champagne." I lead Eric up some stairs to a landing where one of the bouncers is hanging out behind a lectern.

"Shade Lounge, Manny," I say.

Manny gives Eric the rundown and Eric lays down some cash. The eight of us take a right behind some velvet curtains and pass several smaller rooms until we reach Shade Lounge. It has a single red couch running along three of the walls with a table on one side and red lighting that just screams class.

In a strip club, atmosphere is everything. Well, atmosphere and booze, but atmosphere is important. The goal is to transport guys to a fantasy world where they feel like rock stars, where time stops, where money is cheap, and where it doesn't seem completely ridiculous that a stranger is tearing all her clothes off. Whenever I start to think that what I do is normal, I imagine doing it under bright fluorescent lights.

But even though Shade Lounge feels like a private universe, there's a security camera watching our every gyration. Partly for our protection, mostly for Abe's. Some girls will trap if they think they can get away with it, but turning tricks can get a club shut down faster than serving alcohol to a toddler.

The guys sit down along two of the walls. Jewel is across the room talking to Eric, Zach, and two of the others. I park myself between the last two, and place my hands on their thighs.

"You all been here before?" I ask, even though I know the answer.

The guy to my right, a blond wearing a Phillies jersey, is playing it cool. "Not this particular club," he says. "I'm Kenneth, by the way."

"Fantine."

"Awesome," he says.

"What about you?" I say to the guy to my left. He's dressed sharp but subtle, in designer jeans that fit just right, and a black Henley.

"Adam," he says.

"The first man."

"No, that's Eric over there."

"I meant like in the Bible."

He doesn't get it, which is probably for the best.

"He's the one who set this up without telling any of us, even though Zach explicitly said no strip clubs."

"What's wrong with strip clubs?" I say, moving my arm around his shoulders. "Who doesn't like looking at naked girls?" He folds his arms and stares at the ceiling so I back off. "You guys live in the city?"

"He does," Adam says, pointing to Kenneth. "I'm visiting from Michigan."

"Oh my God, what part?"

Then he does the thing every Michigander does. He holds out his right hand, which is roughly the shape of the lower peninsula, and points. "Chelsea."

"No way. I grew up just south of there." I realize I've gotten carried away. In the half decade since I left home, I haven't told anyone where I'm from, but this feels safe. And, besides, if for some weird reason he tells someone, I can always say I was playing him.

"Nice. Where abouts, exactly?"

"Clinton," I say. It's a lie, but not by much.

"Okay, okay. The big question. Spartans or Wolverines?"

"Spartans," I say.

"You're killing me, Fantine."

"So, you guys want a dance?" I don't know why I say it. I guess it's just programmed into me.

Adam looks Kenneth.

"Yeah, okay," Kenneth says.

The sound system is pumping the room full of Justin Timberlake's "Don't Hold the Wall," and the slow, hypnotic rhythm feels like a striptease paint-by-number. For a while I'm in my own world, pretending like I'm dancing alone in my bedroom. Clothing vanishes and soon it's just skin and high heels.

When I do allow myself to notice the guys, Kenneth is watching my body, afraid to make eye contact. Adam stares into my eyes, afraid to look at my body. Both of them are frozen, fists tucked at their sides, like they're worried their hands will start groping me of their own volition.

I duck between Adam's legs, my hands on his thighs, and propel myself up until my boobs are eye level. Something about it feels off. Not degrading, or embarrassing, just unnecessary, and I realize I did this on purpose—not to put them at ease but to kill the flickers of a human connection.

When the song is over, I put my top back on. I make a decision. I'm not going to be a dancer anymore. Not for the rest of the night, anyway. Tonight, I'm going to be a girl at a club, just talking to some guys.

Eric walks over with the bottle of champagne and three glasses. "Time for a toast, boys." He pours us all a glass and then stands in the middle of the room and shouts over the music. "To Zach and Megan. May they enjoy too much success, too much happiness, and too much dirty, dirty sex. Cheers!"

We drink up. Eric makes another round filling our glasses, and I find myself accepting, swept away by the pure fun of it all.

"So, how do you all know the groom?" I say.

"Most of us went to college with him at UPenn," Adam says. "Eric and he grew up together in Pittsburgh."

"That makes sense."

"Yeah, Eric… he's a bit of a character. But he's a good dude. What about you? What's your story?"

That's a good question. "I'm a student."

"What do you study?"

"Psychology."

"That's awesome. I'm going into childhood psychiatry. I'm just finishing up my residency at U of M. What do you want to do after school?"

"I have no clue. I thought maybe law. But my life is kind of a mess right now." I can sense Kenneth feeling neglected, but I can't make myself care. Adam starts telling me about different careers I should consider, but soon the conversation spirals in a thousand different directions. Sports, music, movies.

"So, Fantine. *Les Mis*, right?"

"You don't buy that's my real name?"

"I just assumed."

"Yes, *Les Mis*."

"Book or musical?"

I wrinkle my nose. "Oh, book."

"Yes, totally." He gives me a high five.

"It's Justice, by the way."

"What?"

"My real name. You can call me Justice." He's watching me and I can see him inhale deeply, like he lost his breath for a moment. I place my hand into his and he squeezes it gently, and we just sit there for a long time, not looking at each other.

I've never been in a relationship. I tried dating a few times and messed around with a couple of guys my second year of college. But the closer I got to any of them, the lonelier I felt. The more intimate the conversation, the more the lies weighed on me. I was cut off from love by the wall between my past and my present. I found myself resenting the guys the more I liked them and the more they liked me. Things would inevitably fall apart, and I would hide in my room, crying for days.

Will that ever change? Can it?

I whisper into Adam's ear, "We can get a private room if you want another dance."

He doesn't move, but I feel his grip slacken. "Oh, no. That's fine. I'm going to get another drink."

I sit there hating myself and wondering what made me say it, even though deep down I know.

I rush out of the room, past Manny, in the direction of the dressing room. My vision is blurry with tears, and I don't stop moving until I'm inside the bathroom and the door is shut. I sit on the toilet as ugly sobs pulse through me, and I'm just relieved the music is loud enough to drown them out.

For years I've had one goal—*normal*. It's the thing I wanted, the thing that I envied whenever I saw people walking through the mall holding hands or sharing a meal. You wake up, you go to school, you spend time with friends. And then you build a life. Find a job, fall in love, buy a house, maybe have some kids. You live and you die, and no one dies because you live.

And I could have it. Nothing's stopping me, not after Dax. Only I know I can't. Because something is stopping me. The same thing that has always stopped me—stopped me from connecting with boys and being real with Cadence and taking down the Exiles and allowing Izaak to hold me in his arms and reassure me that I had the strength to fight another day.

A contradiction.

I've been trying to have it both ways—to expose the truth and cover up the truth. And, before that, to be normal and prepare for war.

I've been living my life halfway, each foot stuck in a different universe, too afraid to commit to either of them. Afraid that if I commit to a normal life, Pop will track me down—and afraid that if I commit to rescuing my sisters, all three of us might die. And so I've let myself live a lie. To pretend that I'm normal and prepared. That I'm going to save my sisters—just not today.

Now I realize it's either/or. Halfway doesn't exist. It's just an illusion that keeps you from seeing that the two worlds you're stuck in are really two sides of a guillotine.

What was it Dr. Harper said? About how we need to live for something besides our own desires and wishes… for truth and for justice? I've been so afraid of the truth coming out, but now I realize what really terrifies me is that the truth might stay buried.

If I'm going to die, I'm going to die fighting. Not for security or vengeance. I'm going to fight for the truth because it is the truth—for justice because it is just. If it takes my last breath,

I will find who attacked Terrance and Warren and Cadence. And if, by some stroke of fate I don't end up in jail or buried in some forgotten cemetery, I'll return to Michigan, and I will free my sisters and face down the man who terrifies me more than death itself.

And after that? It's a question I don't yet feel prepared to answer. Not while so many other riddles are left to solve.

What do I *know*? I know that Vic Michaels died by my hand. I know that Terrance and Warren did not. I know that Pyke is connected to the Exiles. And I *think* I know that he was with Terrance and Warren on the night they died.

And what about Cadence? I haven't wanted to think about it because every thought feels ugly and disloyal. But I can't put it off any longer. I need to face her, to look her in the eye and ask her why she gave Pyke an alibi. And then I'll know whether I still have a friend.

CHAPTER TWENTY-THREE

CADENCE'S LAST INSTAGRAM UPDATE WAS two hours ago—a picture of her and two girls from the Black Students' League having drinks at The Grog. I text Andy to see if Cadence is still there, but Andy doesn't answer.

By the time the Uber drops me off, it's inching toward one in the morning, and The Grog is packed with college students. Amazing how no matter how broke you are, you're never too broke to pay for overpriced beer.

I squeeze through the crowd but don't see Cadence. Despite it being twenty degrees outside, inside it's half a sauna, which only intensifies the smell of old beer and fried fish. I can feel the sweat from people's shirts rubbing against my arms and cheeks, and I say a silent prayer that I'm not much of a drinker. Who would do this willingly?

Eventually, I fight my way to the bar and wait for the bartender to see me.

"Is Andy here?" I have to yell it a couple times before he understands me.

"The new girl? Haven't seen her."

"She said she was working tonight."

"She came in yesterday but left with a bunch of guys halfway through her shift."

Andy.

I prop myself up onto the footrest of a barstool, even though some girl with hoop earrings and a tube top is sitting there. She shoots me a dirty look, which I ignore. I scan the room and there's Cadence, sitting in the very back corner in one of those high bar tables. She's got one girl next to her and one girl across from her, and they're all laughing and guzzling beer.

I dive back into the crowd and work my way to her table. When I get there, she looks up at me, and I see a coldness in her eyes.

"We need to talk," I say.

"I don't think we do."

Her coldness throws me and my first instinct is to ask what I did wrong and search for a way to win back her smile. I don't fight the desire. I stand there, allowing myself to feel every inch of it along with a sadness so deep I'm terrified it will overwhelm me. Then I remind myself why I came here and of my vow to place no consideration above the truth. I ask, knowing what it will cost me, "Why are you lying about Pyke?"

She motions for the two girls to give us a moment. I sit across from her. Her face has mostly healed, and what hasn't healed is covered with exquisitely applied makeup. She looks like herself again—not college cute, but striking and fierce.

"You think I'm lying," she says evenly.

"I saw him with Dax Morrison. He's part of the Exiles."

"Right. Yeah, I heard about that. Funny how Miss Breaking and Entering is going to accuse me of lying." Every word is bitter, but I force myself to ignore it and push forward.

"You know about that?"

"Girl, the things you don't know. Mathis is no racist. You know what he is? He's a goddamn war hero who ran into the middle of a firefight to save the life of a *black* soldier. Took two bullets and still carried the poor guy on his shoulders for a mile and half before they were rescued. Oh? You didn't hear about that?"

"That doesn't prove anything. You know that."

"No? What about the fact he sleeps with *me*?"

I don't have an answer for that so I say, almost offhandedly, "The boys were going to meet him that night."

"What?"

"Vic, Terrance, Warren—they were going to meet Pyke the night of the murders. In Phoenixville. He must've been throwing a party after you two hung out."

Her eyes narrow and she doesn't say anything. I've got to her.

"How do you explain that away?" I say.

"I don't know. Why don't we ask Mathis?" She looks up and smiles at someone behind me.

Pyke sits down beside her. He leans back and smiles a chilling smile.

We study each other for a long moment. He's older than I had thought. Early thirties, with a sharp jaw and prominent veins on his neck and shaved head. His eyes are deep and sunken, but softened somewhat by the rings of hazel. He's wearing a black t-shirt under a black jacket and his hands are large and powerful. I'm sure he could snap my neck as easy as snapping his fingers. I want to run, to get as far away from him as I can. But sometimes the only way to safety is running toward the danger.

"Justice Winters," he says. "In the flesh. I hope this time I won't have to watch you dive out a window. You're lucky to be alive."

"How do you want me to take that?"

"I was just telling Justice about how she's full of shit," Cadence says, not taking her eyes off of me.

"Don't be too hard on her," Pyke says. "Think about it from her view. She sees me with this guy who it turns out was white supremacist scum, and since she pulled some insane Superman shit rather than wait around for an explanation, what other conclusion was she going to draw?"

"She says you knew the guys. The dead ones."

"Clients. Don't look surprised, Justice. Down and Armstrong were two of the biggest college basketball stars in the country. You don't think they had to deal with stalkers? Now *Vic*. I can't say I knew him. I had nothing to do with him."

I see mockery in his eyes but no hatred, like we're sharing a secret.

"Happy now?" Cadence says.

"Who's 'big man'?" I say. "You and Dax weren't talking about security. You were talking about 'big man' saying you all needed to lay low. You aren't going to tell me Jack Jackson is a client of yours too?"

Pyke laughs. "Big man? That's Darryl. He's my employee. The guy's a refrigerator—like six foot eight or something. He's the one Dax was mostly working with. Come on, Justice. You're sounding paranoid. Like Cadence says, I was with her. And even if I wasn't, I may be a lot of things, but I'm no racist."

"I think we're done here," Cadence says.

"Hold up, hold up. I've got some questions for Justice." He looks at Cadence. "You don't mind?"

"I'm starting to," Cadence says. "This is definitely not how I wanted to spend my evening."

"All right. Just one then. Justice Winters, from Orange County, California. You must've led a very sheltered life."

"You could say that."

"Because I did some digging, and the weird thing is, I can't find any online presence for you up until a few years ago."

"Like you said, I was sheltered."

"Yeah? Sounds like you had great parents. What were their names again?"

"Why don't you tell me? You know so much about my past."

"Humor me."

"Chad and Lisa Winters."

"Chad and Lisa. Yeah, there are quite a few Chad and Lisa Winters out there. And what about your grandparents? What were their names?"

"What's your point?"

He leans toward me and the look on his face is frank and sincere. "Who *are* you, Justice Winters?"

I lean forward until our noses just about touch. "Pray to God you never have to find out."

CHAPTER TWENTY-FOUR

MY PHONE RINGS AND THROUGH blurry eyes I make out the time. It's just past noon.

"Did you get my message?" I say.

"Yeah. I got it." Izaak hesitates. "Did a Google deep dive and… did I just wake you up?"

"Don't be a Judgie McJudgerson."

"Fair. Anyway, just war hero stuff. I even tried to pull Pyke's rap sheet. The guy's clean." My stomach sinks, but then he says, "But… J, there's something you gotta see. Can you swing by my place?"

"Ten minutes. And, Izaak… I'm sorry about yesterday. It's just—"

"Don't worry about that. Just get over here."

I pull on a dirty pair of jeans and a wrinkled Deftones t-shirt and rush down the stairs. As I reach the floor, I see Andy on the couch watching an old episode of *The Office*.

"Look at you, up and about," Andy says, as Winston bounds off the couch and paws at my knee like I'm Beyonce. "How's life among the living?"

"You really want to know?" I say, trying to sound casual as I futilely try to call an Uber and put on my coat at the same time.

"Absolutely not."

"You working tonight?" It's my passive-aggressive way of asking her about the disappearing act she pulled at The Grog. She doesn't seem to notice. And if she does, she doesn't take the bait.

"Honestly? I'm going to spend the day sitting here, eating my Cheez-Its, and living vicariously through Jim and Pam until I fall asleep."

"Stay safe."

I spend the ride over trying to think of something other than how Izaak and I left things yesterday. But I just keep seeing his face when I told him I worked at Night Shade and it wasn't even surprise or hurt or anger but just this quiet acceptance of something he already knew but didn't want to admit. I resented that. Or maybe I was just frightened by what it meant.

I go to knock on Izaak's dorm room door but it swings open before my fist connects. I guess he heard me walking down hall made of centuries-old wood.

"Get in here," he says, pulling me gently by the arm. He sits me down on his bed and pulls up next to me, thrusting a thin pile of photocopied pages paper clipped together in my lap.

"What is this?"

"That's a police report from a few years back. Seems Vic was involved in a car crash—"

"On prom night."

"You knew about that?" Izaak says.

"It ended his basketball career," I say, hoping he forgets his question.

"Yeah, it did more than that. It also killed his girlfriend and nearly took out another passenger." I think of the photo of the young girl and the cat I found in Vic's safe.

"What does this have to do with Pyke?"

"Read it."

I do read it. I read the dispassionate account of an officer getting called out to some remote backroad on Vic's prom night. Of finding a car totaled after smashing into a stone fence. Of a seventeen-year-old girl, Joy Cassidy, sprawled out on the pavement, already dead, and two eighteen-year-old boys, Vic Michaels and Levi Tyson, on the ground next to her, fighting for their lives. Of a witness who saw the girl driving the car, swerving this way and that before the inevitable collision, and who called in the wreck to the police. The witness was a man named Mathis Pyke.

"Jesus Christ."

"It can't be a coincidence," Izaak says. "But what the hell *does* it mean?"

I flip through the pages as if they'll give me the answer, but I'm not even looking at the words. "For one thing, it means Pyke lied to me."

Izaak's eyes narrow in confusion.

"I spoke to him last night. He said he didn't know Vic. No, don't worry. We were in public. I was safe." I don't mention Cadence.

Izaak starts to say something, but nods—not like the answer satisfies him but like his mind is flooded with so many questions he doesn't know which one to ask.

"So, what are we talking about?" he says finally. "A guy sees a kid nearly get killed. Maybe they become good friends. After that he tries to indoctrinate the kid into white supremacy, but maybe the kid decides he likes his black friends too much, so all three of them get killed to shut them up?"

"I mean, maybe. But then why make it *look* like a hate crime? It's a step away from leaving your name and number at the scene." Okay, it's not the only flaw in Izaak's story, but I can't tell him that. I flip through pages again and point at a name. "Him. Levi Tyson. That's who we need to talk to."

Izaak slides one of his knees onto the bed and faces me, taking my hands in his. "Justice, I know what I said yesterday. But you don't have to do this. This right here? This is enough. We show this to the police, and they'll have to look into it. If you're doing this because… I'm not trying to push you into something you don't want to be a part of."

"Izaak, I'm going to say something to you, and it's not going to make much sense right now. But someday maybe it will. Last night, when I was coming back from the city, I was thinking about all the people I saw. Heading to work. Or dinner parties. Or first dates. Or home to see their kids. I was thinking about how they all had their lives—simple lives with fun and frustration and love. And I thought: That's why Jack Reacher and Lisbeth Salander are just stories. That's why heroes don't exist. They can't—not without throwing all that away. And for what? So other people can go on living and enjoying life, not having to risk everything chasing down killers. Who would make that trade? Only someone who had nothing to give up. I'm not doing this for you, or those three boys, or even Cadence. I'm doing this because it's what I choose to do. Because, for me, the equation is different."

We sit there watching each other for what seems like a long time, and it feels as if he's repeating my words in his mind, not understanding them, but wanting to hold on to them for the day when he will understand them. Then he tucks my hair behind my ear, kisses me on the head, and goes to grab his cell phone from his desk. A minute later, he pulls it to his ear.

"Yeah, I'm looking for Levi Tyson... No, a friend from high school... Oh, really? Which one?" Izaak jots down something on a piece of paper. "They say how much?" He pockets the phone and gives me a smile that looks more like a shrug. "Well, the good news is, I found our boy."

"The bad news?"

"We're going to need my check card."

CHAPTER TWENTY-FIVE

I ARRIVE AT NARBERTH BOROUGH POLICE JAIL just before two. Izaak wanted to come, but I told him we'd have a better shot of success with just me. It costs me a few hours of waiting and four thousand dollars of Izaak's money, but they finally release Levi Tyson around five. He comes walking out to where I'm waiting for him in the lobby.

I recognize him immediately from the picture in Vic's bedroom. *The Fourth Musketeer.*

He's tall, and the handsome face from high school has hardened and decayed. His clothes are a mess, marred by stains and tears. His sunken eyes dart back and forth as he searches for someone he knows. I raise my hand, and he sulks over.

"Who are *you?*" he says.

"I'm the one who paid your bail."

"Yeah, but who *are* you?"

"The one who's out four thousand bucks if you don't show up for court."

"Don't count on that."

"I wasn't."

"Can you give me a ride?" he says.

"We need to talk first."

"I got some place I gotta be. We can talk on the way."

"Yeah, well, I don't have a car, so we're going to talk here."

He looks me up and down, then walks off toward the parking lot.

I catch up to him. "I just need ten minutes. After that, I'll take you wherever you need to go."

"I need a drink first."

"You can't wait ten minutes?"

"You want to talk. I want to drink. It sounds like a win-win to me."

"Fine, there's a bar down the street."

"Nah, not here," he says. "There's a place in Garrett Hill, has the best bar food on the Main Line."

"Flip and Bailey's?" It's a bar and grill on my block and kind of reminds me of that show *Cheers*. But since I don't really drink and they don't really serve vegan food, I've only been inside a couple of times.

"Yeah, Flip and Bailey's. That's where I want to go."

I try to grill him during the Uber to Bryn Mawr, but he keeps stonewalling: "Not until my meal."

The Uber drops us off at Flip's, and we grab a table in the back room, which is empty except for a couple video games and a shuffleboard table from the 1930s.

"You're paying, right?" he says when our waitress arrives.

"Sure."

"Bring me out two Golden Monkeys."

"I'm fine," I tell Levi.

"No, for me." He turns his attention back to the menu. "And then let me have your Philly cheesesteak and some of that lobster mac and cheese. And then, for an appetizer, get me some of that crab dip. But instead of the toasted pretzels, can you do your soft pretzel bites?"

"Sure thing, hun," the waitress says. "Anything for you?"

I shake my head, and she disappears into the kitchen. "Now can we talk?"

Levi's lip grows into what's meant to look like a playful smile, but really looks like a snarl. "How do I know you're not going to skip out on the tab? Or give me a ride home?"

I toss five twenties across the table from the extra cash I'd gotten from Izaak's account. I figured it might come down to money.

"I plan on having a lot of beer," he says.

I peel off another five as the waitress brings out Levi's drinks. The first one disappears in an instant but thankfully he nurses number two.

"Okay, okay. What you got for me?"

"You went to Lower Merion."

He stiffens, and then the second beer vanishes. "Yeah. I guess I did."

"You were friends with Vic, Terrance, and Warren."

"Waitress! Two more Monkeys!" he screams loudly enough to be heard in the main bar area. "Yeah, I guess I was."

"You all played ball?"

"Sure."

"Coach Michaels gave me the impression they were all pretty good but you mostly rode the bench."

"Who cares? It's high school basketball. Even when it matters, it don't matter."

"But didn't you resent that? I mean, maybe you could've gotten a scholarship if you had the chance to really play."

"Why would I resent it? That's life, right? It's all who you know."

"But it was so unfair."

"Who said life's fair? Look at Terrance and Warren. They were headed to the NBA. And now they're dead. And me? I should've died plenty of times. A bunch of people probably wish I had. And here I am. So, you ask me about fair, I'd say all things considered, I'm doing pretty good."

The waitress returns with two more drinks and Levi's crab dip and more or less tosses them onto the table. Levi is digging into the crab greedily before the echo of the plate clattering onto the wood fades. "How we doing on that cheesesteak?" he says, food spraying from his mouth.

The waitress looks at me, and I mouth an apology.

"Have you ever heard of Pyke?" I say.

"Pyke? What the hell's a Pyke?"

"Or the Exiles?"

"So, which is it? The Exiles or Pyke? For someone willing to shell out four Gs, you sure ask some strange-ass questions." More food, more beer, and I'm starting to feel about as nauseated as I am frustrated.

"Are you happy?" I say as Levi licks the remains of the crab dip off his bowl. He licks his fingers for good measure and rubs them on his shirt.

"Happy? Who's happy? You happy?"

"No."

"Okay then. Why ask?"

"It's just that you say you didn't resent Vic, yet I'm watching you pour down drinks the day after you get a DUI."

"What's one got to do with the other?"

186

"You tell me."

He points a pretzel bite at me. "Everyone thinks you like to get fucked up because of some fucked up thing that happened in your fucked up childhood. But why can't it just be that it's fun to get fucked up?"

"Tell me about the accident. On prom night."

"Why you doing this? Why you so interested in dredging up the past?"

"Do you remember anything? Maybe about the guy who pulled you out of the car?"

"I don't want to talk about this. We're done." He swallows drink number four and starts to get up but sees his main courses coming out and slinks back into his seat.

"Fine," I say. "We don't have to talk about the crash. But let's talk about money."

"Hey, there's a conversation worth having. It ain't smart, you know, carrying that much cash around. Someone gets the urge, they'll grab that like it ain't no thing."

"I'm not worried."

"Should be."

"The last person who tried something like that? It didn't end well for them."

"Yeah? Me, personally? I would never rob from no one. Unless I needed it. You got to have principles, you know?"

Apparently. "From what I hear, Vic did pretty well for himself. Did he have money in high school?"

"Oh, no doubt about that. All of them did. You should've seen Warren's ride. It was sick. This Audi S5? Man, we racked up some tickets in that thing."

There's an explosion of sound from just behind me. I jump

out of my chair expecting to see a gunman firing off rounds, but in the space of a heartbeat I realize the sound came from one of those heavy metal shuffleboard pucks being hurled against the wall. The man who hurled it is Ron Michaels.

He stumbles toward me, eyes glassy. "You bitch!" he screams. "You let him get away. That kid who killed my boy… he should be behind bars. But you… you put him on notice, let him take the easy way out."

"I'm sorry… but he—"

Ron grabs the collar of my shirt, but I don't fight him or back away. Behind the anger I can see the sadness in his eyes, and I know his goal isn't to hurt me.

"I never had a chance. Never had a chance to look that sonofabitch in the eye and let him know what he took from me." He's not yelling anymore but sobbing, his head pressed against my neck, and all I can think is: *If he only knew.*

"Hey, you need to go." It's one of the bartenders pulling Ron Michaels off of me.

Ron doesn't resist but takes a step back and composes himself. I think he's going to say something to me but instead he squints in the direction of Levi. "I know you," he says.

The bartender yanks on Ron's arm. "Buddy, I'm not asking again."

"Okay, okay. I'm sorry about…" he points to the dent the puck left in the wall, "all this."

I say to the bartender, "I'll cover the damages." Well done, Justice, what a hero. Yeah, you killed the man's son, but at least you saved him some pocket change. I'm sure Ron Michaels will sleep real soundly tonight.

The moment passes and I try to remember where I am and

why I'm here. When I turn back to the table, Levi is standing up, looking over my shoulder.

"I'm not done," I say.

"You ain't pissed off enough people for one day?"

"Where'd the money come from?"

"Why do you care where the money came from? Man, you shouldn't be asking such nosey questions."

I start to count out another grand but he shakes his head.

"You can save your money this time. And make sure anyone asks, you tell them I didn't say nothing. How Vic got his money, that was between him and God and his therapist."

"What? He saw a therapist?"

"Maybe it's just a saying."

"Maybe."

"Look, wouldn't you see somebody after some shit like we went through? Vic paid for me to go, too. I tried it once, but it wasn't my thing."

"What was the therapist's name?"

"Man, I don't remember how I ended up in jail last night. How the fuck I'm supposed to remember some dude's name I met five years ago?" He chuckles. "Funny thing, though. I *do* know his name."

It's like I know what he's going to say before he says it.

"That guy they been showing all over the TV the last few days? That college professor from Vic's school?"

I close my eyes. "Dr. Harper."

"Yeah. That's the guy. Harper."

CHAPTER TWENTY-SIX

IN BRAZILIAN JIU JITSU, you don't spar, like in kickboxing or karate. You roll. It's an apt name, because you're literally rolling around on the floor with your partner, trying to submit them with a choke or a joint lock. And it's also incredibly intimate. You're skin to skin, sweat to sweat, and it's no rare event you'll find your face between their thighs.

And that's cool, except that sometimes you have a partner where it's not. A few weeks into my training, my physics professor came in for his first class, and we had to roll together. If you have never mounted your teacher before, let me tell you. It's pretty much as awkward as it sounds.

The thing is, I remember what it felt like when I saw him walk into the gym. I couldn't quite make sense of the experience, almost like I thought he just lived in the classroom and had no business being seen in the world.

That's kind of how I feel now. Dr. Harper's name had no business coming out of Levi Tyson's mouth.

And on other hand, it makes perfect sense. If Dr. Harper knew Vic's deepest, darkest secrets, wouldn't he see right through the murders?

I stay at Flip's after Levi leaves, finishing the pretzel bites and trying to piece together a puzzle that seems to get more complicated the more I learn.

What do I know? I know that Dax wasn't the killer... maybe. I know that Pyke knew Vic and is involved with the Exiles... maybe. I know that Cadence is covering for Pyke... maybe. I know that a bunch of high school buddies had more money than they should have... maybe. I know that the killer has my bag... maybe. If maybes were margaritas I'd be dancing on the bar of Flip and Bailey's topless, wondering why people weren't stuffing bills into my g-string.

Whenever you're stuck on a problem, you either don't have enough information or you're making at least one wrong assumption. I know for sure I lack information. But what assumptions am I making? My brain fizzles out, and I look out the window and think a margarita would taste pretty good about now.

I push the thought aside. I need to see Dr. Harper—and I need to pray to God he'll be willing to talk to me.

It's already dark when I leave Flip and Bailey's and walk in the direction of my house. But as soon as I round the corner, I see a light in the distance. Not the light from a window or a streetlamp or leftover Christmas decorations, but a molten stew of orange and red dancing in the sky. I'm running again and now there are more lights, the pulsating strobe of red and blue from emergency vehicles parked around my burning house.

I'm still running toward it when I feel powerful arms seize me, and I hear myself screaming. "Andy! She's in there! That's my house! Andy!"

"She's safe. She's safe," a washed-out voice says. "He got her out."

I look up at the fireman who's holding me, beads of sweat and rain dripping from his walrus mustache.

"What? Who got her out? Where is she?" I'm screaming, and for a second it feels like he's shaking me, but then I realize it's me trying to twist out of his grip.

"Now, calm down. Listen to me. She's going to be okay. We're taking her to Bryn Mawr Hospital. But you need to go with the cops while we go to save this poor guy. He was inside when we found him half dead, trying to save your dog." He nods toward an ambulance. The door is shut, but parked just ahead of it is a car that belongs to Izaak.

I step back trying to slow my thoughts, but then I see the fireman motion for someone, and I know there will be questions I can't answer. I slip behind a firetruck and into the shadows of a neighbor's driveway, and before anyone can find me, I'm gone.

CHAPTER TWENTY-SEVEN

I HIKE THE ENTIRE THREE MILES and change to Minella's, a twenty-four-hour diner not too far from where Conestoga intersects Lancaster. I spend the evening drinking too much coffee and waiting for the sun to rise. After a couple of hours, the server asks if I'm all done. I tell her I'm a student, and does she mind if I stay and study until morning? She says it's fine as long as I keep ordering food and drinks every now and then. She doesn't seem to notice I don't have any books and spend the evening staring out a window.

The sun is starting to rise when I order some oatmeal with fruit and trade the coffee for orange juice. I'm as refreshed as I'm going be. I settle my bill and walk the five miles to Bryn Mawr Hospital, making sure to follow back roads rather than walk down Lancaster. It adds time, but that's better for me, anyway.

Bryn Mawr Hospital's main building is a tower made of red brick that feels more suited to the 1960s than the 2020s. I loiter out front for a while until I don't see anyone approaching, then ruffle through a trash can, salvaging a used stick-on visitor's pass, the kind that includes a black and white printout of your license. The picture is of a woman two decades my senior, whose long, curly hair looks nothing like my chin-length locks. But it's not like I'm entering some top-secret facility guarded by Navy SEALs or TSA. It'll do.

"Excuse me," I say to the woman manning the welcome desk, making sure to lean against it so she can see I have an ID, but not the photo on the ID. "I keep getting lost. I just stepped out for breakfast, and now I can't remember what floor my friend's on."

"Name?"

"Andrea Simmons."

"Looks like they have her in the Inpatient Unit on floor five. Five thirty-four."

I start for the elevators.

"Hold up, miss. I need to scan you in again." I give my best smile while she scans my badge and waves me on without a problem.

A lot of people say they can't stand hospitals, but I find them comforting. Millions of dollars and hundreds of people all devoted to keeping you alive—keeping you alive regardless of who you are, what atrocities you've committed, how much money you've got in your pocket. For all the contentiousness in the outside world, in these walls, we're all just people.

I take the stairs and head up to the fifth floor. Inside, I find Andy propped up in bed watching an episode of *LIVE with Kelly and Ryan*. She looks washed out and restless. I throw my arms around her and she startles. "Jesus. I didn't know you were here."

"You're alive." I wrap my hands around her shoulders and enjoy the warmth of her cheek pressed against mine. "What happened?" I say.

"Honestly, I don't really know. I went to sleep, and the next thing I knew I was on the pavement."

"Do you remember seeing Izaak?"

"I just know that some guy was trying to talk to me, and when I saw the fire I just started screaming that Winston was in there, and the guy ran back into the house."

She turns off the TV with a remote, tubes dangling from her arm.

"Where are your parents?" I say.

"My dad's in Europe. He said he's catching the first plane home. Mom had to take Winston to the vet. He's going to be okay, though, the little trooper."

"You don't remember anything else? How did the fire start?"

Andy tries to pull herself fully upright but winces. "The cops say our neighbors saw some guy run up to the house and throw something through our front window."

"Who?"

"Honestly, I was going to ask you." There's a hint of judgment in her voice, but I can see she regrets it instantly. "It was dark, so who knows? Hey, is he here? Your friend? If he is, maybe I could see him. You know, to say thanks."

I nod absentmindedly, trying to connect the puzzle pieces.

"The police are looking for you," she says.

"I figured as much."

"They gave me a number for you to call." She tries and fails to stifle a moan as she rolls over and reaches for her purse. She digs through it and pulls out a business card. "I said I'd give this to you if I saw you."

I pocket it. "You need anything?"

"They're pumping me full of narcotics, so I'm doing just fine for now." She sits up, half-startled. "My DVDs. Did my DVD collection survive?"

"How much morphine do they have you on? Learn to use

streaming, girl." Before I can stop myself, I add, "I heard you walked out of The Grog."

Her face goes red and I feel like an ass for saying it. "I was afraid to tell you. But really, it's just for the reason you said. I didn't need to be around all that drinking and partying. You wouldn't believe how many guys offered to buy me drinks. But I was a good girl. Thanks, but no thanks."

I squeeze her hand. "I'm proud of you, Andy. You've been through one too many levels of hell."

"We should hang out more, once I get home," she says. Then we look at each other for a long time, sharing the same unspoken thought. Eventually, she breaks the silence. "Where are you going to go?"

"I haven't thought about it, to tell you the truth. I don't know. Maybe some friends from work, until I can find a new place."

"We have room at our house. I'm sure Mom won't mind. Not like she's ever around, anyway."

What I want to say is, "No thanks, I'm not going to risk your life a second time." But instead I just squeeze her hand again and say, "Don't worry about me."

"Justice Winters. Chick of Steel."

I kiss her on the forehead. "I'm sorry all this happened."

The guy at the nurses' station outside of Andy's door tells me Izaak's on the fourth floor. I head for the stairs, pausing in the stairwell to clear my head and build up the courage to face him.

I find Izaak's room and enter without knocking. I'm standing there surrounded by Izaak and a man and a woman I don't recognize. He's alive. Hell, he's more than alive. When he sees me, he sits up easily in his hospital bed, beaming.

"Surprise?" I say in history's worst attempt at nonchalance.

Izaak spreads his arms out. "Welcome to my new digs. Mom, Dad, this is Justice."

Izaak's mom shoots him a look that I imagine must mean, "As your attorney, I strongly advise you not to talk to this girl." If he notices, he doesn't acknowledge it. His mom is elegant and severe, the kind of woman where you find yourself pronouncing every letter of every word you say.

Izaak's father looks like Izaak with a little less muscle and a lot more gray hair. He smiles broadly and reaches out a hand the size of a ribeye. "Dick Lane. My wife, Vanessa." Then he points to my chest. "That badge. That's not your face."

"Can we have a moment alone?" Izaak says.

"Remember what we talked about," Vanessa Lane says as they exit and close the door behind them.

When we're alone, I say, "Should I be worried?"

"The police are looking for you. They say you ran last night. Mom's just watching out for me. She's not going to snitch, though, if that's what you're asking."

"What happened last night?"

He bows his head sheepishly. "I had this bad feeling about you going to see Levi alone. So… I kinda followed you. Then while I was waiting outside Flip and Bailey's I saw this Crown Vic circle the block a couple times. I started following it when I saw the driver jump out in front of your place. By the time I got down there, he was already around the corner and your house was on fire."

"I owe you," I say, bowing my head.

"How about we're even?"

"No. I mean I owe you the truth." I take a deep breath and close my eyes. Okay. No going back now. No more secrets. No more lies. "That dancer who got into a fight with Vic? That was me."

"I figured as much."

"He took a video of me dancing. He said he was going to share it with the whole school."

"Piece of shit," he whispers. "You could've told me, you know. I wouldn't have judged you."

"You don't understand. If that video got out, it would have made headlines. The girl who falsely accused a basketball star of attempted rape is a stripper?"

He nods, thinking he understands, even though he has no idea.

"After Vic threatened to show people the video of me dancing, I asked him to meet me at the golf club. I was going to pay him off. All three of the guys came. Then… I don't know. Things just sort of happened and he attacked me and… well, you know what happened to Vic. The others, though? What we wrote was true."

Izaak's face is tears and anger. He's squeezing my hand so tight I think my fingers are going to break.

"After Vic died, the guys ran and I ran. I ran because I didn't want the truth to come out. And it sounds so awful, like I let all this happen just to avoid some embarrassment. But that's not it. It wasn't about that. Izaak, there's something else."

"What?"

I search for words I've never voiced. The words come slowly, like I'm reading a court transcript. "My name isn't Justice Winters. My real name is Paige Marie Rexroad."

"I don't get it."

"Have you ever heard of the Day Thief?"

"No."

"It's kind of this myth where I'm from out in Michigan. Girls have been disappearing for years. They're never found. Police try to say it's a bunch of unrelated incidents. Sex traffickers kidnapping people and taking them over the border into Canada. But everyone else talks about the Day Thief, the man who will grab you right off the sidewalk in broad daylight."

"What are you telling me?"

"The Day Thief is my father."

"Jesus Christ."

"Most of the girls, he kills. A few he keeps. They became my sisters. I left them behind, Izaak. Five years ago, I escaped, but I left them behind." I'm a puddle, but Izaak just wipes away my tears and sits there, listening.

"Why didn't you tell the police?"

"I can't. Pop always said that if the cops ever showed up, we would all commit suicide. But it's worse than that, Izaak."

"How can it be worse than that?"

"The Heiden—that's what Pop calls the girls he takes—he keeps them for a year. For the first six months, he rents them out, you know, to guys. Then he purifies them so they can die in a state of grace. Anyway, the thing is that I don't know who all is involved. Some really high-powered people, I think. They'll never let the truth come out."

He pulls me toward him and I rest my head on his chest, both of us crying for what feels like a long time. Then I wipe the tears away pull myself erect.

"So, you see? It's all my fault. And once the cops get a clue? It's over for me. I can't turn myself in. Even when this is all over, I can't go back to my life."

He pulls me in for a hug, pulling my head down to his shoulder, then whispers into my ear: "It's not your fault. None of it. But you do what you gotta do. And you need anything—ever—you let me know."

"I will," I say. Even though I won't.

CHAPTER TWENTY-EIGHT

I WALK OUT OF THE hospital and into the sun. For the first time I can remember, I feel safe—safe because I know that even if I die, my story will live.

I travel down State Road toward Lancaster, and despite no sleep, despite walking for mile upon mile, I'm energized and alert, and my past doesn't feel like a weight dragging me into the abyss. It feels like stops on a map leading me on a journey that's filled with pain and hardship and regret, but one that's worth taking.

For the first time in my life, I feel seen.

Dr. Harper talks a lot about the soul. My soul was an invention, stolen from a thousand different sources and patched together into a quilt designed to cover up the truth. Me? I did not exist. I had to be invented.

I was not a totally blank slate. Pop trained us to steal, fight, and kill. And he also saw to it we were educated. We studied math by reading Euclid, science by reading Newton, history by reading Thucydides. Everything else we got from the Bible. But we were not real people; we were receptacles, designed to be filled, but never free to speak our own words.

And who would we speak them to? For us, there was only

Pop and each other and the animals that scurried across the farm and in the woods. The outside world didn't exist, and to the outside world, neither did we.

Our only glimpses of life beyond the farm came on nights when Pop would watch college basketball in the living room.

Most games he would sit silently, nursing a single beer over the course of the evening, reacting to nothing. It was different when the University of Michigan played Ohio. He would pace and curse and once polished off an entire six-pack.

My sisters and I would join him, but the game was only an excuse. It was the commercials we loved. Images of little girls playing with Barbies and couples eating romantic dinners and house moms becoming giddy over soft toilet paper. That's what kept me alive—the belief that there was a world beyond our farm, where people were free and happy. For my sisters, it was only a fantasy—the kind of escape you get from reading a romance novel. For me? I knew that someday I would live in that world.

And then I escaped.

After that I realized just how impossibly demanding freedom really is.

I spent the better part of a year in California, living out of my car and scraping together cash by doing day labor, along with the immigrants who would congregate by U-Haul outlets, flagging down patrons in need of cheap workers. They gave me odd looks, but left me alone, which was all I wanted.

If you want to know the meaning of surreal, that was it. I felt like one of those characters in a fantasy novel who gets transported to another land and time. Only I never had a guide to introduce me to the world. I had to figure it out on my own.

When I wasn't working, I was watching. It's all I did. I would spend hours at the Irvine Spectrum, people-watching and eavesdropping in the hope of learning how to be a person. I would watch fathers promise to take their daughters onto the enormous Ferris wheel and then march toward Target in the hopes the girls would forget. I would watch old men sit outside of The Coffee Bean drinking tea and reading the paper and complaining about taxes. Most of all, I liked to follow couples my own age. It was mystifying. I expected them to talk about love and kissing and sex. Mostly, they just teased each other and talked about celebrities.

Occasionally, someone would try to strike up a conversation with me. At first I'd freeze up and run away. But over time I learned to string together a few sentences about the weather or an upcoming holiday.

The one thing I couldn't do was feel. Aside from the panic that would grip me in random moments, there was only a quiet emptiness. I wondered if I was a monster because no matter how hard I tried, I felt neither remorse nor regret nor even guilt for my crimes.

Eventually, I saved enough to buy a phone. It transformed me. I would spend days watching movies and TV shows. It was my light, and for the first time I could feel emotions stir: excitement, sadness, anger, lust, serenity, joy.

It came at a price. The closer I felt to the world, the more I was overcome by a gnawing shame. I would spend entire evenings staring at my hands and wondering how they committed so many atrocities.

The movies became my instruction manual, my escape,

my Bible. I constructed my past and my soul from pieces of characters dreamed up by some Hollywood screenwriter and brought to life by the actresses I adored. One month I would be Jennifer Lawrence. Another month Angelina Jolie. Another month Katharine Hepburn.

That's how I was born. Piece by piece. Through imitation of girls who were sharp and sexy and fearless and feminine. I'd watch every movie and every interview of theirs I could find, memorize my favorite lines and practice them in a mirror, not as if I was preparing for an audition, but as if I was preparing to go undercover in a war zone.

Suddenly, I found myself able to talk to people, and it was so easy because it wasn't me talking—it was Hollywood.

During my Hepburn month, I decided to go to college. I learned that Katharine went to school at Bryn Mawr College, and that became my goal. I saved for the rest of the month, then took off across the country in my Saturn.

The car broke down in Chicago, but I was able to buy a cheap, fake ID and an Amtrak ticket to Philadelphia. The ID was atrocious, but it got me to Philly, and to Abe.

After that, things were easier. The toughest part was trying to get into college without high school transcripts. I pretty much aced the SATs and told the Bryn Mawr admissions officer I was homeschooled but no longer had contact with my parents, for personal reasons. He was sympathetic, but in the end the school rejected me. And so off I went to Haverford.

That's when it really started to sink in, the deepest reason I could never live a normal life. Because even though Hollywood had saved me and allowed me to blend in with humanity, I was stuck in a role. No matter how hard I tried, no matter how hard anyone else tried, I felt cut off and isolated—like when someone laughs at your joke, only you know you stole it from some YouTube video you saw the week before.

But Izaak? Izaak *sees me.*

And I realize something has changed. The reason I'm continuing to fight, the reason I will not disappear until the Exiles are thrown into the ash heap of history, is not to avenge what happened to Cadence. I'm doing it for Izaak.

For a moment I feel as though I'm betraying Cadence, but the feeling evaporates and what I feel isn't guilt but a ruthless conviction. Whatever role my lies have played in straining our relationship, she dealt the deathblow the moment she chose Pyke over me. Maybe I can still fix things. Maybe once I set things right and tell her the truth, I can leave two friends behind instead of one. I hope so. But all that will have to wait. First, the Exiles have to pay.

But time is working against me. The longer I'm on the Main Line, the more likely I'll slip up. Whether it's the police, or the Exiles, or some unseen force I can't imagine, they will get to me and that will be all she wrote. I need to get to Dr. Harper. Soon.

But what I feel isn't the frenzied need for quickness but a quiet serenity of knowing I'm on the right track.

As I near Ludington Library, I stop in front of a park with an ornate gazebo and, far behind it, an empty playground. I try to see the path ahead. To anticipate what Dr. Harper will say, what I will do if he won't talk, and what I'll do if he does. I try to decide what to leave to law enforcement—and what has to be done by my own hand.

Suddenly, I'm floating through space, my phone slipping out of my back pocket and falling to the pavement, and by the time I realize I'm being carried, the door of a van slams shut. I don't recognize the guy holding me down on the floor of the van, but I recognize the driver.

It's Arnold Lyons—Jack Jackson's right-hand man.

CHAPTER TWENTY-NINE

I'M STRUGGLING WITH EVERY MUSCLE FIBER, but so is Lyons's goon. Although he's not particularly large, I'm particularly small. Not exactly a fair fight.

At first, he's behind me, pushing down my shoulders, and I'm able to swing my knees back strong enough to get in a couple of shots. None solid enough to do any damage, but it keeps him off balance.

But as he goes to grab my wrists, I free my right arm and jam my fingers as hard as I can underneath his jaw. He falls back gagging, and I twist around and dive on top of him, sinking my teeth into his lip and yanking my head with all my might. I feel the skin tear as blood pours into my mouth.

I lunge for the door, but Lyons slams on the brakes, and I'm thrown into the back of the passenger seat. The goon is back on top of me again, slamming his fist into my jaw. He relents but then throws his full weight behind his forearm, which is shoved against my neck. I'm choking but more concerned he's going to outright crush my windpipe.

"Don't kill her," Lyons says. "We need to talk to her first."

"She's trying to kill *me*," he says, though he lets up on my neck just enough so I can breathe again. Then he manages to seize my hands, and using his chest to keep my pinned, tightens a zip tie around my wrists.

"Look what she did to me," the goon says, moving to the other side of the van, his words nearly indecipherable. His bloodstained hands are pressed against his mouth.

"Nothing that can't be fixed," Lyons says calmly.

I try to see where we're going, but from my vantage point all I can make out are trees and the tops of buildings. We stop at a light, and I start screaming, hoping that someone walking by will hear. But the goon dives back on top of me, pressing his hand over my mouth.

We start moving again, and soon we're picking up speed. We're on the interstate, heading west, I think. I let my body relax. I need to conserve my energy until I get another chance to fight. After a while, he takes his hand off my mouth.

"Don't be screaming, girl. You won't be the first person I've killed."

"Oh, Ethan," Lyons says, his voice casual. "Don't threaten the girl. She's had a rough morning. You know, Miss Winters, I warned Jack about you. But he didn't want to listen. It's too bad. You can't lead a team if you won't listen to your advisors. So, I really wish things could have been different. But here we are."

"So, it was you? The boys? Dax? The fire?"

"I'm afraid not. I'm sorry to say that you made enemies with us for absolutely no reason. It's just like we told you. Our agenda is much simpler and much more intellectual. We're thinkers. Not thugs."

"Could've fooled me."

"You backed us into a corner, Miss Winters. When you went to the press. Things are going to be much tougher for us, now.

The police. The press. Even your bodyguard friend seems to be under the impression we owe him money."

Bodyguard friend? He must mean Pyke.

"Jack is going to have to be extra careful, and the thing about Jack is, he likes to run his mouth."

"So, why am I alive? Why not just gun me down on the side of the road and move on with your lives?"

"We need to have a… conversation."

The van slows as we exit the highway. The best I can gauge, we're about thirty minutes west, well past the Main Line and into rural Pennsylvania.

We drive for another fifteen minutes and then turn onto what feels like a gravel trail or driveway. Samurai used to have this idea of dying before you go into battle. The thinking was that if you accepted your own death, you would fight with total focus and ferocious bravery. I close my eyes and try to die. It doesn't work. Despite everything, I want to live.

The van comes to a stop and Lyons exits. I hear his footsteps on the gravel, and then the clanging of metal as the old door swings open. "Take her to the back," Lyons says.

Now's my best shot. While Ethan's moving me. But as soon as he throws me over his shoulder, the best I can do is wiggle a bit. In the distance I see a farmhouse, two stories with clean siding. The only other building in sight is an old barn, tall and red, with paint peeling off the sides like the one that housed Pop's office. I catch an address on the mailbox. We're somewhere in St. Peters, which I vaguely recall being south of Pottstown.

Ethan takes me around to the back of the barn, where uncut grass swallows a pile of rusty farm tools and an ancient tractor rots in the weeds. He dumps me onto the muddy ground next to an old water pump. I prop myself up against the barn as the two men surround me.

"I need to run inside. My lip won't stop bleeding," Ethan says.

"Do your job," Lyons says. "I apologize, Miss Winters. My friend is a mercenary, not a true believer. A fair-weather friend, you could say."

"What about you?"

Lyons walks toward me, stopping a few steps away, mud splashing onto his heavy boots. Then he kneels so we're eye level. "Oh, I believe. Do you know what it's like to believe in something? To devote your life to a great cause? Men need a great cause. Otherwise, what's the point in living? I can think of no greater tragedy than to be born in an era of peace." He reaches out and tucks my hair behind my ear.

"For a long time, I thought that was my curse. And then—and you're too young to remember—and then this country was attacked. I'm not ashamed to admit, I celebrated. I had a cause. But, alas, my country didn't want me." He gives an ugly chuckle and cracks his knuckles.

"They said I was mentally unstable," he continues. A grin reveals large, yellow teeth. "But then I met Jack. And he taught me the way things were. That there was a war right here at home. They're related, you know? Have you ever asked yourself why the greatest military power in history can't defeat a few primitive fanatics?"

"I assume you're going to tell me."

"*Shame*, Miss Winters. We are not proud of who we are. In World War II, we didn't hesitate to drop two nuclear bombs on Japan. And then," he brushes his hands together, "that was the end of that. But today? Today we put our own soldiers on a leash and prosecute them for war crimes."

"It's called decency."

"It's called shame. Well, we're going to put an end to that. When we're done, this country will be proud again."

The sun is giving way to heavy clouds, and in the distance I see a couple of squirrels inching out of the woods that mark the end of the field. If I get a chance to run, that's where I'll head. I'll be totally lost, but if I go back to the road, they'll be able to hunt me down regardless of any head start I get. Besides, we're not all that far from civilization. There has to be another house within a mile or two, regardless of which direction I go.

"Now, down to business," Lyons says. "Here's what I need to know, Miss Winters. Listen carefully. I need to know everyone you talked to about us. I need to know exactly what you said, and I need to know who they might have told. I need to know whether you recorded any of your conversations—with Jack, Dax, anyone." He doesn't mention Pyke. "I need to know about anything else you might have gathered. Photos. Notes. Computer files. I need to know it all and where I can find it."

"I guess we're going to be a here a while, then."

That grin. "There it is. Pride. I can't say I'm surprised. Not after what you did back there in the van. Well, good for you, Miss Winters. Good for you." He stands and says, "Take her clothes off," and disappears into the barn.

Ethan steps toward me and I slam the edge of my boot into his shin. He crumbles and almost collapses on top of me. I roll left and dig my nails into the barn. Splinters sear into my skin as I pull myself to my feet and I take off toward the woods.

Then my vision goes blurry as I feel a hand grab my hair and yank me to the ground. Ethan is on top of me and I feel like my chest is going to cave in. He's tearing off my clothes and soon the cold air rushes over my skin.

He drags my naked body to the barn, then he backs up so he's out of reach. Lyons returns. He's carrying a black shaving kit.

"You're really starting to annoy my colleague," he says. "I'll have to ask that you not lay your hands on him again."

He unzips the shaving kit and pulls out a pair of latex gloves, setting the kit gently on the ground.

"I'm sure, of course, you won't listen. It's that pride again. But here's a secret. Pride is fragile. It can't outlast simple pain. But do you know what's even worse than pain, Miss Winters? Humiliation. Proud men resist. They fight. Torture them, and when they gather their strength, they'll fight again. But humiliate a man? Shame will make him docile. If you want total control, you combine both."

He finishes pulling on the gloves and nods at Ethan.

"On your knees," Ethan says.

"You first," I say. Before the words are out, I feel the weight of Ethan's foot slam into my chest, slamming my head back hard against the barn wall, and tearing flesh off my breast.

"Kneel, bitch." The words hardly register. I'm trapped in that place where you're paralyzed by pain and the world seems out of reach. Then I hear Lyons's voice.

"No, Miss Winters. Not that. If that's what you're thinking?" Lyons leans down front of me, grabbing my hair and yanking my head back. He runs his hand over the flesh of stomach and thighs. Then he spits in my face. "I'm not an animal."

A shattering pain explodes from the bottom of my left foot.

It feels like a sledgehammer pounded my heel and nearly sent my tibia ripping the skin of my knee. Before I can process the agony, Ethan powers another hard kick into my right shin and I feel it more in my temples and jaw than in my leg.

I'm rocking back and forth, trapped by nauseating pain, when the world goes black as another kick lands in my back. I'm still conscious, not of people or objects, just shuddering waves and the sickening feeling that my kidney has been torn to shreds.

"When peace like a river, attendeth my way..."

I'm breaking, crumbling into shattered pieces, and all I want is to crawl into the arms of my friend and have him hold me and tell me it's going to be okay.

More blows, but now they seem distant, almost as if I've journeyed miles from my body and the sensations are more like echoes than pain.

"When sorrows like sea billows roll..."

Another blow, then another, each act of violence bleeding into the next.

I'm disappearing and when I open my eyes I see faces. Faces, not from this world, but from my past. I wonder what Anna Claire's child looks like. I wonder if Laudie Mae still draws her pictures. I wonder if they ever think of me. I wonder if they're still alive.

"Whatever my lot, thou hast taught me to say..."

"It is well, it is well, with my soul..."

"It is well, with my soul."

Hours pass. Or maybe minutes. Or maybe seconds. I'm so lost that when I come to, I'm surprised to see that I'm not a child and the man in front of me isn't my father.

"You, Justice Winters, are a heretic."

Arnold Lyons is standing a few feet away, holding an object that looks like a collar with a piece of black iron running through the front. The iron looks like an H, with two sharpened points at each end.

Lyons continues and there's a sickening pleasantness in his voice, like a kindergarten teacher welcoming her class on the first day of school. "During the Spanish Inquisition, heretics would, eventually, confess. Don't believe Hollywood, dear girl. Every man—and woman—breaks. But, you know, the heretics would sometimes recover their courage before they would face their execution. This, of course, was…counter-productive. So the Spanish invented a device they called the Heretics' Fork."

He unfastens the collar and holds it up against the sky like a woman admiring a diamond necklace.

"*Abiruo*," he says, as if he's reading something engraved on the iron. "It means: I recant. You see, once the heretic confessed, he would be put in this collar, two of the prongs dug into his chest, two dug into the flesh under his jaw, so he would be forced to look up at the Heaven he denied. Any motion and he would experience a pain unlike anything you can imagine. He could not sleep. Could not swallow. He would stay like that for hours, his muscles cramping, every movement sending shudders of agony through his body, every shudder making the pain worse, until it was time, finally, for him to be burned at the sake."

Lyons hands the collar to Ethan and chuckles.

"No, Miss Winters. No one will be burning you at the stake. I'm offering you a much more humane choice. Tell me what I need to know and this will all be over. Or…"

Ethan takes a step toward me, malice in his dark, dead eyes. "Or it's going to be a long night for all of us."

I lay on the ground looking up at them, the taste of blood and dirt caking my mouth, my body quaking from the cold wind blowing across my naked skin. I feel empty, like a starved animal wandering across an endless desert. I think of Innocence and wish that she were here to scream at me: Get up. Run! Only I'm glad she's not here. Because I can't run, and I can't live with the knowledge that I failed her once again.

Is it really wrong to surrender? When you can't fight, isn't there dignity in giving up? In accepting your fate and welcoming a quick death? Where's the victory in suffering? Where's the heroism in pointless martyrdom? There's something wicked about shaming someone for refusing to endure the unendurable. We sit in a movie theater, looking down on the prisoner of war who gives up—and then we go home, driving past the gym and thinking: No, not today. I'll work out when I'm not so tired. It's so easy to be a hero in your head.

But isn't that the whole trick? To will yourself forward, even when you are too tired? To find the energy, even when it's not there? People waste their lives waiting until they feel like working out, feel like taking action, feel like telling the truth. But they've got it backwards. You don't feel then act. You act then feel. You move forward, not because your emotions make you, but because you mind decides.

Ethan reaches down to clasp the Heretics' Fork around my neck and, with my bound hands, I seize his arm. This is it. My last stand.

I twist onto my side and fling my legs around his head, trapping his arm across his neck in a triangle choke. Then, knowing I don't have the energy to hold him or the time to strangle him, I dig my thumb into his eye and tear it from its socket.

He yanks himself out of my legs, hands covering his face, as he crawls away from me, unable to do much more than howl.

Lyons doesn't move. He watches me, eyes wide with what looks like surprise. Or admiration.

Every part of me feels engulfed by pain, as if a welding torch is trying to split me into two. I turn to the barn, once again digging my nails into the old wood, struggling to pull myself to my feet. I slip, but catch myself and keep struggling.

I'm on my feet, but they won't support my weight, and I lean desperately against the barn, trying to put distance between me and Lyons. I know it's hopeless. He knows it, too. He's toying with me. Letting me build up hope, only to be torn away by a few easy strides.

And then those strides come. He marches at me and thrusts his boot against my knees. They buckle and I collapse again, my head crashing against the old wheelbarrow.

"I can end this for you," he says. "Answer my questions and it will all be over. No more pain. No more fear. No more humiliation."

I grope around for the wheelbarrow so I can pull myself up, but all I can find is grass and rotted wood. Then, buried in the grass, I feel something damp but sturdy. I curl my fingers around the handle of a steel rake and when I hear the sound of Lyons's boots move toward me, I lift it and twist and heave it in his direction with the last of my strength.

Two sounds come in quick succession—the sounds of a rusty rake blade digging into flesh and bone. And a thud, as Lyons collapses onto the ground.

I jerk my head, expecting Ethan to come hurtling in my

direction, but he's moving away from me, a hand cupped over his face as he stumbles into the van and drives off.

Lyons's arms flail around his face, trying remove the blade, which has cut through his cheek and obliterated an eye. I crawl toward him and seize the end of the rake handle, flinging it back and forth over and over again for seconds that feel like an eternity.

I want to keep going but I know that if I do I won't be able to move and will die here in this field.

I pull myself next to Lyons's still body and feel through his pockets. I find his phone, which unlocks by facial recognition. Not helpful.

I look at the farmhouse. It's more than a football field away and I'm not sure I have the strength to make it.

So what, Justice? You're either going to live or die trying.

I push my body up and for a few yards I'm able to crawl on my hands and knees. But the throbbing pain in my legs and back is too great and my arms are too weak. I collapse onto the ground.

My movements come slowly. I pull my knees forward, then push with my feet and pull with my fingers. Every inch feels like a marathon. But every inch brings me closer. I stop to catch my breath, but I feel like those Himalayan mountain climbers who talk about how at certain heights you're always out of breath, even if you're perfectly still.

Anxious thoughts rush past me. What if the house is locked? What if it's abandoned and there's no phone service? Part of me wants to give up, to rest, to wait for some passerby to see the glint of my body from the road and race over and help me. But a car hasn't driven past since I started, and it would never see me from this distance.

I push the questions out of my mind and keep going, slow movements summoning pain that reaches deep in my core.

The sun is setting and I still have fifteen yards to go. I need to hurry because the temperature is plummeting. If I can't make it inside, the cold will finish me off, not in hours, but in minutes.

As the last hints of light disappear, I reach three stairs that lead to the porch. I pull myself up each one and then collapse against the door. I fight my way to my knees, my fingers clutching the doorknob. I turn and it opens.

Inside I can smell lingering hints of barbecue, and warmth flowing from radiators. Through the hallway I can see into the kitchen and, mounted on the wall, a phone.

I am not going to die tonight.

CHAPTER THIRTY

I OPEN MY EYES and through blurry vision see Anna Claire watching me from the doorway. I try to speak but the words don't come and she vanishes.

The darkness swallows me again once more and when I awake, I'm being pinned down and I'm fighting again, blank figures I don't recognize holding me and barking orders I can't understand. Am I dreaming? Am I even alive?

My body relaxes and it's as if I'm floating in space, an unexpected euphoria holding my hand and walking me down a tunnel made of color and light. When I look down, I see Laudie Mae at my feet, five years old, coloring in a book filled with pictures of ducks and rabbits and gators and snakes.

Then she starts crying. "You left me, Paige. Why did you leave me?"

And then Anna Claire is there again, holding Laudie Mae and taking her away from me as she watches with icy eyes. "You abandoned us," Anna says. "You didn't fight. You left us here to die. Why aren't you fighting? Fight! Fight!"

The voice becomes more vivid and changes shape. "Stop fighting, babe. Stop fighting." I take in a sharp breath as I realize

I'm lying in bed, Brenda looking down at me. I let my muscles relax and I fall back into a pile of silky pillows.

"It's okay," Brenda says. "You're safe."

Minutes pass as I try to recapture existence. I'm dressed under the blankets of the bed in soft pajamas. I can move, but my body feels half numb, and I see a tube running from my right arm to an IV bag beside the bed. Then I catch the aroma of cinnamon, and when I turn I see a tray beside me with a bowl of oatmeal and sliced fruit.

I prop myself up in the large, lush bed, sinking deep into a half-dozen oversized pillows. The room is small, but tastefully decorated, with green skirting board rising from the floor and white crown molding lining the ceiling. Pieces of memories re-emerge, and I say to Brenda, my voice hoarse, "Abe. He got me."

"Yeah, babe. He got you."

"Where is he?"

Brenda hands me a glass of orange juice from the tray. "He's here. He wants to come in. It's just… hard for him. But never mind Abe. How are you feeling?"

"How long have I been here?"

"Four days."

"I don't remember much."

"Oh, it was bad. That first day, Abe had a doctor friend of his come by. We were this close to taking you to the hospital, but you wouldn't hear of it. Thankfully, you seemed to be doing a little better by the next morning. We've had to keep you on a pretty strong dose of morphine, though."

"Did I tell him anything? About what happened?"

She bites her lip. "No. But Abe saw enough of it. He sent some boys down to clean things up."

"You don't need to do all this. You shouldn't be putting yourselves at risk for me."

"Just eat up. Gather your strength." She sets the tray on the bed, and I stare at the plate, knowing I need the energy but sick at the thought of food. As Brenda leaves, I finish the orange juice and, ten minutes later, I'm drowsy again and back to the pillows I go.

It's dark when I open my eyes, so dark that it's minutes before I realize someone is here, sitting in a Barcalounger in the corner of the room.

"Abe?"

He lights a table lamp, which sends soft beams across his face. He looks older than I remember, with new creases branching from the corners of his eyes and his lips. He doesn't smile, but nods in a way that feels like a smile. Then he places his hands in his lap and squeezes his thumb, unsure of what to say—or unsure if I'm prepared to hear it.

"That man. You do that?" he says.

"Yes."

"He hurt you."

"Yes."

"He the only one?"

"No."

"Good. I want a turn."

He turns away from me and rests his chin in his hand.

"My old man was a cop," he continues. "His old man was a cop. His old man was a cop. Cops, all the way down. So, me? Naturally, I wanted to be a cop. But you know what he tells me? He says, 'Brahmie, you don't want to be no cop. See, because a cop can't do the things that have to be done. You want to do something in this world, what you need is power.' Then he says to me, 'Now there's two types of power. You got the gun, and you got the dollar. Cops, see, we got a gun, but we ain't got no power because we got people telling us how to use that gun. Got a sergeant, got a captain, got a DA. So really,' he says, 'it comes down to this. You choose the gun, you best live outside the law. You choose the dollar, you control the law.'"

I can't tell whether Abe's talking to me or to himself or whether it even matters.

"So that's what I did, you know? I went and I made a bit of money. And I told myself, okay, I've got the power. Now what? Well, I try to do something good with it. I buy the club. Try to help you girls. But the thing with money is someone always has more of it. And so I see that it can't be like that. You want to do anything worth doing in this world, you got to have both. You got to have the dollar and the gun. Then…" He points at me. "Then you get to live on your own terms."

I laugh bitterly, and Abe arches his eyebrow. "I thought I was living on my own terms," I say. "When you got me set up, and I was going to school, and living a normal life. I thought: Way to go, Justice. You've done it. But the thing I've learned is that if you're living a lie, you're at the mercy of everyone. I've done everything within my power to set things right—but because I tried to do it while holding on to the lie, all that's happened is that I've hurt everyone I care about—Andy, Izaak, you."

"What lie?"

"I never told you this," I say, "but last year, someone did something to me, or tried to… no, let's just leave it at that. It's over now. But he came from a rich family, and one word from

Dad, and that was the end of that. The world is controlled by those with power. And the rest of us? We can't fight back because our hands are tied. We're bound by laws. They aren't. We have to tell the truth. They don't. We are predictable. People count on us showing up at work and sitting down for dinner. They can be erratic and capricious."

"You got to play their game to win their game. That's what I'm saying."

"But I don't think that's right, either," I say. "Because everyone has to live for something. If they don't, they end up like Andy, trying to obliterate themselves with drugs, or they end up like Scarlett, insatiably pursuing money and attention, or they end up like Dax, seeking some group or cause to give their life meaning."

"I don't buy that. Every person I've seen living for something? They end up taking orders from some psychopath. Me? All I care about is being able to sleep well at night and look myself in the mirror in the morning."

"But what gives you that?" I ask. "What gives you that sense that you're okay?"

"Just knowing I don't owe nobody nothing, and I did right by my own mind."

"Not a cause but a code."

"What's that?"

I shake my head. "Something my professor says. If you live for a cause, you become a puppet. You become like the guy I left out there on that field or, hell, even Cadence, in her own way. But if you live for a code—that's what gives your life direction and meaning. Maybe that's the whole trick, Abe. Maybe what the world needs is someone who is bound by nothing—not friends, or family, or work, or even the law—nothing except a rigid moral code. Maybe that's the only way that the good wins and the evil loses."

"What are you talking about, Justice?"

"Maybe my destiny. Or maybe I'm still delirious. I don't know."

"Well, rest up. You can stay here as long as you like. I'm going into the office soon, but Brenda'll be here. We left a bunch of her old clothes beside the bed. You don't find something you like, just say so. She's got two closets full, so it's no bother."

I swing my legs over the bed and it takes a moment for the dizziness to pass. Everything aches but I can stand. "It'll just be one more night."

"Then what?"

"Then I go back to the world."

"You need anything, you let me know."

"You got a spare car and cell phone lying around?"

He laughs and nods. "Follow me."

We cross the hall into an office. Abe flips on the light and I gasp. The walls are covered with weaponry: knives, swords, axes, throwing stars.

"Jesus, Abe. How many enemies have you made?"

"I'm just a collector," he says, rummaging through a desk drawer. He tosses me a phone. "That's a burner. Don't think I've used it, but double check. Should have a hundred-twenty minutes and the same number of texts."

Then he digs into his pocket and pulls out a key fob. "You can keep the phone. This, I'll need back. It's for the Escalade in the garage." A little flashy for my purposes, but beggars not being choosers and all that. "There's a couple grand in the glove compartment, if you need it to get yourself out of town."

"Thanks, Abe." My eyes are still on the walls. "But I'm not leaving. Not yet."

He presses the keys into my palm. "Don't suppose I can talk you out of it?"

"God Himself couldn't."

"Aside from the antiques—" he waves his hand at the walls. "What's mine is yours."

After Abe leaves, I go on a long walk around his neighborhood, a peaceful cove in the northwest part of the city called Chestnut Hill. Brenda asks to come with me, but I need time to clear my mind and decide what comes next.

But though I walk for hours trying to think about the future, I can't escape thinking of the past. I think of the vow I made to my sisters, that I would come for them. I think of the mornings spent scouring the news for signs of the Day Thief. I think of all the times I started dialing the cops, thinking that maybe they could help those girls—only to toss away the phone, despondent at visions of Pop sending my sisters to the grave.

But that's over. That girl who backed down in fear and clung to existence without life died on a field in St. Peters. I've pretended for five years to be Justice Winters, but the truth is, I was still Paige Marie—a frightened girl who did not understand her own strength. Or who knew it but was terrified by it. But here, now, that fear is gone. I am not Paige Marie Rexroad.

I am Justice.

And in that moment, I see my mistake. I see… everything. I've been blinded, not by ignorance, but by bad assumptions.

I've been assuming that everything is one thing. I was Paige Marie—or I was Justice. The killings were about race—or they weren't. The Exiles are white nationalists—and nothing else. But nothing is one thing.

My address wasn't my address.

Dax wasn't writing down my address back in July. He was writing down Andy's. Because he wasn't *just* a white nationalist. He was dealing drugs over the Dark Web—probably sending them out in cheap DVD cases. Drugs he got from Mathis Pyke, the man who supplied drugs to Vic, Terrance, and Warren.

That's why Terrance and Warren had to die. When Pyke heard that Vic had been killed, he knew there'd be an investigation. The police would look into Vic's background, check his cell phone records, wonder how an unemployed college student was dropping thousands at Philly strip clubs. Unless Vic's background didn't matter. Unless he died for a reason that had nothing to do with who he was or how he had lived.

Even if this wasn't about race, it was.

It's past eleven when I return. Brenda's asleep in the living room, an episode of *The Wire* still playing on their flat screen. "All the pieces matter," says Lester Freamon.

That they do.

I cover Brenda with a blanket and head upstairs to shower, pack, and sleep.

I awake to the first hints of light. I grab my bag, tiptoe down to the garage, and climb into Abe's Escalade. I start up the SUV and send a quick text to Izaak and Andy to make sure they got out of the hospital okay, though really I just want to make sure Jack's goons left them alone. Then I close my eyes, take three deep breaths, and I'm ready.

CHAPTER THIRTY-ONE

THE GOOD NEWS IS THAT finding Jack Jackson is easy. Jackson Trucks is headquartered not far from the Port of Philadelphia, apparently changed to PhilaPort a few years back because, really, who has time for syllables? Its offices are located among other ugly industrial buildings, all painted the same not-quite-white, not-quite-yellow color. I drive by the front gate and park along the street, hidden in a line of other cars.

The bad news is that you can't just go walking into the Jackson building. It's surrounded by high fences topped by razor wire, and security cameras are everywhere. Employees must have a pass or some electronic sensor because a gate opens automatically for them. Visitors have to go through a separate entrance manned by a security guard.

I pull a pair of binoculars out of the bag I took from Abe's. The parking lot is mostly empty. Only about a dozen cars are parked out front, though more and more are starting to arrive as it nears eight o'clock. I don't see Jack's Tesla, but it's possible he's already here. I mean, whose only car is a Tesla?

A security guard wearing one of those Secret Service earpieces drives by in a golf cart just as eight hits. Cars are now backed up at the gate entrance. It's hard to make out the drivers from where I'm parked, but as far as I can tell Jack's not among them. I see the security guard drive by a few more times—about every fifteen minutes. An hour later and I'm looking out at hundreds of cars, trucks, and SUVs parked inside the gates.

I'm beginning to wonder what I'm doing here. In the movies, stakeouts seem kind of cool, but I can't take advantage of jump cuts and montages. I'm living things second by second, and I can feel every one of them. It's not boredom. It's that thing worse than boredom—restlessness. Not just waiting but waiting for something to happen.

I get a text from Izaak. He wants to know if I got out of town okay. I don't answer. I don't know how to answer. I don't know how to tell him the truth, and I'm done lying. So, the phone sits there in my lap and I feel cruel.

Then comes the Tesla. Only instead of coming up from the main road it passes right by me, and I about pee myself when I see Jack's face. But he doesn't look my way, just bites into a McDonald's egg McMuffin while leaning over the steering wheel, the way drunks do when they're trying to stay inside the lines.

I check the clock. 10:12.

Everything depends on Jack having a routine. But a guy who arrives at work at 10:12? I feel so out of my league.

The Tesla vanishes in the sea of cars, and I'm back to waiting. Restlessly.

I figure my best bet is to follow him home tonight. Doubtless he has a gated home, but chances are it's not a heavily guarded compound like this. Then again, if I were secretly involved with sadistic revolutionaries, I just might shell out for a team of crack guards and a panic room.

Transitions. That's what I need. I need to catch him during

a transition. There's a tavern around the corner, and the optimistic part of me thinks maybe he walks there for lunch every day. Of course, the optimistic part of me is the one that makes New Year's Resolutions to not empty an entire bag of chips and salsa every night.

Speaking of which, my stomach is growling, and I consider taking a quick lunch break. That's when I see Jack Jackson walking the perimeter of the fence with a pit bull and snacking on an entire footlong hoagie, shards of lettuce and onion raining down to the pavement with every bite.

I check the time. Just after one.

The gate is only a foot from my car, so I lean down in my seat as he approaches, half expecting that I'm going to sit up and find him staring at me, laughing, pieces of pastrami stuck between his teeth. But when I emerge, he's long gone.

CHAPTER THIRTY-TWO

I'M LEERY ABOUT SHOWING MYSELF around Haverford, but I need to talk to Harper. I pull up to his place, but there's no car parked outside and all the lights seem to be off. I settle in and wait for him to return. Restlessly, as always.

I look out at the campus. I can see Duck Pond from here, and part of me aches, knowing it would be easier for me to get through the fence surrounding Jackson Trucks than to sit beside the water and breathe in the fresh campus air.

Then a blue Corolla pulls in a few spaces away from me. It's Harper—or what's left of him.

He's frail and unsteady on his feet. He stumbles as he climbs the porch stairs, then straightens his back and starts fiddling with the doorknob. I climb out of the Escalade, and as I pass Harper's car, I notice the passenger seat littered with tiny bottles of liquor.

He goes to swing the door closed as he enters and flinches when it doesn't slam shut. Then he turns around, and looks at me, and just says, "Hah."

I march past him without waiting for an invitation. I enter a living room just left of the entrance and lean back against the window, motioning for Harper to sit across from me on a plush sofa. "Let's talk."

"I'm afraid I'm quite a few sheets to the wind," he says, taking a seat.

The room is empty except for the furniture and boxes stacked high against the back wall. "You're packing? I thought the decision wasn't final."

"I submitted my resignation," he says lifelessly. "I think you'll understand when I say that it's better for everyone if I don't prolong things."

"But what if you were right?"

"That is not the received wisdom."

"But what if you're *right?*"

"Whether I was right or I was wrong, it wasn't my place to question what happened. I hurt too many people."

I'm looking at a broken man.

"You treated Vic Michaels when he was in high school."

I've never seen someone's jaw literally drop before. It's not a flattering look. "Justice, you know I can't talk about my patients." He's struggling to pin down a thought and finally gets hold of it. "How did you find that out?"

I lean forward and stomp my boot on the coffee table, folding my hands over my knee. "Here's where we are. Three boys are dead. My house was burned down, and two of my friends were put in the hospital. So I could give two fucks about patient confidentiality."

He rubs his eyes with his hands but doesn't speak.

"Fine. Forget Vic. Tell me, hypothetically, about a high school student. Loses his prom date in a car wreck. What happens if he comes to see you?"

"Well, hypothetically, we'd try to figure out what the problem was." The words come slowly at first, but as his mind clicks into gear the sentences become fluid, and I can almost see the man he used to be. "And you might think, well, obviously the problem is the trauma of the accident. But, no, not obviously. You would want to explore every possibility."

"And what might you find?"

He shakes his head. "Pure evil."

"Evil?"

"People think pure evil's a myth. You won't find it in the DSM. But there's a reason every religious tradition has a concept of evil. It's real. Only it's not what people imagine. They imagine some cartoon villain who acts without any coherent motivation. And they're right. People don't act that way."

"Okay," I say, thinking it's incredible how, despite two pints of booze, a lifetime of pontificating allows him to wax eloquent, even though I'm sure he's going to wake up tomorrow wondering what year it is.

"What would you do if a close friend, someone you respected, criticized an action of yours? If they told you it wasn't worthy of you?"

"Probably feel hurt," I say.

"Then what?"

"Think about it. Try to decide if it had any merit."

"Exactly. Exactly. But what if you didn't want to face the truth about yourself? Then you'd tell yourself a story. A story that absolves you of any guilt. A story that paints your friend as cruel, or jealous, or stupid. You'd begin to resent them, and you would find every reason in the world to justify that resentment. Now, imagine if you did that every time you felt a ping of self-doubt or shame. Imagine if resentment and envy became the emotional stew you lived in. Can you start to see how such a person could act to destroy the pure, the good, the innocent—simply because it was pure, good, and innocent? If you have no moral center, how would you feel about a man of innocence or integrity? Their very existence would be a slap in the face. You would want to destroy them so you didn't have to face the truth about your own soul."

"You're saying Vic was evil?"

"No. Oh God, no. Vic was broken. He was broken by his encounter with the malevolent. That's another trope of religion. That when we encounter wickedness, if we are not prepared for it, if our soul is not in the right state, just the very sight of evil can destroy us."

"So, if it wasn't Vic, who was it?"

"I don't know."

"Would you tell me if you did?" I say.

"I don't know."

"What did they do to him?"

He realizes we've left Hypotheticalsville and tries to walk it back. "We shouldn't be discussing this. I'm, sorry. I'm a little drunk."

"I need to know."

He hesitates.

Then I say: "I know about the drugs. He was dealing, wasn't he?"

He lets out a deep sigh. "I don't suppose it matters anymore... When Vic came to see me, he wouldn't say much at first. Only that he couldn't play basketball and that it bothered him. But I could tell. I could tell something was deeply, deeply wrong. It took a long time, but eventually he began to open up. First in small ways. But eventually, yes, he told me about the drugs, about how most of the narcotics that came into Lower Merion went through him. And then, in our final session, he told me about the wreck."

"So what was it? Were they high when they crashed the car on prom night?"

"No, Justice. No, that wasn't it. His girlfriend—her name was Joy... that I do remember—she had discovered the identity of the supplier."

"Vic give you a name?" I ask, even though I'm pretty sure I already know it.

Harper shakes his head. "He didn't say. But the supplier told him Joy had to go—and if he didn't do it, she would not be the only one to disappear."

"Wait, it wasn't an accident? Jesus Christ."

"They left prom to go to a party."

"Vic, Joy, and Levi."

He nods. "Only Levi wasn't supposed to be there. He was supposed to be in another car, but that one left early. Vic tried to talk him out of coming, but as you might imagine, he wasn't in a position to argue too insistently. Vic had rigged the front passenger seat so the buckle wouldn't work. Then they drove out to some back road and Vic wrecked the car and..." His face is red and he waves as if to say, "You know the rest."

"But it makes no sense. Why a car accident? Why would Vic put himself at risk?"

"I asked him that. He said that is what he was told to do."

"Did he say anything about the witness?"

"Witness?"

"There was a witness there who said he saw Joy driving. I think it was Vic's supplier. A man named Mathis Pyke."

Harper looks at me befuddled. "No, Justice. Mathis Pyke was no witness. He was Vic's brother. His half-brother."

"*What?*" It's weird. Usually we're shocked by things that confuse us and we need to struggle to make sense of. But now? This is the first time I have ever experienced the shock of clarity. It all fits. Every question, every mystery, every puzzle piece.

Then Harper whispers: "He came to see me."

"Who?"

"Vic's brother. Mathis Pyke. After our final session. He asked what Vic had told me. I explained that it was confidential. But he…" Harper seems lost in a memory he's struggling to escape. "Well, he insisted. Let's just call it that. And I told him that even if one of my clients confessed to a past crime, I would not be at liberty to reveal it to anyone."

"You knew. This whole time. You knew it was Pyke."

"No. But I suspected. Only I couldn't say anything. Or, perhaps, I was too afraid." He rubs his eyes again and looks at me with an intense sincerity. "I don't know how you're involved in all of this. I can't say I want to know. But there is something I believe. I believe the question you should be asking right now is: How do I get my soul into the right state?"

"I'll worry about my soul later. Right now, I need to stop a killer." Then I remember my conversation with Abe. "A moral code."

"Yes, Justice. A moral code. Most people try to forgive themselves into a state of grace. But we have to earn our way there." He points to a stack of computer paper three inches thick resting on the coffee table. "I've been writing about this. I've been writing about these ideas for a long time. A few years ago, I finished my manuscript, though I haven't been able to bring myself to publish it. It's called *10 Steps to Serenity*. Hah. I don't suppose I have any right to have written it." Well, at least some part of him is self-aware.

"I don't get it. With everything you know, with everything you understand… how can this be how you end up? I know what you said, about not having courage. But why?"

"I've thought about that a lot. And what I think it comes down to… I'm sorry, I'm getting a headache." He pulls a small bottle of bourbon from his pocket, and I'm too revolted to object as he downs it. "What it comes down to is hubris. Or, not hubris, exactly. But I felt as if I had discovered the most important truths—about what gives life meaning and allows us to make our way through a dark world. And I let that be a justification. Maybe I'm not living right, but that doesn't matter, because I'll share this knowledge with others, and help them live right."

"And so here we are."

"Yes. Here we are." He bites his knuckle so hard I expect it to bleed. "I'm very tired, Justice. I want to be alone."

For a long time I don't move. I'm lost in a thousand thoughts and a nagging sense of guilt. Even though all of this should make me feel better about taking Vic's life, for some reason I can't name, it makes me feel worse.

Eventually, I start for the door, but I can't leave Harper. Not in this state. "You're in no condition to be alone. Is there someone I can call?"

He shakes his head.

"Let me make you something to eat."

"Good. Yes. That would be nice."

I walk to the kitchen and find a bag of Ramen noodles and start boiling some water. I watch as the bubbles start to form, one or two at first, and then it's a roaring cauldron and it takes me a minute to remember to put in the Ramen.

I want to believe that Pyke is threatening Cadence. That he is holding something over her head. Or that she knows nothing and is blindly covering for her lover. But a voice keeps whispering to me that the truth is much worse, and I steel myself, vowing to face the facts whatever they turn out to be.

A sound tears through the house and I'm on the floor before I'm aware of what I'm doing. But an instant later I know what happened. I know it without having to look.

It was the sound of Peter Harper blowing out his brains.

I walk toward him and place my hand on his shoulder. He's slumped over, the gun still gripped in his fingers. Did I know he was going to do it? Did I let him? Could I have stopped him? I stifle the questions and, despite myself, whisper a prayer from my youth.

Death can become common. It never becomes normal. It's not Harper's body that haunts me. It's the incomprehensible fact that he was here, and now he isn't. Life and death. Two worlds separated by a chasm anyone can traverse with the single motion of a single finger in a single instant.

"You wanted to write about the path," I whisper. "I want to walk it."

Then I grab his manuscript and hurry out the door.

CHAPTER THIRTY-THREE

CADENCE STIRS FROM A NAP, and as her eyes open, they widen. I'm standing on her bed, straddling her at the waist, and holding the tip of a high-end Tachi sword to her neck.

I press my finger to my lips. She suppresses a scream.

"You lied," I say, my voice low.

"What are you doing?"

"Pyke wasn't with you that night."

"Justice—"

"No more lies. You understand?"

She nods.

The Tachi is long, almost as long as a Katana blade, but heavier and more deadly. I move the blade from her neck to her cheek.

"Pyke's not part of the Exiles."

"No."

"But he knew Dax."

"Yes."

"How?" I want to hear her say it, so I know she's being honest.

"Business."

"But not security."

"No."

"What was it?"

She shakes her head then closes her eyes. "Mathis sold him drugs."

"Which Dax re-sold on the Dark Web."

"I guess so. Mathis doesn't talk about his work much."

"Vic worked for him."

I can see her weighing her words, trying to assess how much I know. Even now, she wants to protect Pyke.

She nods.

"Tell me *everything*," I say.

She winces as the blade presses harder against her cheek. "You know that, too?"

"Why did Pyke kill them? And why did you cover it up?"

"I didn't know he was going to do it. That night, he got a text and just left."

"What time?"

"After midnight."

"Who was the text from?"

"I don't know." I press the blade into the skin of her cheek and a tiny red dot oozes out. "I don't know!"

"When's the next time you saw him?"

"The next morning. He promised me, promised he was in Philly."

"Even though a witness placed him at the crime scene."

"I didn't know about that until later," she whispers.

"And you didn't tell Ty. When you found out what he did, you covered for him. You let him beat the shit out of you and blamed it on the Exiles. Then, when we published our story, you gave him an alibi. You betrayed *me*."

"You don't know him, Justice. When he got out of the

military, he had nothing. He was broke. Had PTSD. No one wanted to hire him. The drugs? He didn't have a choice. Then things… they just got out of hand. But he's a good man."

I wonder if she believes it. I wonder if she knows how far back the story really goes. "He's a killer," I say.

She laughs darkly. "So are you. I tried to warn you, Justice. I told you to lay low. Everything would've been fine. That would've been the end of it. But you couldn't let it go."

"I was trying to protect you."

"Yeah, well. Didn't work out that way. Did it? And now you're judging Mathis and me? You're no different from us, girl."

"Vic deserved to die," I say. "Warren and Terrance didn't. Pyke's using you. You're as disposable as they were. You're as disposable as his own brother."

"No!"

"Quiet down. I can slice faster than you can scream."

She lowers her voice again. "No. He loves me. He would do anything for me."

"Except apparently tell anyone he's dating you."

"That's not his fault. My dad. I was worried that if he found out about Mathis he would, I don't know, investigate him or something. I kept waiting until maybe Mathis's security business took off and he could stop selling. Go straight. Then we could tell. But don't pin that on Mathis. He never wanted us to be a secret."

I sheathe the sword and sit on the end of the bed. "He's going down, Cadence. You both are."

She's crying and nodding.

"I need to talk to him," I say.

"To Mathis?"

"Yes."

"What, and shove a sword in his face? You don't get it, girl. He wasn't just a soldier. He was *the* soldier. You know what I'm saying? The one all the other guys looked up to. The one all the other guys feared. The toughest dudes in the world, and none of them would have gone toe to toe with Mathis. They told me that. His war buddies? They all said it." She's serious. "Don't be stupid, Justice. Call the damn cops and be done with it. Okay? Shit, I'll give you my dad's number. We'll do it right now."

"Not yet. Pyke has something that belongs to me."

She nods. "Your bag."

"He still have it?"

"As far as I know."

"Where is it?"

She shrugs. "I've never seen it."

"Where does he live?"

She hesitates. "I won't tell you. But I'll show you."

"Not happening."

"It's the only way it's going to happen," she says.

Reckless courage. That's something I understand.

CHAPTER THIRTY-FOUR

WHEN I WAS FIFTEEN, I learned that I was like the others. I had always thought I was special, that Pop really was my father. Then Anna Claire and I got into an argument, and I got so worked up I told her, "You're just mad Pop loves me more because I'm his real daughter."

She laughed, right there in my face. "You're not special," she said. "Pop found you the way he found all of us." She didn't have to say the rest.

I would've been an infant. My mother would have been playing with me in the back yard or taking me to the store. And then she'd have made a small mistake, a moment of trusting a stranger just long enough to find herself and her infant locked in the back of a van. A year later, she would have been cleansed and buried in the earth.

After my escape, I hid out in Ann Arbor for a week. I spent a couple days in the Downtown Library, combing through old news stories until I found her. Audrey Jessica Potter. Born in South Bend, Indiana. Gave birth to a daughter, Carrie Jessica Potter, when she was only eighteen. Moved to Blissfield, Michigan with her fiancé, Paul Cobra, a year later. Went missing, along with her daughter, from the Adrian mall a year after that.

There was a picture of my mother in the paper. She looked like me, but with long hair and wide, joyful eyes. I searched for more information about her, but she vanished before the days of smart phones and social media. The only thing I could find was a low-resolution picture of her on her high school's webpage. She was on the track team, and in the picture she was kneeling in front of a group of eight other girls. Only this time she wasn't smiling, but had a look of fiery determination.

How is it you can miss someone you never knew?

I found out Mom's fiancé had left Michigan a few years after the murders and ended up in Irvine, California. I used most of the cash I had taken from Pop to buy an ancient Saturn I found on Craig's List. Three days later I was in Orange County and tracked him to a Whole Foods at the District in Tustin, where he worked as store manager.

It took me a few days to work up the courage, but finally I saw him eating lunch one day at the dining area and somehow forced myself to sit down across from him. I was sure he would recognize me right away, but he just said he was on break and that the cashiers could help me.

"You were engaged to Audrey Potter."

He pushed his tray away and examined me. "You're a relative?"

"I think you know who I am."

"That's not possible," he said. "Her daughter…"

Her daughter.

Certainty is a funny thing. So often you think you have things figured out, and then you find out that up is down and down is a cheese sandwich.

Only this time is different. This time, I'm right.

"That's it," Cadence says. "The red building."

We stop down the block from Pyke's place in downtown Phoenixville. It's the first in a row of renovated duplexes, just across the street from two different microbrewery bars. Not exactly the best place to smite your enemies, but not the worst, either.

I don't tell Cadence about the smiting part, and I wonder if that counts as a lie. I wonder if honesty means revealing everything or whether maybe there's an exception for lying to your enemies in war. It's something I'll have to figure out someday, and I wonder if Harper discusses it in his book. The thought slips away as I fix my mind on what I'm about to do.

"Walk me through it," I say.

"I mean, you walk up the steps, you go inside, and you're inside."

"Try harder."

She wrings her hands and steals a glance as I sit there, twirling her cell phone in my fingers. "There's a heavy deadbolt on the front door and one of those security cameras on the front door he can see from his cell. You can see the bars on the windows."

"Any other way in?"

"There's a back door, but he keeps it barricaded."

"That never made you suspicious?" I say.

"He's a security guy who lives across the street from one half of a bar crawl."

"Fair. What about weapons?"

"He's certified to carry a firearm for work."

"And he carries one?"

"Usually," she says.

"Just one?"

"Usually two."

"Where does he keep them?"

"Inside his jacket in one of those, what do you call them?"

"Shoulder holster?"

"Yeah. The other's in his boot."

"Right or left?"

"Hell, I don't know," she says.

"Think hard."

"He's left-handed, if that helps."

"It helps. Now tell him you're here and you want to see him."

I start to hand her the phone and she lets out a cynical laugh. "Girl, how you ain't dead yet?"

She's right. Cadence is type A. She schedules everything. She wouldn't show up at Pyke's on a whim. "Tell him your dad is starting to question your alibi and you need to come talk to him."

I hand her the phone so the sentence comes out in her own words.

dads starting to ask questions… can i swing by

"Send it," I say.

We both sit there, neither of us able to breathe while we wait for the reply. A few seconds later Pyke texts back.

I got you, babe.

It's about a thirty-minute drive here from Haverford. A little less, the way Cadence drives. I note the time and settle in to wait. Something is making me uneasy, but I ignore it. I know what I have to do and I have to move forward. What happens after that is out of my control.

Then I say, without quite knowing what I'm saying or why: "Cadence, did you ever love me?"

"What? How could you ask me that?"

"You chose him over me. Seems like a fair question."

"Okay, *Fantine*. Yeah, we know. But that's the least of it. Justice, you've had your guard up since the beginning. I stood tall for you, and still you treated me like some outsider snooping around any time I tried to find out what was going on in that head of yours. Like, I get never meeting your people or any of that. Lord knows everyone's got their story. But you never told me yours. Shit, you never even bothered to make one up. It was just this closed door. We were supposed to be sisters. I tried. It cost me, but I tried. And so, yeah, maybe Mathis ain't an angel but at least he's human. At least he trusts me."

She winces, and for a moment I regret asking her to betray him. I regret that I'm about to leave her to finish out her life feeling responsible for the death of the man she loves. But it's only a moment. Because even though everything she's said is true, it doesn't change the one thing that matters. Pyke has murdered the innocent. And I cannot let that stand.

"I'm sorry," I whisper after a long silence. "I should have been a better friend. It's just… it never felt like hiding. Or I guess it did. But it was only because I thought that if I didn't, you'd think less of me." I chuckle. "That was stupid to say. Isn't that always the reason for a lie? Even the most malicious ones? To make the world think we're better than we are so we can get more than we deserve? But it never works, does it? Because the thing about the world is it's ruled… by justice."

"I'm going to lose everything when all this comes out," Cadence says. "And I'm okay with that. But Dad? Justice, I just keep picturing how he's going to look at me and… anyway, I feel you."

She doesn't look at me, but she holds out her hand and I

take it and we sit there that way comforting each other and saying goodbye.

When I think I'm able to speak without crying I say, "Okay. It's time. Just go to the door and knock."

"What are you going to do?"

"Don't worry about me."

Cadence gets out of the Escalade first and starts for Pyke's. I grab a black Strider SMF knife from Abe's bag. For a second, I consider grabbing a few more items as backup. But the thing is, I win or lose with the element of surprise. If I don't take Pyke out the first instant he knows I'm there, I won't get a second chance.

Cadence hesitates at the bottom of the stairs as I catch up to her. I stay close to the building and as she climbs the stairs, I pull myself up to the top stair from the ground so that I'm pressed next to the door, out of sight of the camera.

I warned her not to make eye contact with me, and she doesn't. But as she goes to press the doorbell, I realize it doesn't matter. Pyke already knows I'm here.

I missed it. I was so focused on the words I didn't see it. But like I said, Cadence is type A. She always texts with perfect spelling and punctuation.

dads starting to ask questions… can i swing by

I dive off the stairs and stumble back toward the street just as Pyke opens the front door. When we make eye contact, I can tell I was right. He knew. He was ready.

"I'm sorry, baby," Cadence says, falling into Pyke's arms. "She held a goddamn ninja sword to my neck."

Pyke's face is pure venom. "Not a smart move, Winters." He scans the street. It's not crowded but enough people are around that he can't exactly come out guns blazing, so he walks down the stairs with Cadence on his arm and takes a seat on the last step before waving me over.

"She knows," Cadence says.

"Yeah?" Pyke says, still with that mocking smile. "Let's see your cards."

I stand on the edge of the sidewalk, far enough I don't think Pyke can lunge out and grab me, though I doubt he'd take that risk anyway. Then I say, "You killed the guys and made it look like a hate crime to cover up a drug ring. Sound about right?"

Pyke purses his lips and glances at Cadence. "Is she recording this?"

"No. I don't think so."

"Let me see your phone."

I unlock the burner and toss it to him. "Happy?"

He checks it and throws it back. "You left out the most important part."

"What's that?"

"The part where you tore a hole in Vic's neck with a broken bottle. You can act all high and mighty, Winters. But Terrance and Warren? They'd still be here if it wasn't for you. You think I wanted to do it? But after you did Vic like you did, Terrance and Warren were ready to go to the cops and tell them everything." He glances at Cadence. "That would have been the end of me. It would have been the end of us."

Cadence is still shaken. She knows she sold her soul to protect Pyke. But I can also see that it's just one more thing—just one more sin to rationalize away, one more transgression to be dismissed as a necessary evil. *A rigid moral code.* Any code that places ends above means or that counsels forgiveness isn't a real moral code. It's a counterfeit check.

"You know the real difference between you and me, Winters?" he says. "It's a small one, but it's important." He leans toward me. "Proof. I have it. You don't. The cops find those clothes, it's going to be hard for you to explain that away. They'll want to know: Why'd you hide? Why didn't you come right in and confess if you're so innocent? And you'll come up with some excuse, but you won't be able to tell them why you went and stole Vic's phone, or why you had an unregistered weapon… or why you're carrying around a lock of blonde hair and clippings about a missing blonde girl."

"Risky move, keeping all that," I say. "I'd have figured you'd toss the bag as soon as we outed you in our story."

"Maybe I did," Pyke says. "Or maybe I just kept it some place real safe. Some place the cops'll never find it. But some place where, should anything happen to me—or to Cadence—it will find its way to her old man's desk. See, that's why I'm not bothered to tell you all this. You won't talk. You can't. You have as much to lose as any of us. If I go down, you go down. You can't afford to let the truth come out."

He's right. It's all or it's nothing.

"So, here's what you're going to do," he says. "You're going to leave town. Not tonight. Not tomorrow. Right now. You disappear. I won't come after you. You can live out your life anywhere, any way you want. Your secrets stay buried. If not… you've seen what I can do. It won't just be you who goes down. It'll be all of them. Andy. Izaak. Everyone you care about."

CHAPTER THIRTY-FIVE

"YOU MADE IT," I SAY.

"You ever doubt?" Izaak and I are standing alone in a Valley Forge parking lot, just across the street from several wooden soldiers' cabins. The headlights of the Escalade shine on the snow that is starting to collect on the frosty pavement.

"I'm a dangerous girl to be around."

"You don't know the half of it. Your face is all over the news. Someone saw you coming out of Dr. Harper's place the other day. What happened back there?"

"Regret. Cowardice. Shame."

Izaak sighs and kicks at the gravel. "So, what is this? Just old friends catching up?"

"Would it disappoint you if I said yes?"

"It might. Honestly, I'm just happy to see you. After the hospital, I thought you were gone for good."

"But here I am."

"Here you are. But not for long," he says.

"No, not for long."

"So, you figured it out?"

"Everything."

He nods, more to himself than to me. "So now you're going to settle things?"

"We are. You wanted your story? Now you'll have it."

"Yeah, well… I don't give a damn about that anymore." He steps over to his car and leans against the side. "See, the thing is, J, my whole life I've been so focused on winning. In the classroom, in the gym, with the paper. But I was never really clear what I was trying to win. Then this story comes along, and what I realized is that the outcome never matters as much as you think it does. Fame, victory, money. All that stuff is fine, but it's the process. And with everything we did, the only thing I enjoyed was the work and spending time with you."

"Izaak—"

"No, don't worry. You don't need to say it. I think we were meant for each other. But maybe not in that way. Maybe in some other, much deeper way. You'll always be part of my life, even if it's just the knowledge that your feet are planted on the same Earth as mine."

He steps toward me and pulls me into his arms and I'm home.

Then a light. I hadn't even heard the car approach, but there it is. A police car flashing his alley light on us.

A uniformed officer steps out, and I pull my scarf over my mouth as Izaak pulls me close. I catch his message. Let him do the talking.

"Park's closed."

"We got lost," Izaak says. "We're supposed to be heading to Phoenixville but our GPS took us in a circle."

The officer stares at us, not responding. Then he shines a flashlight: on Izaak, then Abe's SUV, then Izaak's car, then on me. If he asks for ID, I'm finished. Instead, he shines the light up the road and says, "Just keep heading that way."

"Thanks, officer," Izaak says.

"I'll be circling back around in a few minutes. Don't be here when I get back."

"We won't," Izaak says.

"Okay, we'd better get moving," I say after the cop pulls away. "I want you to record a video. I'll text you when I want you to post it. Can you do that?"

"What, upload to YouTube? I think I can manage that."

"Everything depends on you waiting."

"Of course I'll wait. What's it for?"

"I'm going to tell the world the truth."

He shakes his head. "You do that, you can't take it back."

"I know."

"But it's just that—"

I rest my head on his chest and whisper, "I know." When I look up at his eyes, I see pain and fear and trust. "I've tried everything, Izaak. I've done everything I can think of to put this to rest and still salvage what's left of my life. I was wrong. You can't live that way. You're either all in, or you're all out."

He smiles, and I can tell he doesn't want to smile. "Okay. Let's do it." He pulls out his phone and holds it up, facing me. "Whenever you're ready."

I stand in the parking lot, lit by the Escalade's headlights, snow flurries collecting in my hair and along my collar. For the first time in my life, I feel no fear, no regret, no doubt.

"I am not who you think I am. You think I'm Justice Winters, a twenty-three-year-old psychology student at Haverford who grew up in Orange County, California. But I have secrets. I've told lies. I've lived with shame and I've fought wars.

"The truth is that Justice Winters is a lie—a lie I made up to hide my past.

"Here's another lie. Last year I retracted an attempted sexual assault accusation against Kareem Hanley. I did it under threats from his father.

"I built a house of lies that nearly came tumbling down two weeks ago, when Vic Michaels filmed me dancing at Night Shade, a strip club in Philadelphia. Vic threatened to expose me, and I let him hold me hostage, not with lies, but with the truth.

"I demanded that he delete the video. He refused. When I insisted, he attacked me, and as his two friends, Terrance Down and Warren Armstrong, looked on, I killed him.

"What I did not know is why, the next morning, all three of them were found dead. Now I know. They were drug dealers working for Mathis Pyke. Pyke murdered Terrance and Warren to cover up his crimes, and when it looked like the truth was about to come out, he framed Dax Morrison, one of his dealers, disguising his murder as a suicide.

"How do I know this? Because Mathis Pyke told me. He demanded that I stay silent, or else he would come after me and the people I care about. One of those people is Izaak Lane, who's filming this video.

"If there is a single act of retaliation against anyone in my life—if they should so much as get struck by lightning—Pyke is the guilty party. And he should know that I will come for him."

We stop filming. We stand there in the cold, neither of us willing to be the first one to say goodbye.

In the distance I can see the lights of a car. Probably the cop circling back. I place my hand on Izaak's cheek and say, "You really hate me, don't you?"

He squeezes my hand and tells me, "From here to the moon and back."

CHAPTER THIRTY-SIX

JACK JACKSON TURNS THE CORNER of the compound a few minutes after one, leash in one hand, hoagie in the other. His pit bull has its nose buried in the ground, scampering this way and that, looking for God knows what.

For the last three days, I've watched him. For the last three days, the routine has been the same. Now the only question is if he'll play ball.

I tuck Abe's Strider SMF folding knife into my boot and step out of the SUV, walking so that I'm inches from the Jackson Trucks security fence. Jackson is ten feet away when he sees me. He drops his sandwich, and the dog instantly goes to town.

"Well, I'll be," he says. "I had a suspicion we would meet again someday. But I can't say I expected someday to be today."

"Let's go for a walk, Jack."

He lets out a big belly laugh. "I'm a fool, girl, but I'm not a damn fool. I'll tell you what. Why don't you come in here and we'll talk?"

I look at the razor wire fence and smirk. "I'm a fool, Jack, but I'm not a damn fool."

"Sweetheart, I've got over two thousand employees who work for me in here. I've got security cameras all along the perimeter, monitored by guys who go home every day to daughters not much younger than you. In here's about as safe as you're ever going to be."

I stuff my hands in my coat. Probably should have brought an extra knife. "I have your word?"

"Oh, don't get me wrong. I have the opportunity someday, things may go different. But for now, how about we have ourselves that talk? Besides, a friend of mine has gone missing. I'd love nothing more than to know if you've seen him." He points to the gate entrance a few hundred yards away. "Go on down that way. The guard'll let you through."

I start walking and eventually get to the gate. Four men are talking to the security guard. I try to hang back and look at the ground while I wait. A man in blue shirtsleeves comes up. "Okay, you guys wanted to look at our new EV heavy duties, right?"

"Right."

"You with them?" the guy in the suit says.

Everyone turns around to look at me. "I'm here to see Jack Jackson," I say.

The salesman looks disappointed. "Okay, Charles can help you with that. Charles?" The five men march off, and a sleepy-looking guard pokes his head out. "Yeah, yeah, Jack said you can go on in. You know where to find him?"

"I'll be fine." A buzzer goes off and the gate door swings open again.

Jack's still standing back by Abe's vehicle, and with every step I try to think of what could go wrong. But really, all I can think about is the yellow grin of Arnold Lyons.

"Well, here we are. Together again," Jack says. "So, what did you want to talk about, my girl?" He looks down at the dog. "I hope you don't mind if we walk. Trails needs her exercise. Otherwise she gets cranky. Me?" He pats his belly. "I can't say I relate."

We stroll along the parking lot in the direction of the coast. There isn't any public access to the side of Jack's building, so I'm walking into a blind spot. If something goes wrong, it will go wrong there.

"You're really something else," he says. "You got one of my guys so worked up he hasn't left his house since. And the other one? Well, let's just say I haven't heard from him."

"You won't."

"Didn't think so. But what I'm curious about is whether anyone'll be finding him, if you catch my drift."

"They won't."

"Huh. I have to say, you outsmarted me. I'm not afraid to admit it. You know why most people never amount to much? Too much ego. I learned a long time ago to let all that go. Chances are you're not the smartest man in the room. And if you are, well then that's the problem because that means all the talent is hanging out with your competition."

"I appreciate the advice, but that's not why I'm here."

"Okay, I'll bite. Why are you here?"

"I want this all to end. I'm skipping town. Today. You won't find me. The police won't find me. But there are people I care about. I want to know there will be no retaliation."

"That reporter... what's his name?"

"Izaak Lane. And my old roommate, Andy Simmons. What I'm saying is that we're even."

"Even, huh? My math must be a bit fuzzy, because the way I figure it, you killed one of my guys and disfigured another. And now I've got Rambo blaming me for losing one of his best salesmen. He goes and offs Dax and now's asking *me* for payment. Accelerated depreciation he called it. Can you believe that? Yet here you are just taking a walk in the sun."

"That's my offer, Jack. Take it or leave it."

"You're not going to believe this, but I never set out to hurt anyone. Now, Arnold? He was a sadistic prick, no doubt about that. But a good worker. You know he was taking care of his mother? She has dementia. Ugly disease. It's going to be rough for her now. What was I saying? Oh, right. I never wanted anyone to get hurt. I'm a businessman. Practical, you know? And let's be honest. Violence usually isn't practical. Case in point."

We reach the end of the parking lot and start left toward the side of the building. It stretches out hundreds of yards, lined with those large metal shipping containers they use on ships. "All of this? I built all of this. And I did it honestly. No one can take it away from me. You see on TV, every time someone makes a fortune, you can just be sure they committed some crime. You know that, right? More crimes on TV are committed by businessmen than terrorists? That's the kind of propaganda I'm out to fight. But you went and forced my hand."

"I told the truth."

"You think that absolves you? What's a traitor, except a person who tells the truth to the wrong people at the wrong time? Loyalty, girl. Loyalty trumps truth. What you did is you went and gave aid and comfort to the enemy."

"You think just because people have different political opinions from you, they're the enemy?"

Jack yanks the leash to keep Trails from running too far ahead. "What else is an enemy except someone with different opinions? Don't give me that 'can't we all get along' horseshit.

You're too smart for that. It's a dog-eat-dog world out there. But, you know, people don't understand that phrase. They imagine two dogs fighting like two boxers. *Mano a mano*. But dogs are pack animals. You want to win a fight, you best join up with your group. But you? You think you can go it alone. Look at you, coming here like this. Your balls must splash in the water when you piss."

He turns and faces the ocean in the distance. "Look at that, Justice. You know what's out there?"

"Water?"

"The world. The entire fucking world. And the world? It doesn't give a rat's ass about you or me. And that's what you want to go and fight alone. Me? Like I said, I'm practical. If I fight, it's going to be with my own kind. All of us against all of them."

Jack and I are the only ones on this part of the property. I see a few cameras, but they're pointing outside the gate and at the doors of a warehouse. Not where I wanted to be when I pulled the trigger, but now's the time to pull it. "You're right, Jack. I can't do this alone. That's the other reason I'm here. What happened on that farm, someday you'll have to pay for that. But right now I need your help."

"Yeah? I'm listening."

"I want you to call Pyke. Tell him you're ready to pay your debt. Tell him you have me here and need him to take me off your hands."

"An ambush, right? But why make it so complicated? I'm you, I just set up across the street from his place, take him out the next time he makes a beer run."

"You know better than that."

He laughs. He does know better because my guess is he

already tried it himself. "Okay, okay. Still. Seems to me that's a high risk, low reward scenario for the guy. You're something else, my girl, but maybe not as important as you think."

I check the time on my phone. Izaak should've posted my video by now. "He'll come. Trust me."

Jack Jackson smiles at me, only it's not his usual shit-eating grin. This one is contemplative, and a bit sad. "That's the thing, Justice. I don't trust you."

Something hard connects with my hamstrings and sends me to my knees. I'm on all fours, the pain so intense I'm unable to make a sound. A man I don't recognize looms over me, a night stick in his hands.

"Hurry it up. Hurry it up," Jack says.

The guard shoves his boot under my rib cage, sending me heaving for oxygen, then runs his hands over my body.

"Hell of a knife," he says, pulling the Strider from my boot.

"Now, now, Justice," Jack says. "I thought you were smarter than that." Another kick from the security guard and I'm flat on the ground. He's dragging me into a nearby shipping container. I struggle and try to bite his leg through his boot, but the leather does more damage to my teeth than I do to his leg.

He's dragging me over the pavement and I hear Jack Jackson. "Get her out of here. Then get Parker. Tell him it's a code five-twenty."

I hear the clicks of metal teeth as steel squeezes my wrists. I flail my legs, but in an instant they're bound by cuffs as well. I've got the fight of a cat but the strength of a slug. The pavement tears into my stomach and my breasts as I'm dragged further and further, into an empty cargo container.

Then it's dark and silent and the countdown begins.

CHAPTER THIRTY-SEVEN

MY MOUTH IS DRY, and it's like I can taste the dark. I roll and crawl around to get my bearings but the math is simple. I'm trapped in an empty cargo container by a literal genocidal madman. So much for plan A.

A few minutes later, light pours in, and as Jack Jackson steps into the container, I consider trying to squirm my way to safety. But as quick as the sun rays come, they vanish. Then Jack stands there, shining a light on me with his cell phone.

"I hope you don't feel like I went back on my word," he says. "I said in here's about as safe as you're ever going to be. I never promised more than that."

"Don't worry, Jack. I think you're a killer. Not a liar."

"I want you to know this, though. I'm not Arnold. I don't want to see you suffer. I apologize for what happened at the farm, I really do. This time, I promise it'll be quick."

"You're a real gentleman."

There's a knock at the door.

"I guess our time has come to an end. I like you, girl. I swear I do. But like I said, you backed me into a corner. I hope you understand."

He goes to the door and slides open the lock. In pour four

men. One of them slams what looks like a crowbar into Jack Jackson's knee. He howls and drops to the floor.

"You okay?" Abe says.

"I'm not dead," I say.

"Lost sight of you back there. Next time don't go getting locked up in a shipping container without telling anyone."

"Hey. You live, you learn."

Jack Jackson is holding his knee, moaning and babbling. "Please, please. I can give you money. I've got a safe. It's right upstairs. You can walk out of here. You can have the cash. The girl. Whatever you want. But please…"

Abe lumbers over to Jack and holds his hand out. One of the guys I first saw at the security station gives Abe the crowbar. Abe lifts it above his head and cuts through the air and I see an arm just about split in half. It dangles there, like a tree branch in a storm. Jack makes a sound so ugly and loud that I have the sense it will haunt me for however many days I have left on this Earth.

"This ain't about money, Mr. Jackson," Abe says. "It's just that you done wrong to a girl I know."

"Her?" Jack looks at me, wondering how it is I got the drop on him. It's a fair question. "Come on, guys." The words come out staccato as flecks of spit collect at the corners of his mouth. "It… was never… personal. You know… how… it is. Business… is… business."

"Yeah, it's just business," Abe says.

"Please. You want… me… to say it? Fine. I'll… say it. I don't want to die. I'm afraid. I don't want to die." Those last words don't seem like they were spoken. They sound like air rushing out of a damaged tire.

"Oh, don't worry, Jack," Abe says. "You're not going to die. Not for a long time. Someone unlock her."

One of the guys runs over and unlocks the handcuffs binding my arms and my ankles. I stand up and walk over to Jack.

"You've got a phone call to make."

CHAPTER THIRTY-EIGHT

THE CHURCH OF SAINT FRANCIS is old and feels ancient. A few miles northwest of the Main Line, it's a stone castle only a quarter mile away from suburbia, but it might as well be the middle of nowhere. Surrounded by lush fields and high trees, it reminds me of Dracula's castle, with aging spires framing two steep roofs that jet out from the tower.

This is where Pyke told us to meet—just around back, in a cemetery.

The thing about setting a trap is that your opponent has an annoying tendency not to want to walk into a trap. But I'm okay with that. I've got Abe beside me posing as one of Jack's goons and Abe's got one of his boys already hidden on the hillside overlooking Saint Francis with a rifle that will do its duty to God and country by removing Mathis Pyke from the face of the Earth.

We walk in silence, and though the wind and thunder drown out the sound of our footsteps, the pavement is still dry.

My hands are handcuffed behind me, but I've got a key in my back pocket and the Strider SMF in my front. Tucked into my left boot is a black Gil Hibben Cord Grip throwing knife. I don't think I'll need them, but you know what they say. Better to have it and not need it than need it and not have it.

The parking lot of Saint Francis is empty. The streets feel abandoned, with nothingness stretching out in every direction. I feel small and isolated, even though I'm shoulder to shoulder with Abe and Jack Jackson. But my body is alive with tension, and I have the vitality of a cat, ready to spring across a room and dig in my claws.

There is no moon, and as I round the corner of Saint Francis to enter the cemetery, the glow of streetlights vanishes and the world goes to black.

Abe squeezes my arm. "He won't miss," he whispers.

Better fucking not.

We stand there and I can't tell whether it's been seconds or hours. But just as I can sense Jack about to say something, the wind dies down and I hear the crunch of leaves and dry grass through the darkness.

"Mathis, that you?" Jack calls.

My eyes have adjusted enough that I can make out the lines of what look like shoulders shielded in the foliage of the far end of the cemetery. The shape vanishes and reappears closer to us but still under the cover of the trees. The clouds shift and the glint of moonlight dances off the face of Mathis Pyke. He's calm and that makes me uneasy because there's no gun in his hand.

"What's he waiting for?" Abe says.

"Hell, I don't have all day," Jack Jackson yells. "You want the girl?"

"Send her over," Pyke says. His voice is easy, though muffled by the wind as it picks back up and sends leaves bouncing across the grass.

"Son, just get your ass over here. I can barely hear you over this storm and I got a few words I need to say."

I half expect Pyke to walk off but instead he strides toward us casually and now my stomach is in knots waiting for the sound of the rifle, though I know Pyke will be on the ground before the crack reaches my ears.

I find myself counting the steps. Four. Five. Six.

He's out in the open now, and I realize I'm no longer breathing.

Nine. Ten. Eleven. Twelve.

Part of me wants to look up at Abe, but I don't need to. I can sense what he's thinking. It should've happened by now.

Seventeen. Eighteen. Nineteen.

I slip my hand into my pocket and wrap my fingers around the key to the cuffs.

Pyke stops about ten feet away, hands at his sides. His eyes are on Jack Jackson and though I can't really tell, it seems as if he's smiling. Then he looks me up and down. "I'd have rather had the money."

"I'd have rather had the boy," Jack grumbles, tossing Pyke the other key to my handcuffs.

I can feel the tension pouring off of Abe and finally steal a look. His eyes are scanning in every direction. Why hasn't Abe pulled *his* gun yet? Something isn't right. Definitely. Not. Right.

"How'd you do it?" Pyke says.

"What's that?"

Pyke nods my way. "This one. How'd you get her locked up?"

Jack taps on the makeshift sling holding his left arm. "Don't ask. Anyway, you want the bitch? She's right here." Jack shoves me forward a bit but doesn't let go of my arm. Maybe I'm crazy but it almost feels like he's trying to protect me.

Pyke looks down at me and smiles. "You know what your problem is? You underestimate people."

I feel something tear at my shoulder as two shots ring out in quick succession. Neither shot hit me. The pain came from Abe pulling me into his arms and juggernauting in the direction of the parking lot. As he rounds the side of the building, I look back and see Jack Jackson crumble to the ground and Pyke vanish into the darkness.

"Pyke got away," I say.

Abe pulls me tighter against his chest. I watch his face as he runs. There's no fear in his expression, only the grim determination of a father protecting his child.

"Abe, we have to go back for him."

As we round the front of the church, Abe stops so suddenly that I spill out of his arms and onto the frozen ground. Before I can say anything, I see a light coming from a car parked at the entrance. I inhale sharply as I bound to my feet. Then a familiar voice. "Justice! Justice! That you?"

"Don't shoot!" I scream to the silhouetted figure. "He's with me, Ty!"

Abe pulls me close and I can feel the cool of his sweat mix with the heat from his body against my neck and palms.

"Abe, he's a friend."

"You sure?" I can feel his hand and the steel of his gun pressed against the outside of my thigh.

"Yeah. It's okay. It's okay."

Ty shines a flashlight in my eyes as he reaches us. He drove up in his patrol vehicle, but he's dressed in street clothes—jeans and a North Face Apex jacket. He runs a hand over my shoulders and down my arms until they reach the cuffs. "Cadence said you'd be here," he says. "What happened?"

"She's not safe here," Abe says, pushing me in the direction of Ty's car.

"No!" I protest. "We have to go after him."

I hear another car screech into the parking lot. Ty points his flashlight at his car and orders us to run toward it. Just a few strides and already my thighs burn with exhaustion, but I keep barreling ahead, wanting to look over at the second car, but not wanting to see. Trusting that Abe and Ty will protect me from whoever's inside it.

Then the world disappears from under my foot as I step unknowingly from the sidewalk onto the pavement. My body smashes into the ground, gravel flooding my mouth and nostrils. The taste of flood washes over my tongue.

A gunshot and then the sound of a girl screaming.

I say it, too quietly for anyone to hear me: "Cadence?"

When I roll onto my back, Cadence is on her knees in front of Ty, and Ty, his arms outstretched, is pointing his gun in the direction of Abe.

I can't think. I can't make sense of anything. But it's as if my body knows more than my mind. I roll onto my knees and stumble to my feet, hands still locked behind my back. By the time I reach Abe, he's kneeling, and with what looks like an enormous effort, he lifts his head and we whisper to each other without words. Then he grimaces and I can't tell if it's the pain from the wound that is darkening his beige jacket—or the torment of letting me down.

I press my cheek against his face. His breathing comes in quick bursts, and through painful gasps he murmurs, "Tell Brenda I'm sorry."

Before I can answer, the last of his strength gives out. He falls to the ground and I know I'll never speak to him again.

"I love you. Dad."

A sharp pain tears through my scalp as Ty grabs me by the hair and pulls back my head. "On your feet, Justice. Time to take a walk." Cadence is screaming something at him I can't make out, and he shouts in her direction: "I told you, bug. Get in that car and get your ass home. We'll talk when I get back."

I try to say something, but my throat is closed so tight no words come out. I let Ty push me in the direction of the cemetery, too gripped by shock to resist or to run.

And then the universe vanishes and I know I'm in hell because as we reach the cemetery, I'm looking at Pyke, and Izaak, and the sickening grin of my father.

"Hello, Paige Marie."

CHAPTER THIRTY-NINE

TY SHOVES ME ONTO MY knees then orders Pyke to pat me down. Pyke runs his hands over my body. He locates the Strider and I figure honesty is the best policy, so I say, "There's another one in my boot."

As Pyke finishes disarming me, I allow myself a quick glance Izaak. His face is bruised and his mouth is covered by duct tape. I turn away, worried that if I let myself think about what he's been through, I'll collapse into a place so desolate I won't be able to find my way back.

Pyke stuffs my knives in his jeans and looks at me with an odd mix of contempt and admiration: "Like I said. You underestimate people." Without waiting for me to reply, he leads Izaak to an old telephone pole at the edge of the cemetery. Izaak winces as Pyke forces his hands around the pole and binds them with a zip tie.

I spit blood from my mouth and force myself to meet Pop's stare. He looks older than I remember, with hard lines like cracks in granite running from his nose to his mouth to his jaw. His hair falls in short curls, the chestnut brown yielding territory to ashy gray.

"How did you find me?" I say.

The grin becomes a smirk. "I never lost you."

I swallow hard, knowing he's telling the truth and feeling as if he's stolen something from me I didn't know could be taken. My pride. My self-confidence. My conviction that, whatever else was true, I had liberated myself and remained free through cunning and will. And now, the truth. My freedom had been his gift.

"I have eyes, Paige. Everywhere you could ever think to run, I have eyes. I was with you in California. I was with you on your drive east. And when you settled here? Here I found new eyes, and they watched you, so I could watch you."

"You should've listened," Ty says. "I really was looking out for you—Cadence and I both."

"Do you know who this man is?" I say to Ty. "Do you know what kind of creature you're helping?"

Ty shakes his head. "We all got to make compromises, Justice. You think a single dad can raise a girl on the Main Line on a cop's salary? You think that's possible? And it ain't like I didn't do my job. I was a good cop. But sometimes, you got to let a few things go. It's all about the big picture."

"He murders children. Young girls. Girls like your daughter."

I can see it on Ty's face. The struggle not to hear me, not to let my words become real. That's how it works. It probably started small. Maybe catching a dealer and pocketing a few grand for a job well done. How's that wrong? Who's he hurting? Maybe that's how he meets Pyke. *Hey, no need to go to jail. Just throw a little something my way.* Then Pyke comes to him, says some guy wants someone to look after his runaway daughter. No big deal. Just a small favor. But every lie, every sin, every rationalization to quiet his conscience, drags him down further, until he finds himself ready to kill three innocent people just to keep the lies buried. To kill, not to keep out of jail, but to keep himself from facing the truth about his own soul—and the truth about what he has done to the soul of his daughter. *Hey, bug, meet my colleague, Mathis. He's a good man. He'll take care of you.*

"You're weak, Paige Marie," Pop says. "You can't live in this world on your own. You *need* me. You've always needed me."

"I needed a mother. You stole her from me."

"Your mother was a whore. Unmarried. Pregnant. I did you a favor. I kept you pure. I kept you on the path. But you threw it all away. You gave in to the world and it made you blind to the true and the righteous. I thought you would come to see that. I believed that when you were rejected by the man who was not your father, that when you were defiled by a brute who uses women like objects, that when you had to kill to survive and found yourself tortured and alone, that you would remember me and the life I gave you. I can still save you, Paige. I'm not here to hurt you. I'm here to protect you. Not from the cops, but from the world. From an ugly, malevolent, broken world."

"So that's it? I go back to Michigan and all this ends?" I point to Izaak. "I go back with you and you let him go?"

"Not exactly." Pop vanishes into the brush and returns holding a red gas can. "I can help you, Paige. But first I need to know you're willing to help yourself. You need to prove that nothing comes before family. Nothing comes before your duty." He starts splashing gasoline in Izaak's direction and ends by dumping the remains of the can at the base of the pole, leaving Izaak's shoes and pants soaked. Izaak stands there tall, shoulders back, unmoving, his eyes fixed on me. And even though he can't speak, I know what his eyes are saying. But I'm not ready for goodbyes.

Pop hands the can to Pyke and the two of them stroll across the landscape until they're only inches away from me. Pop holds out his hand and Pyke places a matchbook into his fingers. "Just a simple motion," Pop says. "A flick of the wrist. Then we'll watch, and then we'll go home. Your sisters are there. They're waiting for you."

"You're just going to let him do this!" I scream at Ty. "He was like a son to you. Izaak was like a son. You can't just stand here and watch him die."

Ty steps toward me. "You need to shut your daughter up or I'm going to—"

Before he can finish, Pop slaps him hard on the jaw. "Don't threaten my daughter, Officer. That I will not stand for."

Ty looks at Pop dumbstruck.

"You're a bigger fool than any of them," I say to Pop. "You think I would ever return to that death camp you call a home? If I ever set foot there, it will be to save my sisters and burn the place to the ground. So you can release us both. Or you can tie me up next to Izaak and let me die beside my friend."

No more grin. No more smirk. Pop's face is marred by anger and disappointment. I was his greatest investment, and I just declared bankruptcy.

"Like I said, you've become weak. Maybe it's my fault. Maybe I waited too long to come for you. Be that as it may, you've made your choice." He nods at Pyke. "Tie her up." Then he leans forward and kisses me on the forehead and says, "Goodbye, Paige Marie."

I spit in his face and say, my words sharper than knives: "My name is *Justice*."

Before Pop can answer, Pyke half-drags me in Izaak's direction, shoving me against the pole. As he searches his pockets for an extra zip tie, I turn to Izaak and whisper: "Run."

There are things Pop taught me I wish I didn't know. I

know the look on an innocent girl's face as she faces death without fear. I know how to pick a man's pocket without him suspecting a thing. And I know, down to the centimeter, the difference between a cut that will annoy you and a cut that will destroy you.

It happens so fast it doesn't even feel like motion. As Pyke leans down to latch me to the pole, he's startled when my hands emerge from behind my back, the cuffs unlocked by the key hidden in my back pocket. I pull the Strider from his jeans and run it deep through his femoral artery. I don't wait for him to react but continue turning in one smooth motion, sending the bloody edge of the blade into the hard plastic binding Izaak's hands.

As Izaak stumbles away from the pole I see a flash and then flame traveling toward me, slower than I would have expected, but deliberately, as if it's hunting me. I'm on the ground, tearing off my engulfed boots and trying to keep the fire from catching my jeans, but to no avail. The hunter has its prey.

I can barely open my eyes, the raw stench of fire-singed hair and burnt flesh punishes my nostrils and I'm screaming, consumed by the inescapable pain. I manage to free myself from my jeans, and scurry backward, every blade of grass feeling like the edge of the Strider against my burnt skin.

When I look up, Ty is towering over me, a gun pointed at my face. As he squeezes the trigger a wrecking ball sweeps out of the shadows and I realize it's Izaak taking Ty to the ground just in time to keep the shot from taking off my head. Instead, it grazes my right shoulder, and I feel like I just got bit by a Rottweiler.

I can't breathe. The only thing I'm aware of is pain and the sound of two bodies wrestling. The fire shines bright in my eyes, but it's caused the ground to vanish. I grope in the darkness, searching for my knife, which I dropped in all the frenzy. Then I hear a girl's voice screaming and I turn around to see Cadence pointing a gun at Ty, who's on top of Izaak. "Dad, leave him alone!"

Everything stops.

The first motion I see is Pop, walking calmly, almost strolling in my direction. He stops a few yards away from me and the sly grin returns. He scans the cemetery. "I was wrong. You're not weak. Someday, you'll come home."

Then, I remember. I dive backward toward Pyke, who's lying still, his chest still rising and falling and his hands clasped futilely around his thigh. I run my hands down his left leg until I feel the gun lodged in his boot. I yank up his jeans and grab the Smith & Wesson Shield.

By the time I roll over, Pop has vanished. In an instant, I sweep the gun to my left and take three quick shots. One of them finds its target and Ty Jenkins crumbles to the ground beside Izaak.

Cadence screams. She drops her gun and heads, not for her father, but for Pyke.

"You… okay?" Izaak calls to me, struggling to catch his breath.

"Oh, just dandy," I say, crawling in his direction. I collapse once I reach him, my head resting on his stomach.

"It's over," he says. "Grab Ty's phone and call the cops."

"No," I say quietly. "Not yet."

I struggle to my feet. Through searing pain, I stagger toward Cadence, who's on the ground beside Pyke, her face buried in his neck.

"You saved Izaak's life," I say.

Cadence shakes her head and seizes my hand. "It wasn't supposed to be like this. They promised no one would get hurt."

I think of Abe. I think of Harper. I think of Izaak. I think of Innocence.

I bend down and press my lips against Cadence's hand. "Thank you," I say. Then I step back and point Pyke's gun at Cadence's head.

"J?" Izaak says, rising to his feet.

Cadence stares at me in bewilderment. "Justice? What are you doing? We're sisters, remember?"

I hold back tears and say, my voice raw: "Yes, Cadence, we're sisters. But there are no repairable mistakes. I will always love you for your courage, but I can't forgive you for your crimes."

"Justice!" Izaak pleads. "Please. Put the gun down."

I hear the words but they vanish, swept away by the wind and by the most intense concentration I've ever conjured. In the recesses of my mind, I sense that this is the most important decision I have ever made, and I need every ounce of clarity to make it. I need to not only look—but to see.

I see Izaak. His mouth is drawn and, despite the distance and the dancing of the fire, I can make out the desperation in his eyes. He senses, even if not in words, everything that hangs in the balance. That I'm making a choice between him and something beyond him.

He starts to move but I hold up my hand.

"You don't need to do this," he says.

I think of what Harper said, about confusing justice with vengeance. But I have seen evil. I have lived it and breathed it all my life. And I have seen the system fail victim after victim.

The problem with vengeance is that it blinds and corrupts

the vengeful. Only what I feel isn't rage but peace. Not the un-thinking frenzy of someone overcome by wrath, but the serenity of a conscientious executioner.

I am not blind. I *see*.

I see my future drawn out in a long path that leads into the shadows. The shadows where I'll live and where I'll fight—not for safety, or friendship, or revenge but to protect the good because it's the good, the innocent because it is the innocent. I'll do what no one else can do because no one else is willing to pay the price. I'll give up everything the Earth has to offer, except that knowledge that I am bound by a rigid moral code that gives my life meaning and justifies my days.

Cadence starts to speak. "Justice, please just let me—"

A single gun blast exits my weapon and Cadence collapses.

I don't know how long I stand there, but it's only when I feel Izaak's hand touch my arm that I lower the gun.

Then I'm crying and I collapse into Izaak's arms, drained by an exhaustion so deep I wonder if it'll ever go away. He pulls me tight and runs his hand over my hair and kisses my head and tells me it's going to be okay.

EPILOGUE

IT'S BEEN SIX MONTHS SINCE I arrived in Ann Arbor. I rented a small place about a mile from U of M, and I've spent most of my days wandering the campus and the city and trying to feel at home. A few times I've driven out in the direction of Pop's farm, but I've never come within twenty miles before turning around.

I found an MMA gym that seems decent. After one of the classes, a black belt named Javier started chatting me up while I was guzzling water. It took me an embarrassingly long time to realize he was hitting on me. When he asked me out on a date, I was so caught off guard I said yes. I'll probably cancel, though.

I've heard from Izaak a few times. But our conversations are always a little awkward. It's like we get trapped on the surface and can never really speak to each other. He says that, officially, I'm still a person of interest, but that in actual fact, now that the media's moved on, no one's actively working the case.

"Probably best not to plan any vacations to the Main Line, though."

"I wasn't planning on it. It's onward and upward for me."

"Let the dead past bury the dead."

"What?" I say.

"It's Longfellow. You don't know it?"

"I think the last poem I read was 'I'm Being Eaten by a Boa Constrictor.'"

After the call he texted the entire poem, which seemed less efficient than sending a link. I kept reading two stanzas over and over again.

> *Trust no Future, howe'er pleasant!*
> *Let the dead Past bury its dead!*
> *Act,— act in the living Present!*
> *Heart within, and God o'erhead!*
>
> *Let us, then, be up and doing,*
> *With a heart for any fate;*
> *Still achieving, still pursuing,*
> *Learn to labor and to wait.*

That's the plan. But waiting is so hard. Every day that passes, my sisters are still trapped—so near yet an eternity away. And what about the Heiden? How many more will die before I'm ready? The thought chills me and I blame myself for their deaths, and then I feel guilty for blaming myself.

It's morning now. The light breaches my blinds, and the first thing I do is pull open the nightstand drawer, the way I do every morning. Inside is the manuscript of Harper's book and, below it, a folder with clippings about Innocence and a lock of her hair. Izaak sent it to me after finding my bag stashed under Cadence's bed. I place my hand on the folder and say to a girl I hardly knew: "It's time."

While my eyes are still blurry, I swing my feet onto the floor and slip them into a pair of running shoes. In the time it takes to brush my teeth and down a glass of water, I'm ready for a jog.

I open the door and step into the cool air, and I know I'm ready. This is the day I face my father. This is the day the killing ends.

* * *

ABOUT THE AUTHOR

D. P. Watkins is the best-selling author of several books on moral and political philosophy. For years, he's nurtured a deep passion for 19th century romantic novelists like Victor Hugo and Fyodor Dostoevsky, but has longed to see their depth and beauty combined with the page- turning excitement of a modern thriller. And so, I Am Justice was born. He is also a Philadelphia Phillies fan for some reason.

ABOUT THE EDITOR

Randall Surles is first and foremost a voracious reader of everything. He is also a former Green Beret and Airborne Ranger who served in the Middle East, Africa, and South America on numerous missions. Lastly, though certainly not least, he has a Creative Writing MFA and is a Story Grid Certified Editor who has helped authors make their stories work by applying the Story Grid Methodology. He is currently a digital nomad, traveling through Europe, but can be found online at www.randysurles.com.